DRAGON LEGACY: EPISODES 5-8

SARAH K. L. WILSON

A DRAGON SCHOOL WORLD NOVELLA

DRAGON LEGACY

EPISODE FOUR: TOURNAMENT OF DRAGONS

CHAPTER 1

I HAD a dragon on my side. Actually, I had at least four on my side, even if two of them were far away and making my heart ache.

You know your dragon is alive, Saugdal told me. *So stop making such a fuss. We will go to Dominion City and bring the cure to your Dominar. Everything is better in cities. It will sort itself out.*

I was not so confident, but I was reluctant to voice my opinion. After all, I needed the help of these dragons and they were graciously giving it to me. Did I want to go back to lying on the ground with Saugdal's paw about to crush me, or did I want to be flying to Dominion City with a new friend?

I snuck a look at Krullmark strapped to Imybram's back. I thought he was unhurt, though I couldn't see his face. His position strapped down on his stomach and trussed up like a butcher's cut of meat looked terribly uncomfortable, but I didn't think it would actually kill him. I could beg the dragons to stop so I could free him, but I was worried that if their riders had the chance them might truss us both up or maybe even kill us. After all, it was our fault that their dragons had rebelled.

We aren't rebelling. We're taking a turn leading, Imybram said complacently. *I've been letting Grayshon make our choices for many years. It's his turn to fly quietly while I take the reins.*

It might even make his temperament more sunny, Saugdal suggested.

I have often thought a little humility might make him more attractive to other humans. Don't you think he should have considered taking a mate by now? There was a female in Woeldran City who seemed interested in the prospect, though he showed great distaste for her.

Was she distasteful?

I hardly know. She smelled of the butcher shop where she worked — a very attractive smell, if you ask me. I mentioned it often to Farnesus whose cote was next to mine and we agreed that he ought to find her quite attractive smelling like that.

I tried not to listen to the pair of them as I blushed furiously. "I don't think you should be telling me all this."

Oh, be calm human. We dragons must watch out for our lesser friends, Saugdal said kindly. They were obviously old friends and they weren't going to stop gossiping no matter what I said. *I think there's some kind of rule that keeps the humans who ride us from establishing mating partnerships. I certainly have never seen any of them with young.*

That can't be right, Imybram said, pausing before continuing, *I say, Saugdal, it does make a dragon think. Maybe it's time to return to the lands of Haz'Drazen and choose a different course. I could have eggs of my own by now.*

But what would poor Grayshon do? You've told me before that he's lost without you. He didn't even notice that butcher female's nice scent.

They continued that way until Sky City rose on the horizon.

Those not familiar with the cities of the Dominion always tell me that they are shocked by their first sight of them. This was my first sight of a Dominion City. But to me, seeing the magical city where it hung high above the ground, supported by a stem of Dominion sky steel just made me feel like I had come home. Not home like Dragon School was home, but home like the Dominion where I knew the rules and the people — even if currently I was going to be in super big trouble with them if they found out who I was.

I needed to stay calm, get the cure to the Dominar, and find Reshatharin, and if I could do all those things it would be fine. I hoped. But my heart was torn. I wanted to skip steps one and two and just find my dragon. I didn't feel like a whole person without him. Not anymore.

Do you see them? Saugdal's voice broke into my thoughts.

Who should I be seeing?

The dragons! Look at them! They're competing!

I squinted but even squinting I was no match for dragon eyes.

A relay race! Imybram broke in excitedly. *Look! They're passing a rider from one dragon to the next and she's holding such a pretty silk banner. It's the color of the sunset!*

That's Ankelil on the team with the sunset banner, Saugdal agreed. *She's fast. I've never seen a Red so fast, have you?*

Of course not, but Eyydsach is on the team with the cloud banner and he's terribly quick.

It's not fair to mix the colors, if you ask me. How can a red out fly a purple, hmmm?

So the dragon games were real and if I'd still been a part of Dragon School I might be there watching ... getting everyone water and bringing food to the dragons and helping with tack.

I wasn't sorry to miss it after all. Because flying as a dragon rider — even a fake one — was so much better than just being near the action.

Oh that poor human fell. Oh, oh Saugdal, Imybram said and then they both fell silent.

I swallowed. Okay. Maybe riding a dragon was a whole lot more dangerous than sitting around watching. Maybe people died even when it was just for fun. I still wouldn't trade my Reshatharin for anything.

That's right, Saugdal said, but he sounded upset.

Who was his dragon? Imybram asked soberly.

Elrrmik.

And then no one said anything again until we were close enough that I could see the dragons, too. They'd stopped the games. Would this tragedy mean the dragon games were over? I wasn't sure.

From the distance two black dragons were flying toward us, their riders making hand signs to stop and wait. Likely defenders of Dominion City coming to check that we were no threat.

And just like that my mouth was dry and my fear returned.

Now, human child, don't you fear, Saugdal said. *We have everything in hand.*

But at the same moment Grayshon Bracemender called out, "By your honor and loyalty, Imybram, put me down!"

CHAPTER 2

IMYBRAM FELL to the ground so quickly that I gasped.

Don't worry about him, he's fine, Saugdal said, circling to descend a little more slowly. In his paw, his rider had been surprisingly quiet as if she were merely biding her time but now she spoke very calmly from where she was held.

"I think you should let me handle things from here, Saugdal." Her face was white and I wasn't sure if that was rage or fear that had her face so hard and immobile.

I don't think so, Saugdal said. *No disrespect meant.*

But of course she couldn't hear him. No one could hear dragons — with the exception of purple dragons and their riders — except me. And it was such a new thing for me that I was not sure if I could trust it.

The black dragons racing to intercept us descended as we were landing and their feet hit the ground at about the same time as Saugdal's, kicking up dust in the long grass of the meadow. If I hadn't been on dragon-back the grass would have reached my waist and it blew beautifully in the breeze all tumbled and greenish gold.

Every dragon in the field gleamed in the setting sun and it

caught the grass dust swirling around them, causing it to glow like a cloud of glory.

We are glorious, indeed, Saugdal agreed which proved Reshatharin wasn't the only arrogant dragon.

While their riders dismounted, offering us short, worried nods. Saugdal gently put both Castelan Woeldran — his rider — and me on our feet, puffing out his chest proudly in the presence of two more dragons of his color.

I could barely hear the humans offering the official challenge over the voices of the dragons in my head.

Saugdal, who are these?

This is Imbryam. We fly together.

Imbryam appeared to stretch, but I realized it was a kind of formal bow. My eyebrows rose up. Interesting. Did other humans ever notice this? The black dragons did their own stretch bow and introduced themselves.

Unlkann, Veansyo. Our riders are very agitated. They don't like this break in protocol.

Surely, Saugdal said, puffing his chest even more, *you realize that protocol is also of utmost importance to me and I would never violate it without the most pressing of reasons.*

Nor would I! Imbryam squeaked. *Is there a way to get this human off my back? My rider tied him too tightly.*

Hmmm, Unlkann shuffled closer, titling his head back and forth before nuzzling Krullmark. My friend grunted irritably. *I think I could, but burning the ropes might singe him. Do you think that would hurt? Humans are so prone to injury. I think they don't have scales at all sometimes.*

Please don't flame the ropes! I begged with my mind and all four dragons turned their heads to me.

She can talk? Veansyo asked, head drawing back in horror.

I didn't wait to listen to Saugdal's explanation of who I was and why they were breaking protocol most urgently. Instead, I hurried over to Krullmark.

A glance at Grayshon Bracemender and Castelan Woelran told me that they were too engaged in concerned discussion with the black rider patrol to notice me sneaking over, though I heard snatches of conversation that made me very nervous.

"...very dangerous ... posing as actual riders!"

I slid around Imbryam until I could see Krullmark's red face and put a finger to my lips. He frowned, his green eyes studying me as if I were a strange piece of text in another language but he said nothing as I set to work on the cords binding him. We might not be able to escape but at least I could untie him and make both him and Imbryam more comfortable.

Thank you, said Imbryam.

"...have to deliver them to the authorities immediately," Grayshon Bracemender was saying behind me as I finally unravelled the knots tying Krullmark to his saddle.

I helped him slide down and he shook his head at me but I ignored him, hurrying around to his back to work the knots there. His poor hands were purple from being tied like that.

"Are you hurt?" he whispered furiously at me.

"No," I hissed back.

"What's happening?" His green eyes fixed on me with almost alarming intensity.

"The dragons are on our side."

"For all the good that will do," he muttered, looking away but I thought maybe he was embarrassed. He seemed to think I'd blame him for a predicament that wasn't either of our faults.

Rude! Imbryam said and I worried he would back that up with more than a complaint, but at that moment I got Krullmark's hands free and Imybram sagged with relief as Krullmark strode away from him, massaging his wrists as he went.

"Riders!" Krullmark barked. "I demand you inform Dale Barrowlord, Captain of the Dominion Guard that Krullmark Bachstream of the Purple is being held against his will and kidnapped and his dragon has been stolen from him by these two dragon riders. I demand immediate justice."

The black riders' eyes widened at those words. They were young, I realized. Barely out of Dragon School. I thought I knew one of them — Retich Bowshaper. An unobtrusive student. Friendly, but not gregarious. Not popular, but always with friends. The other one I wasn't so sure of, but he held himself like he might be from one of the great families. They exchanged a worried look.

The one with the noble bearing straightened his shoulders, "I'm afraid this matter requires a higher ranking guard to decide. You will follow me on your dragons to the checkpoint just outside the Tournament of Dragons," he said to Castelan Woelran. "Your prisoners will ride with us."

"That's far too dangerous," Grayshon Bracemender said and I grimaced at the glitter in his eye. He knew perfectly well that we were no danger but for reasons I couldn't fathom, he wanted to keep us with him.

"We will sling them below our dragons," the Retich Bowshaper said stiffly. "They can be no trouble there."

It will be fine, the dragon Veansyo was saying to Saugdal. *We'll fly together. You're going that way anyhow.*

But we don't dare stop, Saugdal said urgently. *When we get to this checkpoint we're just going to have to keep going or the Dominar won't get his cure and then what will happen?*

I ran a hand over my face. Was he going to tell everyone our secret?

How else will they be able to help? He snapped at me.

We'll decide whether to land when we get there, Veansyo said firmly. *There may be higher ranking dragons at the checkpoint who can help make that decision.*

Saugdal hissed, a puff of flame coming from his mouth and beside him Castelan Woeldran cursed.

"Not this again! Get them loaded quickly, watchmen, or we're going to be dealing with a dragon rebellion."

I didn't hear the guard's retort and I lost track of the dragon's argument. There were too many voices at once. I couldn't keep track of them all.

I was manhandled roughly into a net with Krullmark while I was still trying to sort out my confused thoughts. The riders threw long ropes over Unlkann, and then before I could even catch my breath, the black guard dragons were leaping into the air and the heavy net was rising. Krullmark wrapped a protective arm around me, but it wasn't enough to keep a lump of fear from forming in my throat as the ground rushed away and the net swayed terribly, the rough ropes scratching and abrading my skin as we flew toward more hostile people and more obstacles with no one to count on except Ibryam and Saugdal.

Which is more than enough, I must say, Saugdal reminded me. *You couldn't ask for finer dragons.*

CHAPTER 3

"WE'LL BE FINE, SPARA," Krullmark growled as soon as we were in the air. "We're on our way to see real Dominion City officials. Once we tell them our story, they're bound to get you to the Dominar and then we can go free and find our dragons."

I appreciated him trying to comfort me, but I didn't want to be lied to. I shifted in the netting until my bottom was under me and I could sit very uncomfortably and look him in the eyes. The shape of the net pressing down on us put our faces inches apart. It was an uncomfortable thing to be so close while we had this conversation but there was no way around it.

"Krullmark," I said firmly. "I don't want optimism. I want us to be realistic about this situation."

He sighed.

"Exactly," I said. "We're in trouble. Those officials are as likely to believe us as these other dragon riders. I'm probably going to be executed for posing as a dragon rider and if the Dominar is as sick as he told us he would be, then he won't be coming to my rescue unless I get to him first. And that means Reshatharin will die with me." It was hard not to let my voice shake as I spoke but I had to be brave. For my dragon. For my friend. For all of the Dominion. "And who knows what they'll do to you."

"I have friends." He sounded like he was choking on the words. "They'll help us."

"Will they? When it would mean risking themselves, too?" I asked but I didn't expect an answer, I just wanted him to acknowledge that there was no easy way out.

"Don't cry," he said firmly. I was not crying. Yet. And I didn't plan to start. "My friends will help. And if they can't help us officially, they'll help us escape."

"The dragons say they will help, too," I said firmly, "But I don't know what they can do when their own kind oppose this."

We can do plenty. Have a little faith, Saugdal broke in but I ignored him. I needed to have this conversation with Krullmark while I still could. *Sorry, sorry, butting out.*

"What dragons?" Krullmark asked, frowning. He looked so fierce when he frowned, like a bear someone had made angry. It was a little flattering to know all that fierceness was directed toward our joint-cause.

"Saugdal and Imbryam," I said, pointing behind us at my dragon friends who were following the guard dragons. "And maybe these other black dragons, but they aren't convinced yet."

Krullmark's expression went from fierce to disbelieving. "How can you know that?"

"They've told me. I can hear them."

"No." He said it like it was fact. Like it couldn't be questioned.

I nearly laughed he was so ridiculous. "Yes, actually. I can. I do. And they have agreed that our cause is important enough to risk disobedience to find a way to get this cure to the Dominar."

Obviously it is very important, Saugdal interjected. *Sorry. Sorry. Being quiet now.*

"Can this be true?" Krullmark said wonderingly, his green

eyes finding mine and locking onto my gaze. "Can you really speak to dragons of all colors?"

His hand drifted up as if he meant to cup my cheek with it but he snatched it back when he noticed what he was doing.

"It is true," I said, fighting a blush. Why should I feel pleased with myself when this wasn't something I'd earned or figured out, but rather just a gift that had miraculously been granted to me?

If miraculous means you were so annoying that I broke all protocol and spoke to you and somehow opened up a channel of communication between man and dragon that has never previously existed then yes, miraculous, Saugdal said wryly.

"It's true and they're willing to help us, so we need to make a plan," I said firmly. "Saugdal is trying to talk the black dragons into just flying straight to the Dominar and not even stopping at the checkpoint, but he's not having much luck."

"That's why Castelan Woeldran is so upset," Krullmark said, his gaze going inward. "He's not listening to her."

"Exactly. I told you, they're on our side. Now, listen," I said, trying to catch his eyes again. He was looking downward, his face screwed up in thought. "Krullmark."

He looked up. "Yes."

"I don't know what to do." That got his attention. He met my eyes and held my gaze while I confessed. "The Dominar needs this cure. And if he doesn't get it the whole land will be plunged into war with those terrible creatures flooding over the border."

Creatures? I ignored Saugdal again. There would be time to explain to him later.

"And then we won't even have a Dominar to lead us and who knows what will happen. The end of the Dominion, maybe. The deaths of everyone we love. But if I hurry to find the Dominar, that means leaving Reshatharin behind. Wounded maybe, or captured or ... or dead."

I twisted my hands together until Krullmark caught them and held them in his. His gaze never left mine.

"Spara," he said gently. "You love your dragon and he knows it. You've already given up everything for him."

What did she give up? Ibryam interrupted.

Shhh, I'm listening to find out! Saugdal said.

Krullmark was still speaking. "He nearly died trying to achieve this already. He'd want you to save the Dominar and our friends."

I really was crying now. I stole one of my hands from Krullmark's grip to wipe my eyes. It was surprisingly comforting to have him hold my hand. I wished I could do it all the time.

"I will find them," Krullmark said firmly. "Look at me." I looked at him, though he was a watery blur through my tears. "I will go and I will find them while you deliver this cure to the Dominar."

"How can you do that without a dragon to take you? Are you going to walk all the way back to where they were taken? We don't even know where they were."

"Hey," he said. "Hey, don't cry. I can do this. You're going to have to trust me, Spara. I will find a way to get to them, and I will bring Reshatharin back to you. You have been showing us how much you can trust, right? At the Healing Arches your trust saved us. On the Bright Continent your trust bought a cure for the Dominar. Trust me now."

I nodded my head, dashing my tears aside and collecting myself. "I'll trust you," I agreed.

And you'll trust us, Saugdal said firmly. *Because we have promised to help you and you treat that like it isn't enough.*

I'm sorry, I tried to tell him. I'll trust you better.

Yes, you will, he said and when I glanced behind me he had thrust out his chest again even though he was flying and the sight was so funny it was all I could do to hold in a laugh.

CHAPTER 4

My laughter was short lived.

I see the checkpoint! Imbryam called out. *Will you join us and keep flying, black dragons?*

There was silence in response.

Oh no.

You tricked us! Saugdal said, lurching forward as he suddenly picked up speed, his flame flaring out.

Don't flame us or you're going to be in terrible trouble, Unlkann warned but there was hardly need for warning.

From the ground a sudden burst of movement filled my vision and then as we descended, a whole pride of black dragon ascended, like reverse bats, dropping up into the sky instead of toward the earth.

You're going to regret this, you foot-eating hatchling! Saugdal called and then — more faintly as we were separated, *Don't give up hope, Cure Girl. This will only be a temporary delay!*

I could only hope he was right. From where I was being slung to the ground in a rough net, things were looking very rough indeed.

We descended at the edge of the tournament celebrations and in the few glances I managed to snatch before we landed, I could see this tournament was massive. It sprawled out across the ground filling the valley to the west of the sky city and completely surrounding the monuments to Savette — the Chosen One — and her great prince-husband. Pavilions of every color and size dotted the turf, and as night was closing in, roaring bonfires were spaced among them. The closer we got to the ground, the more the sound of music, shouting, and whoops of delight reached up, trying to to lure us in.

For my own part, if it hadn't been for my intense worry over Reshatharin and my desperate need to get the cure to the Dominar, I would have loved to join the festivities.

Banners flew with the colors of the different groups of dragons and huge clumps of similar-colored dragons bedded down in happy heaps while their riders lounged against them, or ate, or danced.

My heart ached a little watching them celebrating together. Reshatharin — the merry dragon — would have *loved* this.

The black dragon patrol set us down in a space between four large black pavilions sporting hanging banners with the Dominar's seal embroidered on them.

The very officialness of the four had me nervous immediately and seeing a few cages on carts and a drunk hanging half out of one of them was not setting my mind at ease. Those were mobile jails. And they were probably my accommodations for the night. Could a dragon pick one up and take it away? I didn't think so. What a fool I'd been to trust these black dragons. Maybe I should have slipped the cure to Saugdal while I had the chance.

No, he told me, his voice still far away. *If the Dominar sent you for the cure, then he'll accept it from no hand but yours. Otherwise he could be tricked and poisoned.*

Good thinking.

Just try to rest easy. We'll soon come for you.

I wanted to believe him, but as they pulled the ropes hastily from the guard dragon's back and opened up the net sack that held us in place, a flurry of guards poured from the tent and surrounded us.

I was more certain than ever that I'd made a mistake. Trust was a wonderful thing. But it couldn't make miracles.

And right now we needed a miracle to get out of this mess.

"What's all this?" a voice barked. From the largest pavilion, a man in a uniform with two silver dragon wings sewn on the shoulder and chest emerged with a frown on his face. He was middling in years and he stroked a thick beard as he watched his guards drag the ropes from over our heads and force us forward.

Right behind us, Saugdal and Imybram landed in the dust and I could hear Castelan Woelran scolding her dragon. They'd caught up again.

Grayshon Bracemender didn't wait for her. He leapt from Imybram's back and strode right past us, throwing up a hand to silence our guards.

"Who's in charge here?" he demanded, as if it wasn't obvious to anyone with eyes.

"I'm Ponden Broadjoist, captain of this checkpoint, and I will be shown respect," the captain said, and for a moment I thought there might be trouble between the pair of them — which could only help me — but Grayshon Bracemender visibly swallowed his pride before giving a sharp nod.

"Fine. Good. We encountered two individuals posing as dragon riders about a day's flight out of Dominion City. We snatched them up before they could commit further crimes and brought them directly here meaning to present them to the proper authorities."

The captain grunted. "And their dragons?"

"There were no dragons," Bracemender said briskly.

Krullmark cleared his throat.

"Well?" the captain asked, turning to him.

His guard were well trained. They remained silent, carefully surrounding all the prisoners and guests, human and dragon alike. Their eyes were sharp and quick to go to any movement. I tried to keep very still and as calm as I could be under the circumstances.

"I am Krullmark Bachstream," Krullmark said and his deep voice held authority. "I am a dragon rider of the purple and I have been unjustly accused of these crimes. I demand immediate release for both myself and my colleague."

Do we fly now? Imybram broke in excitedly so I missed what the humans were saying as the dragons argued.

We're not going to help you escape! Unlkann snapped, flaming enough that the guards near him stepped neatly to the side.

We aren't prisoners! Saugdal shouted and then all the dragons were shouting at once, filling my head with so much noise that I barely heard the captain yelling at his guards to get hold of their dragons.

They were all spouting little gouts of flame and this point and bouncing from foot to foot as they argued while the dragons who didn't know what had happened demanded to be told.

I was grabbed by two guards and hustled forward so briskly that I tripped over my own feet, not even able to register their voices when I was certain they were yelling right in my ear.

It's the right thing to do! It's the right thing to do! Imybram was hooting as an enraged Saugdal roared that they were all a shame to stalwart black dragons everywhere and he would be taking this directly to the silver dragons guarding the Dominar.

I was thrown into one of the waiting cages unceremoniously and Krullmark was thrown in with me, and if he said anything to me then I couldn't hear it. I had both hands — even the crumpled one — up over my ears despite the fact that the sounds deafening me were entirely in my mind.

When they finally died down, and I was left panting from

the intensity of their disagreement, it was clear there was nothing Saugdal and Imybram could do. Their fellow dragons wouldn't listen.

It's not protocol, was the last thing they said and, dejected, my two allies slunk away, their riders following and scolding them roundly.

It was only then in the terrible silence that I came enough to my senses to realize Krullmark was holding me against his shoulder like you'd hold a crying infant and was whispering, "Hold on, Spara, hold on. It will end soon, whatever it is."

Concern laced through his voice and when I glanced at him his wide face was lined with worry. But what I feared most was that it *would* end, and I would never hear a dragon again. Not my new friends, and not my beloved, missing Reshatharin.

CHAPTER 5

ONE THING COULD BE SAID for the cage and that was that with only bars on the top and sides, we could see the Tournament of Dragons very well indeed. Before the sun even came up there were dragons in the sky practicing and warming up for the day's events, flying in tight, almost impossible, formations, speed racing across the sky, and executing wildly complex patterns of twists and turns, flaring at intervals and in patterns as if they were exploding stars rather than massive flying creatures. If I weren't so worried it would have been utterly breathtaking.

As it was, I sat huddled against a dozing Krullmark, worrying at my lower lip with my teeth, and trying to figure out how to not hear every dragon voice at once. Even from so far away the dull roar of them made my head ache. Fortunately, most of them had been asleep last night, so I'd had time to get my own brain back, but as the hours passed my ability to listen only seemed to grow, and my ability to filter what I was listening to was not up to the challenge. If I didn't figure it out soon, I might be the first ever insane dragon rider.

We — dragon riders — didn't usually go insane. Having a dragon to love and tend was a wildly grounding thing. It brought out the best of a person and helped calm them when they were on edge. A dragon's heart was the largest heart of any living thing, and I knew from experience how calming it was to lay your head on your dragon and listen to the certainty of it, but even so, I was running a real risk right now paddling out into waters no other human had ever navigated.

No one bothered us in the cage that first night and it wasn't the same cage as the drunk. I barely heard his calls and jeers. If he thought he could compete with a thousand dragons, he could think again. No one came with food, or blankets, or water and by morning my mouth was dry and my eyes puffy. I wondered if poor Krullmark was going to die with me. It didn't seem fair when he never approved of what I was doing in the first place and only ever just wanted to help.

"Spara?" Krullmark whispered, his breath gusting mist in the cool morning air.

I pushed myself up to sitting.

"Look!" He pointed in the distance and we both scrambled to our feet at the first dragons of the morning leapt into the air, flying almost straight up.

"I've never seen a dragon fly on such a steep angle!" I breathed.

"Neither have I."

For a few moments, we were lost to the wonder of watching a full wing of eight green dragons fly in precise formation straight up and then execute a perfect rise-and-fall turn at the peak of their arc, and plunge toward the ground, scattering in eight different directions at the last moment and fanning out. They were so low to the ground as they arrested their falls that the pale belly of one of the dragons nearly grazed the top of our cage. My breath caught as I heard his rider's laughter.

"I always loved formation flying," Krullmark said a little wistfully as the wing of greens was replaced by a wing of red dragons who were flying a braided pattern together in which one dragon looped and leap-frogged over the next. "You missed that since you didn't go through regular training. I think Reshatharin loved his chance at it. He and Alissi flew in my wing in our Initiate year and he was always right in the thick of it."

I swallowed the thick lump in my throat. For a moment I'd forgotten that Reshatharin was missing. And that Alissi was dead. And that I'd missed out on every amazing Dragon School initiation because of the irregular way I'd come to find my dragon. It all came crashing back now.

I was just composing myself again when I heard a hiss to the side. I turned and saw a huge red dragon head thrust between the pavilions and practically dragging on the earth to peer into our cage.

Are you Spara? he asked, and my mouth was so dry that all I could do was nod and put one hand on Krullmark's arm to forestall the quiet curse he'd started to utter. *I am Yarimal of the red dragons. I'm here with a message from Saugdal and trust me he owes me now.*

"Is he speaking to you?" Krullmark whispered and when I nodded he retreated to the other end of the cage and appeared to be stretching. I frowned until I realized he was blocking us from the view of any guards who might come out of the pavilions.

Saugdal says to tell you that we have a plan to break you out. The minute you see the chaos you need to be ready.

"Be ready how? I'm in a cage."

Just be ready!

He flared irritably and then his head slid away and we were left alone. I repeated his words to Krullmark but my friend didn't look too hopeful.

"There's a lot of a chaos at such a huge event," he said. "I doubt anything would be enough to distract our captors. I think you should try not to get your hopes up."

But despite his sage words, my hopes were up and as each game of the tournament filled the sky, I would watch, hoping this was the one.

Sometime around midmorning, they fed us and let us out one by one to take care of necessary business. I could have used a wash, but I had the feeling that even the guards were hard pressed for wash water with so many people in one place.

"Do you know Dale Barrowlord, Captain of the Dominion Guard?" I asked Krullmark eventually. "The one you asked to speak to?"

He was quiet for a while before he grunted and said. "No. But action needed to be taken. Better to speak to the authorities directly than be left to cool our heels like this."

I shared his rueful expression, but I said nothing. He was right. It would have been better. The hours were ticking away and meanwhile we were so close to our goal but still so far away. And our dragons could be getting farther by the moment.

It wasn't until the afternoon that I saw something that made me freeze, clutching the bars of the cage.

"What is it?" Krullmark hissed. "Is it what you were hoping for?"

"Not in the slightest," I gritted out between bared teeth because there, riding up on a gold dragon, as if he had every right to be there, was a man in rags with long black hair. When he caught my murderous gaze, he winked at me before dismounting and striding into the captain's pavilion. Something glittered from where it hung around his neck. I could barely speak, my mouth was so dry. Instead, I whispered, "What's he doing here?"

"What's he doing on the back of a gold dragon?" Krullmark answered and I felt a stab of icy fear shoot down my spine. "And what is that slung across his chest?"

"The last thing Reshatharin told me was that he had a gold dragon sitting on him," I said in a small voice.

Krullmark gave me a worried look. I was beginning to worry those lines would never leave his face. I loved that he cared about what I cared about … but look at what it was costing him.

"That's what Ursejek said, too," he admitted.

"Could it be possible that an entire color of dragon could be subverted by our enemies?"

"It can't be all of them," Krullmark said, pointing to the sky where a wing of golds was lighting torches as they passed with great precision and tight formation. "Some are competing here today."

"Even one is too many," I mumbled and he murmured a sound of agreement, sitting and hunching over himself as if in deep thought.

We did not get to speak to Jhairen Que'Shal. Or to the captain. Or to a guard. Not even when Krullmark called and yelled that we were being detained illegally and that we demanded an audience before the Dominar.

The guards who fed us and brought us water never said so much as a word.

I had almost given up entirely on our situation when all of a sudden a blast shook the ground, knocking me off my feet while green light filled the air.

I coughed on the dust I'd fallen into, struggled up to sitting with one good hand. When I got to my feet, I saw Krullmark doing the same.

"That must be the signal," I tried to say but the ringing in my ears was too much.

Stand away from the bars! a sudden voice ordered.

It was not an easy request to follow when we were surrounded on all sides by bars, but I hoped they meant the bars of the door.

I grabbed Krullmark with my one good hand and tugged him after me, hurrying to the other end of the cage. He didn't budge at first, looking dazed, but there was no way I could make the huge bear of a man move without his agreement. To my relief, it was only a moment before his eyes opened, he squinted down at me, and then let me drag him across the cage.

There we are! That's the way! The voice said encouragingly and then as a second burst of green light flared and a sound so loud it deafened me broke across the landscape, bright orange light flared at the other end of the cage, leaving the bars red hot.

Something might have squealed — I heard it very faintly — and then water splashed across the cage and I was soaked head to foot and left sputtering, staring at Krullmark in shock.

A hand clamped over my shoulder and I screamed.

CHAPTER 6

KRULLMARK WINCED, shaking his head wildly, and with all my strength I cut off my scream and let him gently turn me so I could see the man who had grabbed my shoulder.

Ystren Cartrender. The Magika.

He was as pale as always, his eyes darting in every direction and a finger over his lips, but I didn't think we'd be seen. Another burst of bright light, this time purple, flooded the air while a third tremor — more powerful even than the previous two — cracked through the air.

I would have been knocked off my feet again but Krullmark caught me. Before I'd even regained my balance, Ystren was pulling us after him. One glance told me the guards were all running from their pavilions, but they weren't coming toward us, they were making for the source of that light further into the crowded field where the Tournament of Dragons was supposed to be happening.

Ystren's lips were moving but I couldn't hear a sound as he tugged and yanked us between the pavilions and into the falling darkness.

Above us, suddenly and silently, since my ears were still ringing, dragons seemed to be pouring into the sky. The dragons were of every color — some riderless, some with riders in harness, or clutching saddles half hanging off, or with mouths open and brows knit together as if they were yelling for their mounts to stop.

They swirled up into the sky and then round and round mounting farther and farther upward like the funnel cloud I'd once seen as a child, or like some of those silvery schools of fish I'd seen with Drazena when we flew out over the ocean.

It was watching them that made me realize that the ringing in my ears that was making me deaf wasn't the explosions after all — or maybe it started as that and then morphed into this — it was voices piled one on top of the other completely deafening me as they spoke over one another all at once.

What was that?

Was it magic?

Where's your rider?

Catch him! He doesn't look well!

Dragon upon dragon upon dragon.

"Spara!" Someone was yelling in my face and I had to blink for a moment before I could see it was Ystren Cartrender.

Somehow I'd lost sense of where I was again and he and Krullmark had pulled me into the crowded tents of the Tournament of Dragons. We were lost in a sea of multi-colored canvas and pressing bodies, though almost everyone was staring at the sky.

Whoever had planned this planned the perfect distraction. Anyone could get lost in a sea of people like this one.

Krullmark pushed Ystren aside and then suddenly he was close, almost nose to nose with me and the sense of relief I always felt when he was close made it possible to focus despite the noise.

"Spara, can you hear me?"

I nodded and was rewarded by one of his small smiles.

"Listen, it's time for the plan. Ystren says he's heard a rumor about where our dragons are. He's going to go with me to rescue them and Saugdal's going to take you to the Dominar. Do you understand?"

"Yes," I said though I had no idea where Saugdal was. I was just so relieved that someone might know where Reshatharin was and that they were on their way to save him that I hardly cared about details like that. "Make sure they're safe, Krullmark."

"I will," he said earnestly, though there was a line in his forehead where his brows were pulled together in worry. I knew it would freeze like that. "Are you sure you'll be fine?"

"I'll get the cure to the Dominar," I said.

It felt like someone else saying it. My mind was *still* overwhelmed with voices. I was *still* a prisoner on the run. I had no idea if I'd be fine at all. But I needed to do my part and I needed him to do his.

"Incoming!" Ystren called.

"Krullmark," I started to say, clutching at his arm with my good hand.

His lips parted as if he wanted to say something to me, too, but then a wind whipped up over me and my hair was blowing everywhere, obscuring my vision. Something snatched me up and away from Krullmark, ripping my grip from his arm and then I was aloft in a sky teeming with swirling bodies. I watched his worried eyes until we twisted and I lost sight of him.

Told you I'd come back for you, Saugdal said. It was his black hand holding me tightly in its grip. *Now, where's Imybram?*

Right here! Hurry! We need the human to use the brush.

"Use the brush?" I asked, feeling so disoriented that I hardly knew what was happening.

For the paint, silly human.

Well, there was nothing to say unless they were going to be more clear. I pressed my cheek against the small hot scales of

Saugdal's paw, comforted by the heat there and tried not to think about how very near we were flying to all these other, swirling dragons.

Whatever had burst in bright flares seemed to have stopped and the sky was very dark so that all I saw were dark shapes and the occasional flicker of color. Saugdal's grasping paw protected me from the cold of the wind but I felt anything but safe swirling ever upward in such a precarious position.

Be calm. I won't drop you. We just need the disguise of so many bodies.

Had he arranged all this? It seemed impossible, and yet Ystren had been there at just the right time.

Well of course we arranged it! Imybram squeaked from somewhere close. *We do have friends, you know, even if those solemn gate guard dragons were so stuck on protocol that they wouldn't listen.*

Friends enough to kick off this insane distraction?

Friends enough to start it, Saugdal said proudly.

And their riders?

Are perfectly safe in a meeting with the human guards about how troublesome you are. I hope it's clear that we won't do anything to hurt them.

"Of course," I said aloud, a little breathlessly, but my words were snatched by the wind.

Because they're still our riders even if they're walking around blind to what's happening because you won't tell them what you're doing.

Did you really steal a dragon? Imybram said. *Because that's very* rude, you should know.

Of course I didn't steal a dragon, I protested mentally.

Good. The pair of them said together and that seemed to be it. They didn't ask anything else and the next thing I knew we were going back down the spiral which was decreasing in speed slowly, slowly as it descended.

I craned my neck over the edge of Saugdal's paw — a course of action I do not recommend at such a dizzying height with no safety straps at all — and saw the lowest dragons landing among the pavilions. Humans raced out to the dragons as if they were ants seizing upon spilled honey and some of the first to land were persuaded to light the bonfires below.

At one edge of the field, I thought I could see the students of Dragon School's encampment with the school banner flown above it. My stomach lurched. I could have family there. My mother and aunts might be there.

But even if they'd come to work during the Tournament of Dragons, I didn't dare go to them. I would only bring danger with me. The thought made my heart sad, so I turned my attention to other things.

There were gold dragons descending with the rest all over the field.

Of course there were golds. It's a very popular color.

But I didn't dare trust any golds. Not when I had seen Jhairen ride upon one. Whatever he was doing here could only mean the worst of trouble. Hopefully, Krullmark was telling Ystren that we'd seen him and Ystren knew who to talk to.

Last we'd seen Jhairen Que'shal, he'd been leading an army of those terrible Medusas and quendral creatures into our land — to see him here and now without them, sent a stab of dread through me for two reasons.

First of all, I feared why he might have infiltrated this gathering. If my friends could cause such a stir with a little light and loud pops — how did they even do that? — what could someone who wanted to destroy us do?

It was easy. We found a Magika who knows my cousin, Imbryam said airily.

Shhh, I want to hear the second reason she's worried, Saugdal said.

I hadn't realized that I'd been accidentally broadcasting my thoughts. But it was impossible not to think of the second reason now that he'd mentioned it and it was that this tournament was very large. So large that all these dragons couldn't just be from Dominion City, Sky City, and Dragon School.

There are representatives here from everywhere, Imybram said excitedly. *I'm so pleased we came back to see it!*

Which meant every other Dominon City and fortification would be more lightly defended. While we had hidden raiders flooding across our country, hidden and unknown.

Saugdal's hand tightened around me until I gasped. He eased his grip.

Sorry, he said but I could hear the breathlessness in his mental words. He understood.

Someone would notice that and deal with it, Imybram said happily. *Don't you worry.*

Someone had noticed. It had been Wawrin Tanglefoot of the Red. He and an entire wing of red dragons. And if no one hear had heard of an alarm sounded by them ... had they died trying to defend the Dominion without me?

We were all silent for a long minute and then Saugdal said, *All the more reason to get this cure to the Dominar, then.*

We dropped down from the sky into a spot in the field on the exact opposite side from where I'd been held in a cage. There were several pavilions here all centered around one large bonfire, but Saugdal ignored the fire and the people around it and slipped under a dirty canvas pavilion so large that dragons could fit inside. He did not release his grip on me until we were under the canvas and I began to struggle to get free.

Here we are. Iapozon should have the paint ready.

I clambered from his paw, sweaty and still worried about what they were doing with this paint when a human voice made me freeze.

"Who's this then?"

CHAPTER 7

I WAS HALF IN and half out of Saugdal's paw when he threw his head back in dragon irritation, catching the canvas of the tent against his crest.

"Whoa! Easy! Or you'll bring down this tent on our heads!" the voice chastised.

I dragged myself the rest of the way out of his grip and spun to look at the speaker. She was short and somewhat round with a leather cap on her head that fit quite tightly and tight curls that spilled out from under it. A bandolier of metal tools was slung around her and she wore a long leather coat covered in singe marks.

"I don't know why I agreed to work with you rogues. First, you bring danger into my tent and then you almost destroy the very canvas of it!"

But despite her protests, I knew immediately why she was helping. Behind her, a diminutive purple dragon sat on his haunches, carefully tilting his head back and forth as he watched us with wide eyes. The saddle on his back was very large and also laden with tools and I knew immediately that he was her dragon and she was his very odd human. Their sizes were so mismatched that it seemed a strange pairing — especially as messenger dragons were meant to be very quick and they never carried assortments of tools with them.

What in the world was she?

"You can put your eyes back in your head, missy," she said to me, tapping me on the shoulder to get my attention. Or at least I thought it was a tap. Her finger was very pointy and she jabbed with a lot of force, but I thought that maybe she always moved with force and she didn't mean anything personal by it. "Well, Ryfsmae? Is her claim real? Does she have something for the Dominar? Or have we risked our necks for a criminal?"

She scowled at me, but again, I sensed it wasn't personal. She had the blunt-speaking attitude of someone who was always scowling.

Give me a minute to ask her, Panza. Take a deep breath, her small dragon advised before turning to me. *I am Ryfsmae of the Purple, and this is my rider Panza Boldbrewer. We greet you at the request of Saugdal, most noble black and Imybram, honored white.*

I tried to match his formality.

"I'm Spara Coldrock, rider of Reshatharin of the purple."

Beside me Panza sniffed loudly like she was trying to express displeasure, though it mostly sounded like she had a very productive head cold.

Saugdal has told us an amazing story and demanded we procure for him silver paint. We have no doubt what he plans to use that for.

Silver paint! My eyes went wide. Silver. Of course. He was going to pretend to be a silver dragon.

I glanced over my shoulder at him and Imybram. Imybram looked sheepish but Saugdal was so blatantly casual that I could only assume he was hiding a similar embarrassment.

The only silver dragons in the Dominion were the personal guard of the Dominar himself. If these two dragons were planning to paint themselves silver so that they could sneak into Dominion City and right into the ranks of the Dominar's own guard, then they were taking a wild risk for me.

Obviously we would never aid you if we did not believe in the cause, Ryfsmae said.

"Absolutely right!" Panza said, crashing one palm into the other.

I jumped at the noise, cradling my bad hand in the crook of my good arm.

"What's this then?" Panza asked, grabbing my hand and examining it thoroughly. "I've never heard of a Dragon Rider with a bad hand. Certainly not a purple. And I would have. She paused, her face growing grim. "But there is a rumor running wild through the camp that one of the staff is looking for her daughter. A girl with a bad a hand."

I flinched. My mother really was here! Part of me wanted to run to her right now and beg her to make everything better. The other part just wanted her tucked back into Dragon School, safe and well and away from all of this.

"The hand doesn't matter," I said coolly.

Obviously, Saugdal said with a sniff and another head toss. His pride was very touchy.

"What matters," I continued, "is that I was entrusted with a very secret quest on behalf of the Dominar and I must see it through."

"It's hardly secret now," Panza said with a sniff.

Show me, Ryfsmae said and I didn't want to show him. I was too scared of what could happen if I lost the cure, but he was right — if any of us got caught doing this then all of us would likely be executed for treason, so he had the right to see it.

Reluctantly, I drew the packet from my clothing and showed it to him.

"It's from the Bright Continent," I said by way of explanation.

"And it can cure him?" Panza said, as if she didn't doubt he was sick, only that the cure would work.

"He said it would," I said a little shakily.

"Even now that he's in a coma?" Panza asked.

We all gasped at once and then the dragons were all talking over each other.

You can't know that!

That can't be true!

How can he confirm he sent her if he's in a coma? What if they don't listen!

Enough! Enough! That last voice was Ryfsmae. *That is why we will go with you. So that no one can stop you or doubt your cure. And that is why we agree to do as you have asked and leave at once.*

CHAPTER 8

"At once" it turned out, actually meant once the dragons were painted silver and the paint was dried and hardened with their flames. It took us about an hour, and a very stinky fume-filled hour it was, as Panza and I applied paint with thick brushes.

"Bet this isn't what you thought you'd signed up for, huh?" Panza asked.

She had a hearty, efficient way about her now that she'd given up poking me and manhandling my bad hand. She didn't even say anything when I held my own paint pot braced between my bad wrist and my torso so that my good hand could be free to use the brush. At least she wasn't prejudiced, just brash.

"How do you know about the coma?" I asked as we painted.

"I have my sources."

I lifted an eyebrow at her but she didn't say more.

"You made me show my cure even though that comes at a great risk," I said, boldly. "But you won't tell me how you have secret information about the Dominar? Can I trust you? You aren't the typical purple dragon rider."

She snorted. It was almost impossible not to like her when her every thought came out as a noise.

"Of course I'm not typical. All those fools flying hither and yon with messages. Do you know what I'm doing? I'm inventing a way to send messages a lot faster. You know how all the sky cities are in the air?"

"Yes," I said, wondering why we were discussing this, but it wasn't like I could paint any faster so I supposed we had time for her to talk.

"Well, theoretically they could see each other given a straight line of sight but with the exception of Dominion City and Sky City the distances are too great. However, each city can see far enough to see a tower, and that tower could see another tower, and another in a straight line from one to the other. And if you could see that, then you could have someone up the tower sending the message along."

"That would take hundreds of towers. It's not practical when a dragon could just fly the same distance in minutes," I said dryly. Maybe Krullmark was rubbing off on me. He was usually the skeptical one.

"Not if you used a looking glass," Panza said triumphantly. "I've worked and worked with a lens crafter and we have one that can see leagues in a straight line. So, my plan is to build tall, thin towers — like lighthouses but on land — and in each one place a couple of men and a telescope looking in each direction. When they see a message, they write it down and then pass it on to the next tower down the line."

"Sounds confusing," I said doubtfully.

"It's not confusing," Panza said fiercely while her dragon turned a sudden snicker into a cough. Clearly she'd heard this before. "It's technology. It's the future."

"So do they write the message really big?" I asked, trying to mollify her. "What if someone else reads it by standing between the towers and looking up."

"You use a code," she said proudly. "I've invented five codes already."

"I still think you'd get eye strain trying to read through a telescope," I said.

"Well obviously we wouldn't use written words," she scoffed, flicking Imybram's ears up so she could paint behind them. He shifted uncomfortably and I wondered if her fingers were as rough with him as they were with me.

So much rougher. She's worse than a mother dragon. All teeth and fire breath.

"We would use signals. Flags maybe. Or flashes of light. Or black and white cards in certain orders. I haven't quite decided yet. But the tower protocols are very promising."

"Really?" I asked and I didn't mean to sound horrified but it must have leaked into my tone.

"Not you, too!" She huffed, spreading Imybram's wing out roughly.

Watch it! I'm not a tool, I'm a living dragon!

"It's always the same." Here her voice changed as she imitated her detractors, "'You're trying to replace us, Panza! You have no respect, Panza. You're supposed to be a purple rider, Panza!'"

I felt my face grow hot. "I mean ... it was my dream all my life to fly on a purple dragon and deliver messages. And now you want to take that away."

"It's progress," she growled.

I hid my face from her, pretending to be focused on a patch under Saugdal's foreleg.

"You could still deliver messages. You'd just be in a tower."

"Yeah," I muttered. "Because that's every girl's dream. To be locked in a stuffy tower straining her eyes instead of flying with dragons."

Saugdal snickered.

Don't fuss yourself. It keeps her happy and its no trouble to us. Dragons will never stop flying no matter how many spindly towers she builds.

Exactly, her dragon chimed in. *Besides, what other marvels might she invent from what she learns building this one?*

"They won't train purple riders anymore, though," I muttered. "And then where will people like me be?"

Who knows, Ryfsmae said with a dragon shrug. *Maybe they'll find something even better to do.*

I didn't like it at all. But I supposed I should reserve my judgment until I could talk to Reshatharin about it. After all, he was the one who was a purple dragon and this was his business more than anyone's.

Just thinking about my dragon gave me a great pang in the heart so I painted twice as quickly and in no time all the dragons were coated and were taking turns flaming each other to dry the paint.

"You'll have to wear a saddle," Panza told Saugdal. "No respectable silver dragon would fly around with a human gripped in his forepaw like a cat with a mouse. Don't look at me like that. Tell him, Ryfsmae. He wears the saddle or we don't fly."

Ryfsmae didn't bother repeating the message. Saugdal could hear just fine. But he seemed just as annoyed when Panza replaced the saddle he was wearing with one not covered in tools.

"I hate putting them in the saddle bags, but there's nothing for it," she said sadly. "Silver riders definitely don't carry tools around. Well, are you ready, girl?"

I nodded my assent.

"Good," Panza said, mounting Ryfsmae with the same enthusiastic roughness with which she did everything else. "Because my friend on the inside won't wait."

CHAPTER 9

I MOUNTED Saugdal with some trepidation. He'd carried me so often in his hand that it felt odd to ride on his back again. Especially as there were reins. Would he expect me to use them? I never had with Reshatharin.

Touch those reins and the deal is off.

Well, that simplified things. I looped the leather strands around the front of the saddle where they'd be out of the way.

We slid out from the tent one by one, my teeth clenched the entire time. Dragons do not sneak well. They creep along the ground even less well and there was a great deal of clanking as they knocked over Panza's tools, cursing — from Panza, and disgruntled snorts — from the dragons. The dragons exiting the actual pavilion looked like small children struggling out of articles of unwanted clothing, each one causing the tent to flap alarmingly before they were finally out.

I breathed a sigh of relief when Saugdal was finally in the fresh air.

The night was deepening and the moon had grown smaller and risen higher. While there was no longer a swirling funnel cloud of dragons, there was plenty of activity in the camp — more than enough to mask our movements.

You can't just have a few colored explosions and walk away, Saugdal explained.

"How did you make those explosions?" I whispered.

He sniffed as if it were beneath him to answer. *We left that to the Magika.*

Well, it hadn't been Ystren making them. He'd been with us. Which meant he must have had a friend do it. A very powerful, magical friend. I bit my lip and hoped the friend could be trusted and that Krullmark wasn't walking into some kind of a trap. But there was no time to worry about that now. We were already flying in the direction of Dominion City.

When we get there, Panza does the talking, Saugdal reminded me. *All you have to do is sit still and be quiet until we get close to the Dominar.*

Panza had lent me a dark cloak with a deep hood. It screamed "disguise" to anyone watching, but there was no helping it. We didn't have anything approximating the gleaming armor of a real silver dragon rider. We didn't even have anything we could paint to pretend. We'd have to hope her friend on the inside could slip us through quickly and quietly before anyone noticed.

I tried to keep from worrying as we drew closer and closer to the city. Twice, we encountered wings of black dragons headed the other direction. They had the look of harried guards, as worried about what they'd find at their destination as I was, and they only gave us a cursory glance before rushing by. The paint on our dragons gleamed silver and with the nip of the chilly night, we could be excused as riders for keeping out cloaks tucked tightly around us.

It was only when we began to get close to the city that I realized how wild this plan really was.

I'd never even been to a sky city before. Raised in Dragon School, with only small towns and villages in the surrounded area, it just hadn't been a practical thing to travel far enough to see one. The city on the Bright Continent had been impressive, but this — this great looming home for our people, rising unnaturally above the ground, was a wonder.

Dominion City — capital of the the Dominion and sister city to Sky City — was built in tiers, the lowest tier being at the edge of the city just behind the city walls. I'd been taught that the wall was there more to keep people from falling out of the city than for defense, though it certainly helped with both. Each layer of city was a little higher up and a little higher up. To reach the apex of the city, one would have to follow the long spiral road that wrapped up the tiers like the spiral of a snail. Hanging from the sides and beneath the city were cables and lines with huge baskets dangling from them carrying people and supplies up into the sky city. I'd always wanted to ride in one of those baskets, but riding a dragon was probably much better.

Of course it's better! Saugdal agreed. *Anyone can be yanked up in a bunch of woven willows but not everyone will have a dragon agree to carry her! Can you see the Dominar's palace yet?*

I could just make it out at the top of the city. Bright lights danced all around it, lighting it up in the night. It made the palace beautiful but it also put a lump in my throat. How were we going to sneak in there?

We won't be sneaking from that side, Ryfsmae assured me. *We'll be flying up from underneath.*

And the black dragons who guarded the city would just let us?

Leave that to us. Ryfsmae's voice held an assurance I certainly didn't feel, but what choice did I have but to trust him?

Exactly, Imybram agreed. *Humans. They always think they're the ones who should be in charge even when a task is better suited to dragons.*

The gusting cough all three of them let loose was very

familiar to me — a dragon laugh. But though I frowned at them, they kept laughing right up until we were within shouting distance of the first dragon guards. There were three of them flying a careful circuit around this section of the sky city.

Dominion City loomed over us in massive magnificence, now that we were this close, dwarfing dragons and humans until we were nothing but tiny specks.

Ryfsmae? An unfamiliar voice hailed him and I felt myself tense in the saddle. If this guarding dragon knew Ryfsmae then our disguise was useless. He would know Ryfsmae should be purple and not silver. Even in the moonlight, the difference was obvious. *Ryfsmae? Is that you?*

CHAPTER 10

I TENSED and I felt Saugdal tense with me. There was no turning back now. We just had to keep going and hope we weren't about to all be arrested as traitors.

If that's your friend, Nelilic, another dragon said, *ask him what that commotion was at the Tournament field.*

Did you see it, Ryfsmae? The dragon identified as Nelilic asked as his rider hailed Panza.

Of course we saw it, Ryfsmae said importantly. *And what a wonder it was. Lights dancing so brightly that they had us all in awe. They painted pictures in the sky like what you dreamed of in the egg and there was a sound like music so lovely that it caused us all to take to wing at once — a thousand dragons with one shared thought. It was like the celebrations of our infancy in the Lands of Haz'Drazen.*

The dragons sighed happily, though that wasn't quite how I remembered it.

Tell us more! The inquisitive dragon asked, but the humans were already wrapping up their quiet conversation.

I will tell you all on my return, but for now my task is too urgent! Ryfsmae announced.

And then we were flying again, unhindered, and I bit my lip

hard on my questions, not even daring to think them in case those dragons could hear us. How could one of them recognize Ryfsmae but not see he was the wrong color?

Panza must have had the same thought because the moment the black dragons were out of sight I heard Ryfsmae reply to her, *But it wasn't a risk at all. Nelilic is color blind.* There was a pause and then more. *Well I don't see why his friends would ask what color we were. You worry far too much.*

I was worried too, but there was nothing else we could do about it now.

To my enormous relief, no other dragons stopped to talk to us, despite how many were out flying under the city in the dead of night. Their presence made me nervous, but I tried to keep calm when Saugdal whispered in my mind.

In a city this size there will always be some dragons busy in the night.

When we reached our destination — so far under the city that we were enveloped almost entirely in darkness, the moonlight being blocked by the bulk of the city and only the occasional lantern lit below to shed any light at all — we turned all at once. We'd been flying in a steady, smooth path, but suddenly Ryfsmae disappeared, and then Imybram, and then with a grunt, Saugdal seemed to almost fall for a moment before launching forward. My heart was in my throat before I realized it was only the back half of him that had fallen, and that it had been done on purpose so that he could flap like crazy and ascent straight up and into an opening at the bottom of the city.

The opening yawned wide like a giant creature's mouth, the pair of lanterns set on one side of it like two great fangs.

And then we were passing through, and my breath stuck in my lungs as Saugdal executed a stomach-clenching turn and half-roll. For a moment, I thought I'd be squeezed off his back, but then we were in, and the door was shut behind us, and everything was dark except for one of the lanterns.

All here? A dragon voice asked as Saugdal shifted and crouched lower. I managed to catch my breath again even though my shoulders were still pressed lightly against the ceiling.

The room we were in was wide but short and all the dragons were forced to crouch. Panza whispered curses as she tried to adjust to where she wasn't squashed like a pancake on her little dragon, and Imybram cleaned his claw tips with a tiny gout of flame that I was pretty sure wasn't casual at all, despite how he was trying to make it look, and was instead his nerves coming out.

All here, Saugdal confirmed, and even his voice was tense.

No one knows? the dragon continued. And as he lifted the lantern in his jaw, the golden light splashed across his scales and I couldn't help it. I sucked in a sharp breath.

I had never seen a silver dragon before.

They weren't raised or trained at Dragon School and their riders didn't come from the school either. They were separate from the rest of us, and whatever methods were used to train the dragons and personal guard of the Dominar were as secret as they were highly debated. Some people claimed the riders were chosen from birth and trained to withstand terrible deprivation and difficulty. Others said they were dragon riders who have somehow ascended to a level beyond, their dragons changing color with the impartation of great wisdom.

I asked Alissi what she thought of it once. "I imagine they're just like us," she said with a toss of her head. "They're just trained in a secret location so that they can be protected. I bet they even have dining halls and dishes and too many ladders."

And then we'd both laughed together.

I wished she were here right now. Or Reshatharin. Or Krullmark.

No one knows, Ryfsmae confirmed.

The dragon greeting us nodded slowly. *You have but one mark of the candle. That's all we can give you to get this done without being noticed. I'll guide you up the spire and then you'll have to wait in the rafters while the human goes in. Which human is it?*

The little one.

The dragon's eyes turned to me. *We cannot confirm this story of yours. We are allowing this upon the words and reputation of Ryfsmae and Saugdal and Imybram. Pray you do not disappoint them — or us. If the Dominar did not send for you, then your life will be forfeit the moment you enter his quarters.*

His quarters?

I thought my eyes might drop out of my head but that was nothing compared to the silver dragon. He shuffled back a surprised step, making a half-whine in the back of his throat that I did not think was at all intentional.

She speaks?

She speaks, Ryfsmae agreed. *It is as the prophecy foretold.*

Ummmm what prophecy?

We'll tell you later, Saugdal said in a quelling tone. *If it works out.*

Great. Was there anything else I needed to know?

Be fast. Get in. Give the Dominar his cure. Come back.

Sounded like solid advice. I had no desire to linger.

Oh, one more thing, the silver dragon said grimly. *You'll still have to get past his human guard yourself.*

CHAPTER 11

Just tell them the truth, Saugdal suggested. *They won't want the Dominar to die either.*

But I didn't think it would be as simple as that. Guards didn't just believe people who said they knew something the guards didn't know and needed urgent access to the ruler of all the Dominion in the middle of the night.

We crept through this strange tunnel that seemed like it was the very bowels of the palace.

It's the garbage gate, the silver dragon said as if I'd said it aloud. *It was very difficult to distract the garbage guards. Do not return here without me.*

Sounds ominous, Imybram said with a whole body shiver.

Oh he's probably just saying that to keep us from causing trouble, Saugdal said.

I am not just saying it, the silver dragon said with a testy edge to his voice. *I am trying to keep you two on track. You have blown flames into the entire dragon population of the Dominion. Word is spreading faster than wild fire that you've found the one who can speak to all dragons and that she is the key to saving the Dominar, and now I can't set down in any place in all the palace without a dragon asking for my opinion on whether the rumor is true or wild supposition. And I was only told of this a few hours ago. You should be glad I trust you, Ryfsmae. Personally, I would have sided with those who said it's only the blowing of the wind without a lick of truth to it.*

And then you'd miss out, Ryfsmae said contentedly. *And then you'd be so sorry, and next time we ate together it would all be moaning coming from you. "Why didn't you tell me, Ryfs? I was right there just a sky city away, old friend." I'm doing you a favor here.*

I didn't think I could hear dragon eyes roll but it sure felt like I was hearing it from the new dragon.

Their arguing might have kept on going but then, suddenly, the corridor narrowed and the silver dragon gave the sign to be silent — learning dragon sign turned out to be useful after all! — and we slid through a tight squeeze of a corridor and then straight out onto a mosaic tiled floor at the bottom of a steep shaft. Or, I supposed, an open tower with a roof at the top.

Of course!

The palace had to be full of dragons. In fact, all the Dominars since Amel Leafbrought had had a bond with a dragon so it only made sense that there would be a place for them to easily access every floor of the palace without the annoyance of stairwells. And this tall shaft was beautifully designed. Each floor had wide corridors leading from it with a small lip to keep idle humans from slipping over the edge but more than that, they were ringed with arched windows and those windows had tiny iron-wrought balcony rails cupping them so that humans could lean out and look up or down the great tower. I thought I saw a gleam of the moon from high up in the tower. Likely, in the day light filtered down and bathed the place in a soft glow. Beautiful.

More beautiful than you could possibly know without seeing it, the silver dragon said and he sounded annoyed as if it was personally offensive to him that I had never seen his home in broad daylight. Was this his home?

Yes. Silver barracks adjoin the palace.

That explained a lot.

But what about the Dominar's dragon? He had one, didn't he? I distinctly remembered a black dragon being with him when he visited me before.

Tagermet. No one has seen him in days.

That didn't sound good. Riders didn't just abandon their dragons, or vice versa. If no one had seen Tagermet, something was terribly wrong.

Well, Saugdal said, ever the philosopher. *Up we go then. No point wondering about what can be discovered with a little effort. We'll drop you off, Spara, and then we'll wait in the rafters until you're ready to leave.*

And when you're ready to go, the silver dragon said, *let me know with a sneeze.*

A sneeze? Saugdal looked at him from the side of his eye.

The silver dragon ignored him. *I'll be waiting here on the ground, watching for trouble. One sneeze and I'll come up and get you. Two if it's better that I don't. There will be patrols, and there will be people who aren't sleeping. I must divert their attention.*

And then? I couldn't help but ask.

And then we'll slip away and hope no one noticed three cottage-sized dragons roaming around and won't that be a trick, he said sourly.

Before we go, can I know your name? I asked.

He gave me a long look before begrudgingly saying, *I am Liherun of the Silver.*

I am Spara Coldrock of the Purple, rider to Reshatharin, I said formally, And I thank you for your trouble.

He sniffed and looked away as if he was disguising some

kind of emotion. *Thirteenth floor. Nearly the top. Don't get it wrong or we'll really be in trouble.*

That seemed to be a dismissal, and Saugdal took it as such, leaping into the air as carefully and quietly as he could — though no dragon truly flies quietly with all the wind they whip up. He climbed hard, wings flapping with vigor and I counted floors with him as we went.

One, two, three ... it took hardly any time to go to thirteen.

My heart was hammering. I was sure we were going to get caught, but there was nothing for it now. We had to try. Grimacing as Saugdal grabbed hold of the lip of the corridor and leaned forward, I scrambled down awkwardly from the saddle.

I'll be in the rafters, my friend whispered and I had to swallow as I nodded.

I still had no idea what I'd say, or what I'd do.

The Dominar's personal chambers are down that hall, but a long way down and through a series of twists and turns, Liherun warned from below. *You'll know the one. It has a fancy door and is guarded day and night.*

Great. I still had no idea what I'd say to the Dominar's guards. And I had no idea what the Dominar would say when he realized I'd shown up at his bedroom door with the cure he asked me to bring. The whole thing made my mouth dry.

The corridor was wide enough for a dragon to easily pass and candles were lit in lamps at intervals down the length of it between the many tall doors. Everything was beautifully carved with intertwining figures of dragons and whoever had done the work had a sense of humor for while some of the dragons were fierce and proud, others in the design winked at you or stuck out their tongues.

What worried me was not the opulent palace, though. What worried me was how silent it was. I did not see a single soul as I crept forward, nor did I hear a sound. Not the scuttling of mice or the creak of a floorboard.

This place is made of magic and stone, Spara, it's not going to creak, Saugdal reminded me. *Also, be careful with how you think. You're broadcasting your thoughts and if there is a dragon nearby they'll hear you.*

They'd hear me? Well that made my heart race because I had no idea how to not broadcast thoughts I wasn't planning to broadcast in the first place. Plus, it was still creepy that it was so quiet.

It's the middle of the night, Liherun reminded me. *People are sleeping.*

A good explanation, but even so, a palace like this must have servants up even at night. The staff at Dragon School had a night shift. I've taken it once or twice, handling tasks that can't wait for morning or just staying up to keep the ovens banked or to offer food and water to late arriving dragons. This quiet didn't sit right to me.

The way to keep from broadcasting your thoughts is to think of us specifically when you're trying to talk to us, Imybram cut in. *And the rest of the time, think quietly.*

How was I supposed to *think* quietly?

A thought that sounded like a sigh came from Saugdal.

Great. I was disappointing my allies. I needed to get it together. Think quietly, Spara. Think quietly.

Panza wants to know what's holding things up, Ryfsmae said. *She says to get on with it.*

I was sure she did. But it wasn't Panza creeping down an empty hall with tingles going up and down her spine and no idea how to keep her thoughts quiet.

When I reached the first turning, I slid up to the corner and peered around it first. Still nothing. I turned down the corridor. It didn't branch yet, so it was safe enough to keep following it.

The corridor turned twice more, never varying in decoration or silence down its full length. On the third turning, when I looked around the corner, I finally saw someone living.

Two men in silver armor stood guard with a silver dragon beside each. They bracketed a massive doorway, and carved on each of the closed double doors was the crown of the Dominion — that terrible crown and mask contraption that at one time hid the Dominar's face from any who would wish to see it. These days, the Dominar just wore a simple circlet. I wondered where they'd stashed the other one. In a vault somewhere, probably. It made me shiver just thinking about it.

These were clearly the Dominar's apartments.

I drew back around the corner and tried to think. Should I just march right up to the guard and tell them who I was?

Yes! Saugdal said. *Or better yet, tell their dragons.*

I had a bad feeling about that and I couldn't say why.

A bad feeling about what?

A bad feeling about just marching up to the Dominar's guards and telling them I was here to see him.

Wait.

Who just asked me that?

I did, a sleepy voice in my head said. *And now I want to know why you're here to speak to the Dominar's guards.*

But the end of the statement the voice had gone from sleepy to alert. I froze, eyes flicking all around me looking for the speaker. It was certainly a dragon and it was certainly speaking to me.

She broadcasted, Imybram said and it sounded like a groan.

Do you know who this is? I asked my friends in my mind.

No one answered, which was concerning all by itself. Had I broadcasted so loudly that the Dominar's dragon guards heard me, too?

I held my breath, watching, but the dragons around the

corner didn't so much as twitch and neither one spoke in my mind. I bit my lip.

Come speak to me, little intruder, the new voice said. *Come speak to me or I'll tell them you're here.*

I froze. This could not be good.

I will give you to the count of five.

One.

CHAPTER 12

Two.

But where was he?

I am in the door across from you. Three.

To get there, I'd have to slip right across the hall where the guards could hear me! I'd be caught.

I'll distract them. Just trust me enough to run right ... now. Four.

I didn't trust him at all, but there was nothing for it. I gathered in a deep breath, took one last glance at the guards, who were suddenly looking in the opposite direction, and dashed silently across the hall to the huge door there. I opened it and slipped inside closing the door silently behind me just as the voice said, *Five.*

"I'm here," I whispered, turning slowly.

And there, before me, was a huge jet black dragon gleaming in the bright moonlight that spilled from the open wall on the side of the room. This wall didn't have so much as a lip for safety, it just opened wide to the crisp night air and in the far distance I saw the thousands of tournament fires glowing in the valley like a river of lava.

I had cleaned dragon cotes all my life, but I'd never seen one like this.

This dragon sat on a tufted velvet feather bed and his dish of water was made of burnished bronze and decorated with curling interlinked dragon tails. I could easily believe this was a king of dragons were it not for his color. He was not a silver. Silvers lived and died to defend the Dominar — as free as I had been in my choices as a young person — they could go, but if they did they could never come back and there was no other way into being one of the Dominar's elite guard except being born silver. No, this dragon was a simple black dragon, just like Saugdal. Just like hundreds of others I'd seen come and go at Dragon School.

It had to be Tagermet, didn't it? But why did people think he was missing when he was right here in his cote?

Now, what are you, little intruder? A young human with an injured wing.

"I'm Spara Coldrock," I whispered. "Rider of Reshatharin of the Purple."

And able to speak to dragons, hmm?

He didn't sound surprised.

"I need to see the Dominar. He's expecting me," I whispered more loudly. "It's very urgent."

What does a human with a broken wing need urgently with the Dominar? The dragon tilted his head so I could see one eye glittering in the moonlight. *Perhaps she comes to lay some wrong at his feet? Perhaps she comes to take her vengeance?*

"Of course not!" I whispered, hesitating only a moment before adding. "He asked me to complete a task for him and I have done it and now I must give him the result. And now that I'm so close I can't afford this delay."

You will *afford it or you'll find a greater delay when you're rotting in one of the Dominions lovely sky prisons. All it would take is a single cry from me and your future would be forfeit.*

I supposed it made sense that the Dominar's dragon would be protective of him. But I took a deep breath. I was getting quite sick of threats. I wished everyone could just be a bit more creative in how they got what they wanted. It was grating on my patience.

I pulled myself up to my full height and looked the dragon in the eye.

"I don't know who you are, or what your position here is," I said coolly, though it wasn't quite true as I was pretty sure this was Tagermet. I spoke at full volume, it's hard to be tough when you're whispering, "but what I have could mean life or death to the Dominar and I plan to get it to him. Tonight. And no one will stop me."

The dragon tilted his head, a little gust of what seemed to be a laugh escaping him.

Really, is that so? You mean him no harm and want only to help? And you come now, on this day of all days?

"Yes," I said a little warily. What did he mean by 'this day of all days?'

Then go through the door and tell him yourself, the dragon said easily, nodding to a door that seemed to link his chamber to the one beside it.

I looked from him to the door and back again.

What? You'd hesitate now when you've just told me that the situation is so dire? There was a mocking note to his voice, but this felt too easy. It couldn't be so simple as this dragon just handing me exactly what I wished for with no difficulty at all, could it?

His dragon grin grew as he watched me struggling to accept that he might be helping me. But I'd come all this way through fire and fear, imprisonment, injury, terror and enemies on every side, and what? Was I going to turn back now because a dragon *smiled at me*?

Not likely.

With a deep breath for courage, I spun on my heel, hurried to adjoining door, and wrenched it open.

The room beyond was shadowed and dark. Moonlight

spilled across the floor in long lines from narrow windows not large enough for a dragon to enter, though plenty large enough for a man.

On either side of each of them, filmy curtains danced in the breeze, making the shadows shift constantly and intensifying the difficulty of making out the furnishings of the large room. There were a few wardrobes and tables. Vases and books and small chests were placed on them. One shadow was a desk with an ink pot and a paperweight shaped like something vaguely animal that I couldn't make out in the sharp shifting shadow-and-light of the room.

There were no guards at the door — not on this side of it at any rate — and I held my breath listening for anyone else breathing. There was only the sound of one other, and he breathed long and slow and deep like a dreamer.

In the center of everything, placed just in front of the windows was a wide bed, and it was from that bed that the breathing came, from the figure curled on his side and swathed in patterned blankets.

I frowned when I watched him, though, because while his size and shape were right for Alexandrie, Dominar of all the Dominion, he was wearing the old Dominar's crown — the one that covered the face with a mask. And that couldn't be right, could it?

The Dominar, when I had met him, had worn only a circlet. And who would wear that terrible crown to sleep? It looked incredibly uncomfortable.

Cautiously, I slipped across the floor.

It was so covered in overlapping rugs that my footfalls were entirely masked and there was no sound but the Dominar's breathing as I found his side, reached down, and placed a hand on his shoulder.

His hand flew up so suddenly that it was all I could do not to scream, and then he had used his grip on it to flip me, and I sailed through the air and landed on my back on the bed, my hand pinned all the while in his grip.

When I blinked away the sudden stars filling my vision, the man looming over me had lost the mask and crown, was rumpled from sleep and frowning down on me.

He was not the Dominar.

CHAPTER 13

"WHAT DO WE HAVE HERE, Kirdval? What is this little mouse doing creeping creeping into the Dominar's very bedroom?"

I glanced to the side and saw the silver head of the dragon from the adjoining room thrust though the door. He must be Kirdval. But he didn't speak to his rider, he just looked at me with a cocked brow. In the moonlight he drew a claw down one foreleg and I gasped. The black paint scratched away where his claw had been and under it his scales were gold.

You aren't the only one who can paint dragons, little mousey.

There was a strangled cry in my mind and then a frantic call from Imybram.

Spara, get out of there! Get ou—

His words cut off and I gasped in a horrified breath as the man's hand slammed over my mouth.

"I don't know why you're here, girl, and I don't know what you want, but you're in big trouble now."

He grabbed me and dragged me to my feet by my hair, his hand never leaving my mouth. He marched me toward a second adjoining door, releasing my hair and dragging my good hand behind my back to pin it there. He ignored my bad hand as I batted and swiped at him, tears of frustration and fear filling my welling eyes.

Saugdal? I called. Ryfsmae?

But there was no response.

"This mouse has a broken tooth, I see," my captor growled. "A pity. You won't like it when we break the other one."

And then we were through the door and into a receiving room.

He flung me hard to the floor. The ground came up and caught my chin, stunning me for a moment, but not before I saw it was a room lavishly decorated with small sofas, tufted pillows, tall slender vases and elaborate lamps. The grate in the fireplace was lit here and it had burned down to embers, leaving a dull light in the room.

I was just levering myself up when my shoulder flared with blinding pain and I went spinning across the floor. Kicked, I thought. And this time, I didn't try to get up again. Not yet. Not until I had a plan.

Above me, the man who had been wearing the Dominar's crown loomed, his attention temporarily arrested by a figure coming from an adjoining room.

"What's this?" The other man said. He wasn't dressed for sleeping. And I knew him. My body went cold so quickly that I feared I might pass out. "Torturing the staff, Yulden? Could you keep your grudges down a little? I wouldn't mind my sleep."

I didn't believe he had been sleeping. I didn't believe that Jhairen Que'Shal ever slept. But what was he doing here and where was the Dominar?

"I caught someone sneaking into Alexandrie's rooms," my captor said.

"You're going to have to stop referring to someone else as 'Alexandrie' when that is now your name," Jhairen Que'Shal said coolly. "Or have you decided you are no longer willing to play our great game of crowns and power?"

"I'm willing," the man — Yulden — said in a hurried croak. "I'm more than willing. But we'll need to dispose of this one. She saw me without the mask."

If I had felt chilled before, I was frozen now. This man — whoever he was — was posing as the Dominar, wearing that old crown that made it impossible to tell who was behind it, and in league with both a gold dragon and Jhairen Que'Shal who hated all dragons. Or perhaps, just all dragons who had not bent the knee to *him*. After all, I'd seen him riding a gold dragon, hadn't I?

"Is she staff here?"

"No," Yulden said. "I've never seen her before. She was just there in my room while I slept."

"A lover?"

"Perhaps. Alexandrie never mentioned a lover," Yulden said uncertainly.

Jhairen laughed. "If he never mentioned one ... ever... in your entire fifteen year friendship, then I'd say he has been keeping his lovers cleverly hidden from you."

"Then she must be one of them," Yulden said with distaste. "I could ask her."

"She will only lie to you. Throw her in with your best friend and we'll deal with them tomorrow. Perhaps she'll comfort him in his last hours on this earth," Jhairen laughed a little cruelly. He still hadn't seen my face and with what little hope I had left, I hoped he never would. "There is other chaos in the palace tonight. I just received word of rogue dragons. You will need to tighten your grip on the guard. There must be no more slips, no more sneaking little fools walking in on you sleeping, no more chances of exposure. You know what is at stake if you fail in this. We have spared your beloved gold dragons because you promised they could be put under the yoke. If it turns our our trust was misplaced we will be forced to rectify that mistake."

"That will not be necessary," Yulden said, white-faced.

I stared at him, and I saw nothing of a Dominar there. He looked very young and very small before Jhairen Que'Shal — who was not all that old but carried with him a great attitude of authority.

"Lock her up," Jhairen Que'Shal said. "And tell that useless dragon of yours not to let anyone else slip through his door or my medusas will be happy to escort him to the same end as all the others of his kind."

"Not necessary," Yulden gritted out again and then Jhairen Que'Shal marched out of the room and Yulden dragged me up roughly to my feet. I opened my mouth to speak and he struck me hard across the mouth.

I cried out, cupping my jaw with my good hand. My mouth was full of blood and my head rang with pain. I spat it on the floor and he cursed, striking me a second time, this time on the cheek. I glanced up and I couldn't help it. I cowered away from his raised hand, afraid of being cuffed again.

"That's what you get for sneaking up on me," he said, trembling from head to toe, but I knew it wasn't that.

I'd embarrassed him because he hadn't known who I was and he thought he was closer to the Dominar than that. His best friend. What an absolutely terrible friend he was.

I shivered.

That seemed to satisfy him. He grabbed me roughly by the arm and marched me to another door out of the suite of rooms. This one was very small — a closet almost — but I recognized it as being for a valet. I'd heard of staff who slept close to those they served to attend night time needs or early morning wakings. This one had been gutted of any furniture other than a cot — which barely fit in the tiny room as it was — and another of those tall man-wide windows.

On the cot was a huddle of ruined blankets.

"You've been keeping secrets, Alexandrie. Too many of them by far," Yuldren said, spitting each word.

He threw me roughly and I hit the cot with a painful thump at the same time that the door slammed shut and the lock snicked in place.

Underneath me, someone moaned.

CHAPTER 14

I SCRAMBLED off the heap of blankets as quickly as I could. My head was still ringing, my vision still not quite right and my face *hurt* but I could move. My shoulder ached where I'd been thrown to the ground. I quickly assessed my body. I had no broken bones, no broken teeth, and the bleeding in my mouth had slowed. That was a mercy, at least. My many healing arrow wounds still ached, but none of them had burst open again.

Through the moonlight pouring in from the tall window, I shuffled out of the way of the other person on the cot and pulled back the blanket where a face should be.

The moment I caught sight of the face, I dropped the blanket, my good hand flying to my mouth.

I had expected the Dominar. After all, my captors had plainly told me that that was who I'd be joining. And this might be the Dominar. He was a man of about the same age, I thought. About the same hair and skin coloring, if the moonlight wasn't deceiving me. But this poor man was a mass of bruises from his shirtless torso to his bare head, his face so swollen that I would not have recognized him if he were my brother.

I sucked in a shuddering breath and slowly drew my hand from my mouth.

The man laughed … maybe … a long, hoarse rasping laugh.

"I look that good, do I?" he asked between ragged coughs. He struggled, seeming to be trying to lift his head, and then collapsed against the thin cot again.

He spoke with the Dominar's voice. I had no doubt it was him. But this was not a man who could make everything right. This was not a man who could unite me with my dragon again or restore us to legality, or toss these invaders from our land, or do any of the things we desperately needed him to do. This was a poor soul so terribly ruined by his enemies that I did not doubt them when they said that tomorrow he would die.

"My lord Dominar," I gasped.

"Alexandrie will do, I think," he rasped. "I do not know if I am Dominar now. And I certainly will not be Dominar by morning. They beat me this way intentionally. When I'm found dead, no one will be the wiser and when my dear friend Yulden takes my place as Dominar, masked and crowned, there will be no one to deny it is me."

"That's certainly their plan," I said miserably. Because that was also their plan for me — minus taking my place. And I was not ready to die. Not when my dragon was still at risk. I'd made the wrong decision coming here. I should have gone after Reshatharin while I could.

"Don't look so miserable," Alexandrie said wryly. "We still have options. We could fling ourselves from this tower before they arrive to do it for us."

I did not find that very funny. And his choking laugh was not convincing me. I blinked back a new set of tears and tried to think.

"Did you come here alone?" he asked me when he was done laughing.

"No, but I've lost contact with my friends," I said aloud while trying again to call to them. Saugdal? Imybram?

There was a sound in my mind like far-away shouting and then a roar and then nothing all over again. I swallowed hard.

"At least we can get you the cure," I said with trembling hands as I drew the packet of herbs out of my inner pocket. I thought, perhaps, that his eyes lit a little at that. "And then if ... when ... we get out of this you won't be dying and you can restore my future so that my dragon doesn't have to die."

"Should have done that from the first," he said with a sigh. He seemed less focused than he had when I first arrived and I wondered if so much talking was draining him. "But I have been too cautious, too secretive, too ambitious and it has cost me."

I didn't bother answering that. Of course it had cost him. It was just a shame that I was having to bear the cost along with him.

There was no water in the room except for a little in the bottom of a cup placed by the side of the cot. Frowning, I dredged the herbs in the water. They were meant to be taken as a tea. I could only hope they'd still help like this.

"I'd better eat them," Alexandrie said when he realized what I was doing. "Soaked in the water."

His words were getting more muddled and I was starting to realize that the struggle for him was that his face was so swollen that it was hard to form words.

"Here, let me help," I said, levering him up to where he could sit propped against me. The darkness was starting to fade to the dullness before dawn and I could just see enough to help him take the softened herbs.

"Maybe I'll get my hands back," he said with a gasp as he finished and I realized he hadn't used them at all. They hung uselessly on either side of him.

Only now that he had the cure in him and my promise had

been fulfilled, did it hit me what was happening. It wasn't just that I was losing my chance at saving both my life and Reshatharin's, but when they killed the Dominar — which they planned to sometime today — then the whole of the Dominion would be taken over by Jhairen Que'Shal and his campaign against dragons and magic would be the law of the land. All the dragons I met up until now, all my friends, all my family would be at risk. They might be killed. And all because we'd lose this one man I hardly knew — Alexandrie, Dominar.

I swallowed against a growing dullness in my chest and tried to lay him down on the cot again. His breathing — if anything — was rougher than before, as if we'd made things worse rather than better. I needed to find him a way out and fast. Carefully, I edged toward the open window and let the cool air wash over me as I called out again.

Imybram?

Saugdal?

Ryfsmae?

Liherun? Anyone?

But there was no answer. The window was wide. Not wide enough for a dragon to go through or even find a solid perch, but if a person was brave, they could jump right out the window and possibly a dragon could catch them. If that dragon were very bold. And a very good flyer.

I swallowed. No one was going to do that. Anyone who might have was fleeing for their own lives right now or captured. Or worse. I tried not to think about worse. I was missing Reshatharin terribly and thinking about him was not helping at all.

I looked at the faraway valley and it's faint fire glow and I hoped that out there somewhere Krullmark had been able to find my dragon and free him. Maybe Reshatharin would get lucky a third time and find a second rider willing to try to keep him alive after I died. Maybe she would ride him beside Krullmark and Ursijek. The thought both comforted and pained me, but I wanted them to be okay — all of them.

I was sinking deeper into despair when a flash of light blinded my eyes. I blinked, turning my face, but the light seemed to follow me.

Ridiculous.

The sun was only just rising, a bare edge of gold across the horizon. What was reflecting it so hard into my eyes? I scanned the city below, looking and then there it was again, another flash reflected right into my eyes. This time, I was able to narrow in on the culprit. A small mirror, if I were guessing correctly. It flashed in what felt like a pattern, though of course I couldn't read the pattern.

But it jogged a memory in my mind. Wasn't this what Panza Boldbrewer had been trying to attempt? Communication from far away using a code? And here I was with that mirror flashing right in my face.

The gleam stopped for a moment and I squinted out into the growing dawn. Was that ... could that be Ryfsmae clinging to the wall over there? And was that dark lump on his back Panza?

I tried to squint but they shrunk from sight as a pair of silver dragons flew by with their riders clearly searching below for signs of some enemy.

I hoped hard that Saugdal and Imybram hadn't been captured. I didn't trust Jhairen Que'Shal with anyone in his custody.

There were silver dragons in the air *everywhere* in twos and threes scanning the city, the sky, and the plains beyond, looking for a threat. I already wished I'd gone directly to them to plead my case, but even if I had, and they'd brought me to the Dominar, it would have been Yulden, not Alexandrie, and our Dominar still would't have his cure.

Frustrated, I bit my lip, but the gleam of light hit me in the face again and then immediately hit a spot on the ground below. Face, ground. Face, ground.

They were trying to communicate with me. I was certain of it. They wanted me to get to the ground somehow. And then what? There would only be Ryfsmae — already on the small side — left to carry the three of us and Panza and she was already too large for him.

I wanted to call to him and ask for an explanation. But he wouldn't be talking to me if he could speak to my mind right now, would he?

Behind me, the Dominar moaned and I heard voices on the other side of the wall.

They were coming for us.

I bit my lip as my heart sped up.

What should I do? I couldn't just sit here and wait for them to kill us both. I had to try something. Anything.

"Lord Dominar," I whispered, hurrying to him.

"Alexandrie," he corrected.

"Alexandrie?" I whispered, "Can you trust me?"

It was the same question Saugdal had asked me so recently. The same question Reshatharin had asked me originally. And he was going to have to answer yes or we were both dead.

"Yes," he whispered as I dragged him up to his feet, draping him over me like a cloak. I could barely hold his weight, but I was going to have to.

I thought I knew what Ryfsmae was telling me. I thought I did. But there was a chance I was wrong, and if I was wrong then I was about to kill us both.

A key rattled in the lock and I whispered.

"Hold tight to me."

And then I walked us to the window, one agonizing step at a time while the weakened, battered Dominar clung to me like a small child.

I hoped I wasn't wrong. I hoped I wasn't crazy.

"Please be right, please be right," I whispered as I edged to the window.

"Right about what?" Alexandrie asked thickly.

I moved him to my bad side and clung him against me with my bad arm. If I was right ... oh I hoped I was! ... then I was going to need my good arm to catch.

"Trust me," I said one last time, and then as the door opened, I threw us both out the window.

I caught a glimpse of Yulden's horrified face and then he was gone.

We fell like stones.

I fought as hard as I could to hold onto the Dominar and not to scream and to my surprise, Alexandrie didn't scream either, though I felt his arms wrap more tightly around me. I thought he was murmuring a prayer.

And then, with a sudden jolt that knocked the breath out of me, something caught us. An arm grabbed hold of me as I started to slide over the edge, and after a desperate scramble for balance we were seated just in front of Panza on Ryfsmae's back as the poor tiny dragon careened wildly toward the city below.

"I told you there was a good purpose for the communications system," Panza said smugly.

And I didn't care that I didn't agree with her on new technology. I could have hugged her right there.

DRAGON LEGACY

EPISODE SIX: REUNION

CHAPTER 1

WE FELL TOWARD THE GROUND, my heart in my throat, my knees gripping the sides of Ryfsmae as hard as I could make them squeeze.

Seriously, you're going to break me in half. I'll pop like a grape under a foot.

He was exaggerating, of course, but even if he wasn't, I wouldn't be able to let up my grip. I was so scared that my lungs were growing raw from my breath sawing in and out like Cook Garlin cutting a side of beef with her tiny bone saw.

I held the Dominar clutched tightly to my chest with both arms. He was in a full swoon, not able to stay on Ryfsmae's back on his own, even if he were flying in a gentle straight line and not diving like some kind of insane eagle.

Eagles have nothing on me!

Panza had my belt in one hand and I didn't even know what in the other — certainly not the reins. Ryfsmae was the one choosing our path.

Humans aren't fast enough in moments like this, he said, as he swooped so close to a shop below that the thatch blew off as we passed and angry shouts and shrieks filled the air from the nearby street.

I'd never flown over a city. Likely it wouldn't be so terrifying if we weren't fleeing for our lives.

I was sure we were being followed, but I didn't dare risk my balance and grip to turn and look back.

Panza says they're right on our heels. I must fly faster! Ryfsmae sounded delighted. *Of course I am delighted! I've wanted to fly like this over a city for* years.

Tears dried on my cheeks as he flew and not just from the wind. I was panicking and I knew it. Ryfsmae was a small dragon. And there were three of us on his back. And we were being pursued by silver dragons guarding the "Dominar" and black dragons guarding the city. There was no hope of escape.

Have a little confidence. Panza doesn't doubt me.

Well, good for her. I was all doubts right now. Doubts, doubts, and a few doubts for garnish.

You're killing me. Are there other humans as funny as you? Panza never jokes like this.

If only it were a joke!

We flew like a skipping rock over a still pond, veering wildly, bouncing to where Ryfsmae's tail smacked thatched roofs and splashed through fountains, leaving a trail of furious shopkeepers and home owners behind us. There was no way to escape notice like this!

But I also didn't think that any other dragon would be crazy enough to fly like this. We were descending through the tiers of the city so quickly that we were nearly at the wall, and then the real trouble would come because the wall was carefully patrolled by black dragons and I was certain we wouldn't be able to get through the ring of them circling the edge of the city.

I was just about to voice my concern when Ryfsmae's voice cut through my thoughts.

Hold on! This might get tricky!

He rose up suddenly, executed a half-somersault, and then

dove straight down into a square-shaped opening — that went right through the city floor — with a cable and pulley system stretched through it. I ducked low, dragging the Dominar down with me, while behind me Panza cursed as she tried to keep a grip on my belt. The cable nearly took my head off despite ducking and Ryfsmae's hiss of pain told me it had skimmed across one of his wings.

He faltered, loosing his perfect dive and crumpling to one side around his injured wing and for a moment we were in free fall and I saw well enough to see the face of a silver dragon peering through the hole at us. He spouted a burst of flame as human workers screamed and shouted for him to stop. Their precious cargo — and baskets containing people — were attached to that huge cable, being drawn up into the city.

The fire didn't quite reach us, but a wave of heat did and I flinched as Ryfsmae righted himself and his wings caught the air again with a snap like a sail. This time, when we soared downward it was thorough a cloud of smoke and chaos. No one was paying attention to us. Which is why no one saw when Ryfsmae slid under one of the huge descending baskets, clutched the bottom with his feet, wrapped his wings in tight and tucked himself under like a bat.

Climb around to my belly, he ordered.

I looked back at Panza in horror. We were barely holding on as it was — she was strapped in but we weren't, and when Ryfsmae had rolled upside down I'd lost hold of the Dominar and nothing but Panza's quick thinking had kept him from plunging to his death. She had the reins wrapped around his mid-section and clutched in both hands. One of mine was gripping the saddle but as I tried to hold on, my knees slipped in their death grip, the muscles shaking badly. I didn't think I could climb around. Not even if I wasn't already worn and exhausted.

Ryfsmae grunted, realizing our position and then shuffled

and bucked in a way that threw the Dominar and I up and over almost to his belly. With a desperate scramble, I managed to get all the way up and to reach back, grab the Dominar's belt in one hand and heave him toward me.

It wasn't enough. He was still dangling half off the the edge of Ryfsmae's belly and I couldn't drag him further. I could barely hold him where he was. I held on fiercely, my muscles tight and painful, my grip slipping, and then a cursing, furious Panza was there. I was grateful for all her bulk as she clawed the Dominar up to us and tucked him in on Ryfsmae's belly. The dragon's wings folded ever tighter and we were slowly concealed from view.

We were cheek to jowl in the darkness, our gasping breath gusting hot in the tiny space. The only person not exhausted was the Dominar, and he might have been dead. It was impossible to tell in the darkness and the loudness of our breathing.

"Alright," Panza said eventually and a little hoarsely. "We'll rest here for a breath."

We'll rest here all day, Ryfsmae corrected. *I can hold this position until then and this basket isn't moving. They're likely checking for damage from that flame. What a hot head! No one should flame near ropes. Even ones thick as a dragon's leg!*

But we'd be discovered here for sure.

I don't think so. This basket has a thick base. No one will notice us from above and no one will look up this high from below. It was full of some kind of covered goods. No humans. No livestock. It will be a low priority as they sort out this mess.

I didn't find that very comforting. Besides, I didn't believe him that he could hold himself and three humans upside down for an entire day.

"Stop arguing with my dragon," Panza growled in a whisper. "You're making him upset."

I closed my mouth with a snap and tried very hard to

remain motionless and silent as the minutes turned to hours and the little dragon-cave grew closer and tighter and hotter by the hour.

CHAPTER 2

A FEW HOURS — at least — had passed when the Dominar finally woke. It was close to noon, and though we were in shadow, there was still light filtering in through the semi-translucent membrane of Ryfsmae's wings. It stained the little cave with violet light, making it impossible to tell if the Dominar's bruises were any better. His eyes were still slits, swollen nearly shut, and his breath came in a ragged gasp.

His hand reached out like an attacking snake and grasped my arm. I bit back a startled yelp, but his grip was weaker than a child's and he looked terribly weak.

"Where are we?" he rasped.

"In a precarious situation, and I'll thank you to keep your voice down," Panza said dryly, but she was already readying her water skin and she offered it to him as she was still speaking.

The Dominar drank, choking on the water in his haste.

"Slow down," Panza whispered. "I swear, Spara, you've saved a fool of a prisoner."

Wait.

Had I not told her that he was the Dominar?

I knew, Ryfsmae said.

And he hadn't told her, either?

Does it matter? He's not ruling over anything right now.

It definitely mattered! Ryfsmae had better explain to her. Silently. Where it wouldn't make the Dominar upset.

"We're hiding here protected by Panza's dragon," I whispered to the Dominar. "When night falls we'll move. Our enemies are pursuing us as energetically as you'd expect."

"As energetically as ..." Panza's voice trailed off and based on the scowl she directed at me, Ryfsmae was explaining.

"Your hands are working again?" I asked the Dominar, trying to distract from her irritation.

"Not very well," he gasped, drawing them up to where he could see them both and testing the flex of his fingers.

They only responded half the time, I thought, and his features were still so battered that he hardly looked human. Even his hands were bruised and I thought he might have one finger broken. It was crooked in a way that made my stomach lurch.

"We'll try to get you bandages as soon as we can," I promised.

"There's no point." He coughed roughly. "Either I will heal like this or not. A strip or two of cloth will not aid me. But I think my feet may have feeling again, soon. I feel pain in them. The antidote must be effective. At least a little. I still feel ... very strange."

"But it wasn't the poison that did this to your face, was it?" I whispered. "Who beat you like this? Was it your friend?"

"My friend?" He sounded wary, like he was planning to lie to me.

Good luck with that. I already knew.

"Your friend Yulden and his gold dragon. The one he's painted black to look like yours." I saw him flinch but I kept going. We were past the point of secrets. "Where is your dragon, Dominar?"

"Alexandrie," he said firmly, but he coughed again, long and ragged. "You must call me Alexandrie. Surely you see what chaos will descend if anyone believes that the Dominar has been deposed. I will regain my seat again and restore order, but not, I fear, until the worst has passed."

"Where is your dragon?" I repeated. After all, that was the most important question, for who would help the Dominar better than his own boon companion?

Panza, meanwhile, was staring at me with her mouth hanging open. I swallowed. I could see why she was horrified. I was talking to the Dominar like he was just anyone instead of the ruler of our nation. But I'd sacrificed so much for him — my future, my dragon, my friends. And here he was acting like everything was normal. It wasn't normal. It wasn't going to be fine, either. At least, not unless we found a way to make it all better.

"I don't know," he said in a small voice and he swayed, his head hanging low. Just this much conversation was wearing him out. "They took him when they captured the castle and put Yulden in my place. And I do not know where they have taken him."

That last comment was so heart-sad that I had to swallow back a lump in my own throat to keep talking.

"Jhairen Que'Shal did?" I pressed.

He slumped further, not answering my question, nearly swooning. Only one of his hands twitched as if he were trying to make it move.

I thought he'd passed out again, but then he murmured, "I do not know where my Tagermet has gone. I do not know if they are tearing him limb from limb even now without me to protect or shelter him. And I do not know how to turn this around."

I opened my mouth but before I even spoke our entire dragon-cave rumbled as Ryfsmae growled.

"Easy, easy now," Panza murmured, caressing his belly before shooting a warning look at the Dominar.

"*Alexandrie,*" she said, emphasizing his name as if she wished she was using his title. "If you please, you are upsetting my dragon and as he is our shelter at the moment, I do not recommend it."

"Mmmph," the Dominar said, and I took it for agreement, but this time when I tried to speak to him, he didn't even twitch and I thought his consciousness had finally fled.

"Well," Panza whispered eventually, "I think his friend stole his throne. And possibly," here she mouthed the word "murdered" as if she could hide it from Ryfsmae, "his dragon. And with Alexandrie's face all swollen and bruised he's unrecognizable, so this Yulden is going to get away with it. And then what?"

I sighed, rubbing my hand with my face. Things had gone from bad to worse.

"And then Yulden will give Que'Shal what he wants — an end to all dragons and the Dominion pressed under his thumb forever," I said sadly.

Panza nodded. "In that case, we'll have to teach them that the Dominion is more than one man. They can't take our freedom so easily."

No, they can't. Ryfsmae agreed. *And there's not a dragon I've met yet who will agree to this.*

I hoped he was right, but I had a terrible feeling that Jhairen Que'Shal would not have come this far unless he had quite a few dragons on his side and how would we know who they were before it was too late?

CHAPTER 3

THE DOMINAR REMAINED unconscious for the rest of the day. By the time the sun began to descend from its zenith, the lift operators had the baskets sorted out well enough to begin moving them again and we had a very nervous moment when our basket gave a powerful jerk before it began to slowly lower.

I bit my lip with worry as we descended inch by inch and Ryfsmae must have felt my nerves because he whispered in my mind.

Don't worry! I explained everything to Panza and she understands that you are the one of prophecy and on our side no matter that you've stolen away the Dominar and speak to him like an equal.

I was still confused about the prophecy and I was still worried about the Dominar. Despite taking the cure, he still seemed very ill and weak.

He might not be as weak as he seems, Ryfsmae said. *The Dominar is just upset because his dragon is dead. Mourning takes us all in its own way.*

Dead? I froze, shooting a guilty look to Panza. Was I the one who had accidentally let that idea slip? Weren't we trying to hide that from Ryfsmae?

Of course poor Tagermet is likely dead. How else would they have separated him from his rider? No living dragon would allow such a thing.

But though Ryfsmae had said that to reassure me, it only left me with a lump in my throat and pain in my chest, because I'd been separated, first from my beloved Reshatharin and then from Saugdal and Imybram who had tried to help me and what had become of them all? Were any of them dead? All of them? I could hardly breathe.

Try to take a breath. There's nothing you can do for them right now and we're almost to the ground.

I bit my lip and I saw Panza biting her lip, too, her forehead wrinkled in concentration. She must be concocting a plan.

Panza says we'll descend to the ground like any other cargo but that I should flap my wings at the last second, stir the dust and then use that as cover to slip into the river that runs beside the landing basket. It won't be easy. There are guards and officials and so many barges. But I'm going to try. You won't be on my back, though. The moment I flap my wings, you'll tumble out onto the ground and you have to get out of the way of the descending basket and the guards as fast as you can. Meet me downriver.

If I'd had questions, I wouldn't have had them answered. The moment he was finished relaying his message he shifted and then suddenly the dragon belly I'd been resting on all day was gone and I was tumbling through the air and landing hard on the gravel below.

The dust was so thick around me that I coughed hard. I couldn't see the basket or the guards or anything else, but someone else had fallen on my leg and I grabbed at them with my good hand, dragging them with me as I stumbled blindly in what I hoped was the right direction.

I could tell it was the Dominar by the fact that his feet wouldn't move properly and I had to half sling him over me, dragging him every step as I wobbled and tried to run. My good hand held his arm over my shoulder while my bad one desperately tried to brace him against me. It was not a good arrangement, but there was no other way.

By the time we stumbled outward to where the dust was clearer and we could see, everyone was scattered and covered in the same dust so that I couldn't tell the difference between guards or workers or barge operators or anyone else. That camouflage was probably the only thing hiding us from capture.

I held firmly to the Dominar's sleeve and ran toward the water, dodging someone who had lost their footing and someone else who shouted, "Hey!"

The last thing I needed was to try to explain myself to anyone — especially with Alexandrie relying on me. I glanced at his puffy face, worried that this eyes were still closed and he was barely clinging to me.

We reached the bushes along the bank and slid into where it was thickest as Ryfsmae called into my mind.

Success! I'm hidden in the water. I don't think anyone saw me. Stay put until dark and then we'll float the river together.

I suppressed a cough and turned to find the Dominar's battered face just inches from mine.

"Where are we?" he whispered. "Explain yourself."

There was a note of confused panic to his tone. I didn't think he recognized me or his surroundings but I was exhausted, and dusty, and afraid, and I couldn't quite bite back my retort.

"I'm the one that you blackmailed into getting you a cure — which I did. I'm the one who you needed my help to save your life — which I did. And I'm the one who you need me right now to help you escape your friend who wants you dead," I hissed back and I hardly knew why I was so snappish. But the strain of hiding and being hunted and dealing with the

Dominar in this state was too much for me. Especially since he'd forced my hand in this and now hardly seemed to remember enough to clear my name and make me a legal dragon rider like he'd promised. "We're hiding in the long grass and you'd better be quiet or they're going to find us both and do who knows what to us."

He froze, running a hand over his battered face and his expression — so hard to read behind the swelling — seemed to crumple. I knew he was much older than me — in the prime of his life, if I had to guess — but he seemed younger in that moment as if he was looking to me to take care of him and make everything turn out instead of the other way around.

"I'm sorry," I said, guilt flooding me. "I'm so sorry. I'm just scared. And I've lost my dragon, too. And now it feels like none of it was worth it."

"No," he breathed eventually. "I'm the one who must apologize. I could say it was the strain of being poisoned and paralyzed, or the fear of being in this exact situation — powerless and on the run for my life, or I could say it's the trauma of losing Tagermet, but none of that is an excuse. Thank you for your help and for risking yourself for the Dominion."

"Is there anyone we can go to who will recognize you like this," I asked a little uncertainly. "Anyone you can trust?"

"Castelan Midin Abyrynth. Castellan Ki Abadar. Trachan Avatlar, Dragon Rider of the Red, Ystren Bracemender. Raolcan, Dragon of the Purple." He sighed. "But we can reach none of them right now. Not without being caught by Yulden. Subterfuge must be our choice."

"We can't just hide and wait," I whispered urgently. "We need to get rid of Jhairen Que'Shal and Yulden before they kill or enslave every dragon in your Dominion."

He said nothing, but his breath was heavy and I thought he might be working through some deep emotion.

"Alexandrie," I whispered. "Alexandrie! We have to find someone. And quickly."

"Yes," he said shortly. "I'm listening. I must think."

I wanted to snap at him, and push him, and tell him he should have known his friend was going to betray him and he should have done something to stop it and that he'd put us all at risk. But what good would that do? He needed kindness and understanding from me right now. Just like I'd needed that from Krullmark when I'd been the staff girl who stole the dragon and he'd been the one with the big problem of deciding what to do about it.

"We'll get your throne back," I said as gently as I could. "And we will find someone we can trust to help us. If you have no one, then I will call on those I trust."

He collapsed against me. Just talking this much had been too much for him. I caught him and tried to lower him to where he could be propped up against the trees but still remain unseen. I was starting to worry. If the cure was going to work, shouldn't it be doing it by now? And if he was passing out from pain and physical ill, then maybe that's why he couldn't think of a solution or a person to trust. Maybe his brain was too tired and injured to work properly.

Which made this up to me.

Again.

Life had been a lot easier when I was staff — cleaning Dragon School, feeding dragons, and serving tables. My mother had a point when she said life would be simpler and freer staying exactly where I'd been born. But I didn't regret my choice for a moment. Even if it was so much harder.

I looked upstream and though I couldn't see the tents for the tournament, I thought of my mother there, working hard and worrying about me. It would be nice to see her if I could. And maybe she could give me some advice about how to handle difficult children. Like Alexandrie and like me.

When darkness finally fell and the workers went home for the night and the barges tied up until morning, I was exhausted from waiting and being on the alert. So exhausted, that I nearly jumped when Ryfsmae's voice whispered into my mind.

Spara? I have news.

CHAPTER 4

Come out quietly and slip down the side of the nearest barge and I'll find you in the water.

I shook Alexandrie awake and repeated Ryfsmae's instructions. He was wobbly as a new kitten, requiring all my strength to help him stand and then to half-carry him as we snuck down to the bank of the river where the warm evening breeze was stirring the rushes.

"Here," Panza said, looking water-logged and breathless. "Don't ask me about hiding in water up to my neck all day. We'll swim up the river as quietly as possible. Quickly, now."

She dragged us up onto Ryfsmae's back — he was trying to crouch in the shallows, but even with a tied up barge for cover he stood out too much. He must have been hiding in the water, too, because he smelled of algae and had bits of clinging water plants hanging from his ears and wingtips. The silver paint had washed away. He glanced furtively back and forth, but even though he was a small dragon, he overwhelmed the river and cast a long shadow.

Panza was right. We needed to hurry.

As soon as Ryfsmae had found the middle of the river and

was swimming with only the top of his back — where we were seated — and his eyes out of the water, Panza passed around her water skin. I helped Alexandrie drink, but as soon as he'd had a drop his head was bobbing again with exhaustion.

"No food, I'm afraid," Panza whispered to me, cloaking the sharp look she shot at the Dominar and the questioning look she aimed at me. I shrugged. I couldn't tell if he was getting worse or not.

Until Panza had mentioned food I hadn't thought of it, but now my stomach growled.

Spara! Ugh! Ryfsmae complained. *Now you're making* me *hungry!*

But other than the single complaint, we slid quietly up the river under the cover of darkness, finally reaching the edge of the camp when the air was beginning to get a bite of cold in it.

Quiet! Quiet! Ryfsmae reminded us as we got closer to where a pair of guards stood watch on either side of the river, fires lit to see intruders better. But as I peered into the darkness, I saw one of the guards was slumped, standing against a tree. He must be asleep on watch. That was a stroke of luck.

Did Ryfsmae see?

I do.

He angled his body and we drifted closer to that shore, passing the fire and the perimeter and sliding into the reeds beyond to where we could clamber up the bank and into the camp.

My heart was in my throat. I'd been so intent on getting to the tournament camp that I hadn't thought about what I'd do once we were there.

Panza says we'll try to make our way to where the Purples are clustered together. If we can find a dragon rider high up in our own color they can speak for us and find support for the Dominar.

And we had to tell someone about Saugdal. And Imybram.

And I didn't know who I should tell. Should I find their riders?

No!

They'd just turn me in. Should I be talking to some other dragon? Since I *could* talk to any dragon I pleased it seemed like maybe I *should* do that.

Why don't you leave that to me? Ryfsmae said.

"Spara," Panza whispered at the same time. "Listen, we might have to ..."

The reeds beside us rustled and then, swelling up from them came two reeking creatures. They swelled up as large as dragons, steaming in the night air, dark and indistinct.

My heart was in my throat, fear slicing through me. I'd never even thought that there might be some kind of river monsters here. And I should have.

I swallowed my scream, trying to see some way out, or even just some way that we could hide Alexandrie while we kept them distracted, but a third monster rose behind us, penning us in on every side. Despair washed over me.

Now what?

Beside me, Alexandrie gave a harsh grunt and Panza made a disapproving sound in the back of her throat.

It only took a second for me to realize why and then relief flooded over me.

These weren't monsters at all. They were dragons — slick with mud and water plants, but dragons all the same. And the laughter coming from the creature riding on the back of one of them told me the next piece of the puzzle. Students. These were students of Dragon School.

"Who goes there?" The nearest one asked, trying and failing to sound formal. There was far too much laughter in that voice.

And it was a voice I recognized.

"Grexin?" I whispered hoarsely. He'd scared the life out of me. "*Initiate* Grexin?"

There was a long beat of silence.

"What are you doing in the mud, Initiates?" Panza snapped, sounding every bit a school teacher at the same time that Ryfsmae asked the dragons, *And who are all of you?*

Badrmo.

Haxajael.

Eyapty.

Their answers bubbled out so quickly that I had a hard time distinguishing one from another.

Greens, Ryfsmae said and it sounded in his mental voice like he was rolling his eyes.

That's right, Badrmo said. *The only color that can liven things up around this dull river bank.*

You're here for a Tournament. There are races and activities all day. It's the most fun you'll ever have and you have to "liven things up?" Ryfsmae rolled his shoulders in irritation.

Our riders are high-spirited, Haxajael protested. *Just out of the egg, basically. We need to run them hard to keep them in line or they'll cause trouble.*

"We're guarding the Dragon School camp, honored Dragon Rider," Grexin said with a snap to his voice and a saucy grin I could only just make out in the dull light from camp.

I saw Panza open her mouth — to snap at them no doubt — but I hurried to speak ahead of her. This was exactly what we needed. Three people and three dragons with a sense of adventure, a willingness to break the rules, and too unimportant to gain any kind of notice. This was better than a camp full of purples.

I flung a hand up.

"Can you help us?" I said in a carrying hiss. "Panza Boldbrewer is a purple dragon rider and she's been helping us, but her dragon is growing tired."

Hey! I ignored Ryfsmae's protest and kept going.

"And we need somewhere to hide this poor man. He was

beaten by the guards for being where he shouldn't be but he was only trying to find his lost dragon."

It was partially true. Enough true that I didn't feel bad about saying it.

"A lost dragon?" Hasten asked from beside Grexin. I remembered he was always hanging around Grexin at Dragon School. Did either of them recognize me as the girl they used to sweet talk into giving them more hot rolls at the table? His dragon — Haxajael — shook like a big dog, spraying mud everywhere and he just managed to get him to stop as he leaned forward, concern filling his face. "Is he going to be alright?"

"We don't know," I said soberly. "But he needs to hide until the trouble passes. And you seem like people good at hiding."

"How did you lose your dragon?" A clear voice asked from behind us and I swiveled to see a mud-drenched girl with a straight back and intense posture on the back of a sheepish looking green dragon.

I remembered her. She had been there on the cliffs applying for Dragon School during my last attempt to be taken in as a student. She must be very talented to already have achieved the rank of Initiate and be allowed around her dragon without supervision — or she was breaking even more rules than the boys.

"Someone took him from me," Alexandrie gritted out. I was grateful that he was conscious enough to answer at all.

Six throats gasped — young humans and young dragons united in horror.

"Well, of course we have to help," Grexin said after a moment.

Of course we have to help, the dragons agreed.

"Good," Panza Sid briskly. "Start by washing this gloop off yourselves and your dragons. You can hardly help us sneak our friend into your tent to hide if you're being scolded by the Grandis for being filthy with mud."

The Initiates shared a long look and then Grexin saluted — an act that almost made me laugh, but I suppressed it well — and they slid into the water to clean themselves while Panza leaned in close and whispered.

"We have to talk. Quickly."

CHAPTER 5

"WE'LL SPLIT UP," Panza whispered, throwing up a hand when I opened my mouth to object.

Alexandrie had fallen into a slumped silence and I didn't know if it were pain, or exhaustion, or just despair leaving him passive while we figured things out, but none of those was a good excuse. He ought to be the one leading. He was the Dominar! How did the fate of the nation rest on the shoulders of one girl and an eccentric purple dragon rider?

"I know, it's a lot to ask to beg you to wait here with him while I go get help, but they'll be looking for him, Spara. And you seem to know these students, don't you?"

I nodded.

"Because you're the staff girl whose mother is looking for her."

My eyes went huge. Had she known all along?

I didn't confirm that. But I didn't need to. Panza's wry expression told me she already knew. She shifted awkwardly in the saddle and then whispered fiercely.

"I'll just come out with it. Something's wrong with this one." She poked Alexandrie in her rough way. He only swayed, not responding or objecting. "Maybe it's the poison. Maybe it's the paralysis he suffered, or his dragon stolen, or something else. I don't know. I'm not a white dragon rider and I'm not devoted to healing. But they'll be looking for him and in order to get help I need to make my way through the camp a little less obviously than with a dead-eyed ruler trailing around behind me. You understand?"

I nodded.

"But someone needs to stay with him. Watch him. Keep him out of trouble until Ryfsmae and I return with help. You're the best one for that job because you know these people and frankly, you look like you could be a student."

I didn't bother to tell her that I'd been rejected from the school four times, or that I still would be staff if Reshatharin hadn't chosen me himself despite every rule that existed.

"But my dragon," I started to say and Panza cut me off with a chopping motion.

"Will have to wait. Again. I'm sorry, but for all that this man seems to be losing himself, we need him or we'll lose the whole of the Dominion, won't we? Ryfsmae has filled me in on everything that Saugdal told him. We know this is true, and you know it's true."

You know it, Spara, Ryfsmae reminded me. I put a hand on his warm back, comforted by his presence. He'd been through a lot rescuing us and staying faithful when we could have died at the hands of our enemies.

I grimaced because Panza was right and I glanced at Alexandrie, wary. Why wasn't he saying anything? How injured was his brain?

"Poisons are like that sometimes," Panza said. "They do things to the mind. On top of that he was beaten very badly. You'll have to take care with him."

"Can you hurry?" I begged her. "Every moment I spend apart from Reshatharin makes me more and more worried for him."

Ryfsmae shifted uncomfortably under me. He must understand.

"We'll do our best," Panza promised. "But you've come this far, Spara. Don't throw it all away now. Keep him safe."

A splash and furtive footsteps told me this conversation was over. The student dragons and their riders were coming out of the river, freshly washed.

"I'm leaving my friends in your care," Panza told them solemnly. "See they're taken care of and not discovered and I will be back for them tomorrow."

The students nodded.

"Promise me you will be faithful in this," Panza pressed while in the background of my mind I heard Ryfsmae charging their dragons with the same responsibility.

"We'll be faithful," the girl Initiate said. Her shoulders straightened even more — which felt impossible. She must have been their ringleader because the others nodded as she spoke.

Wordlessly, I slipped from Ryfsmae's back, drawing the Dominar after me. He let me lead him as if he simply didn't care. I pressed my face against Ryfsmae's side, stealing one last moment of security before he was gone.

I kept losing people. Reshatharin, Krullmark, Saugdal and Imybram, and now Ryfsmae. I wasn't sure I could handle anymore losses. Despite these new dragons and people, I felt very alone.

All will be well, Spara, Ryfsmae said in my mind. *I'll ask about Saugdal and Imybram and find a way to make sure they are safe. And I'll be back before you know it. Panza gets things done.*

That, I believed.

Then trust us now.

And I'd have to. I had no other choice.

We said our last farewells, and then Panza and Ryfsmae slid

into the dark and I grabbed Alexandrie's hand and led him to where the green dragons and their riders waited.

"How did you slip down to the river without getting caught?" I whispered.

"We're masters of deception and disguise!" Hasten said, but the girl rolled her eyes.

"Everyone thought we'd be too tired to sneak out. Besides, the other students are still freaked out about the lights and the ground shaking. They aren't going anywhere and the Grandis thought we'd be the same way. Come on. You can bunk with me and your friend can bunk with the boys. We'll keep you hidden until the dragon rider gets back. She's really something, isn't she? A full dragon rider! And a purple! They're almost as amazing as a green!"

Her dragon nudged her affectionately as she said that and I let my gaze flick from dragon to dragon. They were awfully quiet. Obviously, they didn't know I could speak to them, but I would have thought they would speak to each other. Maybe green dragons were just more quiet in their minds.

We slipped silently back into the camp. It turned out that these students had tents side by side that backed onto the river and their dragons were meant to form part of a protective ring around the camp to keep the students safe.

"Come on," the girl whispered to me as the dragons slipped back into their places in the ring. I heard the ones nearest them grumbling.

You slipped away, Eyapty. Don't think I didn't notice.

Pipe down. I'm sleeping!

But no humans seemed to have noticed and we reached the tents without being caught.

"He needs to stay with me," I hissed, still holding onto Alexandrie's hand.

The girl looked uncomfortable. "We're not supposed to ... fraternize. I have my own tent, but it's supposed to have three girls. It's just that Fressa and Trilida both got the cough and are with the Whites."

"It's the beating," I whispered back. "That's why I have to keep him with me. He's hardly conscious and his mind isn't right. I need to take care of him."

The three students exchanged looks I couldn't read in the faint light of the dying fire outside their tents and then they shrugged.

"We'll give you our extra bedding," Grexin hissed, heading into his tent. When he emerged he had a blanket he thrust at me. "Here you go, Spara."

I gasped. He *had* recognized me.

He leaned in so close that I didn't think anyone else could hear. "You should talk to your mother. She's crazy with worry."

And then he was gone, ducking into his tent with the other boy and leaving me gaping with a blanket in my hands and Alexandrie clutching my hand dully.

Worry knotted my belly. I had more problems here than I expected, but there was nothing I could do about it and now that I was so very close to a safe place to sleep, exhaustion was overwhelming me and making my limbs heavy.

"Come on," the girl whispered, leading us into the tent. She settled us in the pallets that had belonged to her bunkmates and then said, "I'm Shelbren. If you need anything, wake me up."

"Thank you, Shelbren," I whispered. "I'm Spara."

I tried to stay awake as we settled in our beds. Someone should be watching over the Dominar — especially the way he was acting — but within moments I had slipped off to sleep.

I woke what felt like moments later to a voice.

Spara?

CHAPTER 6

I SAT UP WITH A GASP, not recognizing this dragon voice.

Spara? It said again.

I'm here, I tried to say. Who is this?

It's Eyapty, green dragon to Shelbren. It is a wondrous thing that you can hear me.

It was certainly wondrous. But I badly needed my sleep.

I was told to pass a message on to the human who could hear — to Spara — if she came my way and when you told Shelbren your name I thought it must be you.

A message?

It's from Imybram, dragon of the white.

I inhaled sharply. Imybram! I'd been so worried about him.

He tells you that Saugdal, dragon of the gold, was gravely injured and is captured by the enemy. He has gone in search of their riders but he is uncertain that he will be able to communicate the situation to them. He asked that we tell you since you can speak to the humans on his behalf. Saugdal is being held by a man called Jhairen Que'Shal. Does that make sense to you?

It made perfect sense, and it made my blood run cold. But who could I tell and what could we do? Jhairen Que'Shal had seized the Dominion. And I was as powerless against him as all the rest.

Well there's nothing you can do tonight, girl of prophecy. Get your sleep.

I nearly laughed aloud. How was I supposed to do that now that I knew my friend was hurt and in need?

You'll be no good to anyone if you don't rest.

It was sage advice, but I found it hard to follow. My mind raced and worried for at least an hour before I fell into a fitful sleep.

I woke just as dawn was breaking to a pair of eyes staring right into my face.

It was Alexandrie. He clamped a hand over my mouth as I hissed in a breath and then he bent low over me so that he could whisper so quietly that I could barely hear his words.

"I am having a moment of lucidity and I must speak to you while I can. Nod if you understand."

I nodded.

"When Jhairen Que'Shal and Yulden Peaceholder subdued me and took Tagermet, they had with them a strange item. I believe it is this item that has sapped the health and strength of my heart and mind. Most of the time, thought is lost to me."

Well, that explained a lot. It was almost a relief to hear him say it. A magical item that could possibly be reversed or destroyed was easier to believe than that the ruler of the Dominion was falling apart under the strain. I wanted to believe it. Badly.

"You and your dragon are owed a great debt and I will see it paid."

I sighed with the relief of those words.

"But I must beg your help a little longer. I do not know when I will again succumb to the influence of this terrible item — an article I am told is from the days of the Dusk Covenant, a shameful time in our history. I will need your help to persevere through this dreadful curse and to explain to others how it can be broken. "

He sounded so formal. But maybe that's what this was — a formal request from him as Dominar.

"I can do that," I whispered back, matching his gravity, but I knew perfectly well how these things worked out for me. It was unlikely I'd be explaining this to anyone but myself. If my luck ran true, then it would be me breaking this curse. Just like always.

I flushed. That was arrogant, wasn't it? To think that the problems of the world would have to be solved by me. It was just that everything always worked out that way.

"If he can use this on me, he can use it on anyone — everyone, maybe. I don't know the full extent of the item's power."

"Did you see where they kept it?" I hissed back.

"He keeps it on his person," Alexandrie whispered. "A rod about the length of your forearm and as thick as your thumb. It is carved all over with the spiral symbol denoting the Dusk Covenant. It must be destroyed."

I'd add that to the list of impossible things I was trying to do.

"We'll do what we can," I assured him.

He nodded intently and then crawled back into his blankets and when Shelbren woke us a little while later, he was unconscious again and even when he was roused, he seemed to barely know where he was.

"Poor man," Shelbren whispered to me. "He won't survive long with his dragon dead. They told me that no one does."

I felt a little wave of nausea at that. Where was my Reshatharin? He'd been gone for far too long?

We slipped out of the tent into the morning air and I kept a close eye on Alexandrie. He was able to walk on his own today, a lifeless shuffle, but he did not eat when I offered him food and his mind seemed confused.

There was an air of festivity around the proceedings and to my guilty delight, the students of Dragon School embraced me without question, offering me fruit, crispy ham, and fry bread that the Dragon School staff had made that morning over their open fire. I ate heartily, having not been fed in far too long, but I kept the hood of Panza's cloak up when the staff were around and my heart nearly skipped a beat when Cook Garlin bustled through our knot of trainees.

"Eat up! Eat up! There's plenty more where that came from," she trilled, moving too fast for a woman of her bulk as she always did.

I had to blink back sudden tears at the sound of her voice. For most of my life that voice meant it was time to wash up and start passing out food and if I hadn't leapt into Alissi's saddle bag and flown away with her, I could very well be here this morning with a basket of fry bread in *my* hands distributing it to everyone.

Did I miss that? A little, perhaps. I wanted, almost more than anything, to throw myself into Cook Garlin's arms for a hug and to ask her where my mother was, but I held my tongue and kept my head down.

It used to feel like adults could solve any problem — like I could just hand my troubles to them to take for me. But I knew now that was not true. Cook Garlin couldn't save Reshatharin, and the Dominar couldn't save our Dominion, and throwing myself in her comforting arms wouldn't get the job done. I had to stay the course.

Something nudged my arm and I turned to find a dragon snout knocking against my elbow and a large, kind eye looking at me. It was Shelbren's dragon Eyapty.

It's a tournament festival. Be of glad heart. Soon we fly!

I smiled and patted his snout absently. Of course, that solved everything in his mind. I just wished it solved it for me.

Someone gasped and I looked up. Shelbren was staring at

me, while behind her everyone else was still laughing and joking as they ate, occasionally wrestling or performing some clever trick as green trainees are prone to do. But Shelbren was frozen in place, staring at my hand on her dragon's snout.

"Oh, I'm terribly sorry," I said, drawing my hand back. "I didn't think."

Her mouth dropped open. "Last week he tried to bite Grexin."

I shot a wry glance at the gawky trainee who was trying to impress his friends by walking on his hands — he'd already fallen into the sooty dust around the fire twice and he was streaked with black.

"That's unsurprising."

She laughed, but it sounded forced, and I shrunk lower in my cloak to avoid her penetrating looks.

It's hard for humans when they don't know, her dragon said sagely.

When they don't know what?

Everything. They don't know everything. But in this case, she does not know that you are the Clawsinger.

It took every ounce of my will not to turn and stare at him.

It's not my name for you. That purple dragon Ryfsmae came up with it but it's what everyone is saying, all through the camp. The Clawsinger is here — she who can speak to dragons.

It's annoying, a dragon from across the fire said in a put-upon voice. *I'd like to discuss how we're going to win that relay race, not* endlessly *debate if the end of the world is here.*

The end of the world? I thought that maybe my eyes might fall out of my head.

That's the prophecy, isn't it? "Behold, the one who speaks to all dragons comes. She brings in her wake the winds of change and the enemies of dragonkind quake for the end of the earth is near."

That sounded terrifying.

Half of us think so.

And the other half?

Well, we aren't really of the earth, if you know what I mean, the other dragon said and I heard the snorting dragon version of a laugh from where he was standing behind Grexin.

We were called to order by one of the Sworn a short time later and led to a huge clearing in the field for the morning's announcements. Jokes and laughter and cheers were called out from one trainee to another. And I wished I could be light-hearted with them. I wished I could rejoice. But I just kept thinking about the anonymous dragon's words and how it might be me who ruined all of this.

I held tightly to Alexandrie and hoped that saving his life hadn't been the first step down this terrible path. After all, that was the one thing I'd done that might be considered meddling with fate. Well, *one* of the things. Getting him the cure was another one. And deciding to save the life of Alissi's dragon was maybe the first one. Okay, fine. I meddled a lot.

Someone had built a central platform out of storage crates piled up high and as we waited a full dragon rider with gold scarves and decorations mounted the platform and called for attention.

I looked up and looked again and a stab of fear shot through me.

It was Gurenthal Hasclip.

CHAPTER 7

SHE DID NOT APPEAR SO aged or stooped now — that had clearly been a performance for our benefit. I scanned the crowd almost automatically, thinking of Ystren and how the last time I saw Gurenthal Hasclip, rider of the gold, she had been torturing him.

"Dragon Riders, Colors, Sworn, and Initiates," Gurenthal said in a loud, carrying voice. She was addressing every rank of Dragon School. "Before today's Tournament we have a dire announcement and we beg your attention in the fullest."

Behind her, her gold dragon seemed almost smug. He coiled up in a knot like a snake and his tongue flicked out as if he were tasting the festive air.

Around me, the crowd quieted.

"The Tournament of Dragons has been a wonderful testament to the power of the Dominion and the Dominar has charged me to thank you all for your participation."

That got a cheer.

"However, we are pained to announce that in your midst is a pair of escaped criminals." Her tone turned foreboding. "One of them is claiming to be the Dominar himself, claiming to have had his throne stolen and his birthright snatched away. This is a dangerous lie and treasonous and anyone who aids this man is guilty of treason." She paused to let that sink in. "With him, is a dangerous woman who has stolen a dragon and claims to be a dragon rider of the purple. She is young enough to be a student, with dark hair, skin and eyes."

Good thing I hadn't told these students I was a dragon rider. They were looking around wide-eyed but none of them were looking at me.

"Be on the alert," Gurenthal continued, "You will find her without a dragon of her own, but with many terrible lies she will try to fool you with. These two evil doers have killed both men and dragons and must be treated with utmost caution. If you suspect you have seen one of them, you must report them to the Black dragon rider guards immediately so that the proper authorities can deal with the situation."

Shelbren was very carefully not looking at me. Okay, so maybe she suspected.

I dropped Alexandrie's hand as cold flooded over me. We dare not look like a pair right now, but Hasten and Grexin were staring at us with frowns on their faces and I knew that the coincidence of us arriving in their camp the night before was not lost on them, even if we had never made claims to be the Dominar or a dragon rider.

"Anyone found harboring such dangerous people will find their position and rank stripped, their wealth seized, and their families taken in for questioning," Gurenthal continued. There were no cheers this time. Instead, a collective breath was drawn inward. The Dominion was a peaceful place. I'd never before heard of such strict punishment enforced on anyone. "We will be searching through every tent and around every fire. Rest assured, these dangerous people will be found."

She opened her mouth to say more, but to my surprise,

Grandis Childra had mounted the podium and joined Gurenthal Hasclip, and it was she who interrupted in a cheerful, booming voice, "The relay race begins at the blast of the horn. All participating dragons and riders or trainees must assemble in their places and stand ready!"

That got her the cheer I'd expected. It seemed Grandis Childra, for all her sterness at Dragon School, was not interested in tolerating Gurenthal Hasclip for long.

Without further discussion, everyone was scrambling to their places and the entire field fell to a chaos of humans and dragons.

I spun in place, grabbing Alexandrie's hand again.

You're in trouble now, Eyapty said as Shelbren tried to snag his reins and draw him away from me. The look in her eyes was one of torn indecision.

Uh oh.

Who is in trouble? Another dragon voice asked — Haxajael, Hasten's dragon. *Are you in trouble, little purple rider girl?*

I'd never said anything about being a dragon rider of the purple and yet somehow he knew! I swallowed down a gulp of fear.

I can smell purple on you. Smells of arrogance and cunning.

Great.

She's the Clawsinger, you fool! Eyapty said.

Oh! Then she can ride with me, Haxajael said happily.

Eyapty snapped his jaws in irritation and Shelbren let out a little cry of surprise. She had been right beside her dragon's snout.

She's being hunted by that gold rider and her smug dragon, Eyapty said. *And they're looking for two dangerous people. Look, she won't stop clutching at that other one. Anyone who sees them will know exactly who they are.*

That's not good, Haxajael said, his head drooping a little.

Eyapty let out a burst of flame to show his frustration — a very ill-advised thing to do with a crowd scrambling all around him. The flame lit a passing boy's tunic on fire. He shrieked and Shelbren ran forward, smothered the flames, and apologized profusely.

"I don't know what's gotten into him. He's usually so calm," she said as she helped the boy to his feet. He was badly singed but I didn't think he was burned.

I'll take one, then, and you can take the other, Haxajael said as if making a great concession.

We're about to fly a relay race, you sheep's brain! Eyapty snapped. *We're not taking anyone anywhere except our own riders.*

Well that won't work. Look, there are guards heading this way, and I don't want to be the one who lost the Clawsinger. What would other dragons say?

And my heart was in my throat because when I followed his gaze there really were guards headed this way. But between me and them was something much worse.

My mother.

She was frozen in place, a basket of food in her hands and her eyes wide and locked onto my face. I saw the recognition flash across her expression, the relief, and then the growing horror as her eyes flicked from me to Alexandrie and then back again.

I took and unconscious step forward, an apology already on the tip of my tongue, but I was yanked back by Alexandrie and he whispered in my ear. "Don't move."

Fine, I heard Eyapty say. *But this is the last time I do you a favor!*

Think of the glory! Haxajael protested. And then he hopped — one huge dragon leap that made Hasten squeak from his place on Haxajael's back — and he landed beside the Dominar, scooped him up somehow with his snout, and sent him flying through the air to land on his belly in front of Hasten.

"Are you flying with us?" the Initiate asked, a little shakily.

But I didn't hear the response because at that moment the guard surged forward and Eyapty stepped to put himself between the guard and me and there was nothing for it but to leap up onto his saddle in front of Shelbren and hope for the best.

CHAPTER 8

We were in the air in moments. I heard a shout from the ground, but Eyapty and Haxajael were already speeding up to where a cluster of green dragons had formed a kind of a knot.

"What are you doing?" Shelbren hissed at me, her face white with fury. "No wonder they're looking for you. You're making my dragon crazy!"

I swallowed, but I had nothing to say. I *was* making the dragons crazy. I could hear the ripple of voices going through them all and on the edge of it was the same word repeated again and again, *Clawsinger.*

I felt my cheeks flame but what could I possibly say to Shelbren. She'd never believe that I could speak with dragons and that somehow they had a prophecy about me that endeared me to them. If I tried to tell her I would sound like someone who thought the world revolved around them.

"Did you really pretend to be a dragon rider? You know that's a big deal, right? I was there when they wouldn't let you into the school."

I felt my cheeks heat, but I didn't answer that, either. I was collecting a long list of things I didn't want to talk to people about.

"Just hold on and don't get in the way," she said in a frustrated voice. "Our three are supposed to kick off the first leg of the relay and I swear, Spara — or whoever you are — dangerous criminal or not, wanted by the authorities or not, I'll wring your neck myself if you lose this for us!"

We reached the knot of excited Greens — five in total if you counted Eyapty.

The dragon nearest us spouted fire. His rider called out a warning and then a second one flamed, too.

Eyapty seemed just as excited, his muscles tense under us, his posture low. Then the horn sounded through the valley and three of us shot off from the mark while the other two were left behind holding a banner. They must have been marking one of the starting points for the teams because all across the sky other teams of three had launched, leaving two dragons behind them marking their spot just as we had.

Beside us, Haxajael flew with Alexandrie and Hasten on his back. He seemed just as excited as Eyapty, and if I wasn't in a flight for my life, and if I hadn't just glimpsed the horror on my mother's face on the ground, I'd be excited, too.

We flew with speed in a formation of three, flying low to make a turn around a huge ribbon-decorated pole and then ascending back into the heavens. A team of white dragons were right on our flanks, their riders leaning so tightly into their backs that they were practically painted on.

I had no idea what this relay race involved, but we were well on our way out of the valley, racing toward the rising hills nearby and a team ahead of us plunged down into the countryside there and came back up wet and shining in the sun.

The wind was in my hair, Shelbren's excited whoops were in my ears — she'd lost the will to hold a grudge in the excitement of the race — and every sensation was of flying at speed and the exhilaration that came from it.

We dove down to where a platform in the middle of a pond

had been set and I realized why the team ahead of us had been soaking wet as we dipped low, low, low and Shelbren leaned half out of Eyapty's saddle to snatch up a baton from the platform. Eyapty's wings caught the edge of the water, spraying us with the smell of algae and a sharp chill, and then he took off into the air just in time to avoid crashing into the white team on our tail.

There was a moment of confusion — of wings flapping and tails suddenly inches from our faces — and I had to paste myself against Eyapty's neck, my eyes squeezed tight. I panicked for a moment when my good hand couldn't find purchase on anything and my bad hand beat wildly trying to hook something — anything — but then Shelbren grabbed my belt and yanked me back into the seat. I drew in an unsteady breath as my hand finally found a place to hold tight.

"Hold on!" she yelled in my ear while in the background Eyapty's voice was hooting with delight.

We climbed at speed. Eyapty was very fast even with an extra rider.

Fast! Fast! he hooted.

I checked over my shoulder anxiously, but Alexandrie was still on Haxajael's back. Meanwhile, the sky was so full of dragons — near, far, competing, spectating — that I couldn't tell if we were among friends or enemies, so lost was I in the tournament.

They'll never find you like this, Eyapty laughed. *Maybe we should toss you from back to back like that baton!*

It wasn't the worst idea. But I was already dizzy from trying to keep an eye on the Dominar and to keep my seat at the same time, and while I was very safe here on Eyapty's back, I wasn't doing anything useful to save Saugdal, or find Reshatharin, or snatch back our stolen Dominion.

"Just keep flying, just keep flying," I said between gritted teeth.

We were headed out overland in the stream of racing dragons to where the hills thickened and rose to the foothills of the mountains. Ahead, I saw clumps of dragons waiting for us. That was the next stop in the relay, obviously.

The team ahead of us reached their clump, handed off their baton, and a new group of dragons burst away from the others, climbing hard.

Clawsinger, I heard at the edge of my mind as we approached our clump of dragons. *Clawsinger, clawsinger.*

And then Shelbren was passing off our baton, and Eyapty was hooting with glee, and while I was still trying to catch my breath, hands seized me and jerked me from his back to the back of another dragon.

CHAPTER 9

"SHHHH," a familiar voice whispered in my ear as a hand clamped over my mouth. I nearly sagged with relief. "It's me. Krullmark."

But even though he'd identified me he didn't take the hand from my mouth as we dropped away from Eyapty. I reached up, clawing at his hand, but his grip was impossibly strong.

What is this? What's happening? Eyapty asked, spinning around while a frantic Shelbren looked for me. Her eyes grew wide and then she plunged after us, leaving Haxajael with Hasten and Alexandrie behind.

It's a friend, I tried to tell Eyapty, but he had no way to tell Shelbren what was happening.

I bit my lip at the others of her wing — including Haxajael — leapt away in the other direction carrying the Dominar with them.

Haxajael! We need you back, I thought desperately but under the steady thrum of *Clawsinger, Clawsinger,* no one was listening to me.

Finally, I managed to wrench Krullmark's hand from my mouth.

"You big lug!" I spat, not even turning to look at him or see who the dragon we were mounted on was.

"Shelbren!" I called, "we need Hasten and Alexandrie! Please!"

What is she doing? You're supposed to be hiding! The desperate voice of the dragon under me cried. But it was only when Shelbren nodded and wheeled her dragon that I was able to turn, too.

"Krullmark!" I exclaimed, meaning to scold him for ripping me away from Eyapty without hearing what I absolutely couldn't leave the Dominar, but he surprised me by folding me into a huge bear hug. His breathing was ragged with what seemed like relief. I slowed my own breathing to match it.

How could you be angry with someone who seemed so desperately elated to find you again?

"Spara," he breathed, "We thought you were dead."

"We?" I asked hopefully, but when I looked past him there was a stranger with a resigned look on her worn face and behind her a frowning Ystren.

Oh. That "we."

We are Ceopkihn, purple dragon and his dragon rider Emla Spinwell, who you ought to know is the highly honored secret head of the purple dragon riders and who has been begged most prettily by this bear of a human to rescue his friend and his dragons.

Was it a secret if he just told it to people he'd only just met?

How rude of you to mention that.

But really ...

Well, it's not a secret among dragons and since you have thrust yourself into our ranks, you will hear it eventually, so it seemed wise to make it known to you from the start so you could pay Emla her proper respect. No one ever does. Would a bow hurt you? Would respectfully lying prostrate on the ground render you ill unto death?

It would rather spoil the secret.

Hmmph.

But to my relief, we were dashing toward a ripple in the hills below — all of us — where a small creek meandered through the trees. I thought that perhaps it might provide us a little privacy for a moment.

"We thought they'd killed you, or captured you," Krullmark was saying into my hair.

I dragged my thoughts back from speaking to Ceopkihn and back to what was happening right here.

I had to swallow as the emotion in his voice registered. He really did care. He really was worried for me. As I'd been worried for him.

I might have clung to him for a second too long — I saw how Ystren rolled his eyes from behind Emla Spinwell — but I recovered myself and drew back.

"Our dragons?"

He flinched and my heart sank. I nodded miserably. He had not found them. But then why was he here?

Demanding, Ceopkihn scolded. *Rude. Arrogant.*

He could just go on judging me. We'd see what he was like if he ever lost his rider. Ceopkihn sniffed loudly as he folded down onto the ground by the creek and to my enormous relief, Eyapty and Haxajael landed a moment later, both out of breath and panting. All three dragons dropped their heads immediately into the creek, causing a sudden cloud of steam to fill the tiny opening in the forest.

Both Hasten and Shelbren dismounted at once, practically shaking with what I imagined must be fear because they bowed their heads toward Dragon Rider Emla.

Did they know who she was, then? This secret was very poorly guarded.

More likely they have simply realized they are in the presence of a real dragon rider and that they could be in trouble for flying you and your companion around when they are only students.

Oh. I hadn't thought of that. But *I* was a real dragon rider.

Ceopkihn lifted his head for just long enough to give me long dry look before plunging it back into the water.

Sure you are.

"Have you found no sign of them, then?" I asked Krullmark a little desperately.

It wasn't until Emla looked pointedly at my hand that I realized I was clinging to his coat. Flushing, I hurriedly let go.

"We've heard rumors," he said earnestly. "Rumors of not just Reshatharin and Ursijek but also of other dragon prisoners hidden underground in a secret place known only as the warrens."

Behind him Emla hissed with displeasure and this time it was Krullmark's turn to flush.

"My apologies, Dragon Rider," he said to her. "But Spara will find out this secret eventually and she will be more willing to go along with us if she isn't suspicious that we are hiding something."

Not much of an argument since the only reason we've agreed that you should go with us is because this young Magika thinks you have some kind of unique power.

I sighed. It felt like I was forever meeting new people and dragons and having to prove myself all over again. I brought my fist to my chest in a dragon rider salute.

"I am Spara Coldrock, purple dragon rider," I said it with my cheeks burning bright for if anyone knew how little truth there was to those words it would be the head of the purple dragon riders — the only person with any real right to declare someone a full dragon rider.

Emla Spinwell gave me a very long look as she dismounted her dragon.

"Alissi Coldrock I knew, and Reshatharin I knew, but Spara I know not."

"I inherited Reshatharin," I said in a very small voice but I made it firmer when I said, "And I intend to get him back from wherever he is being held with or without your help, and with or without your approval."

She smiled at that. "While I won't agree to call you a dragon rider, I must admit that is admirable. Now, have you brought the Dominar his cure as Krullmark here claims you were busy doing or are you still tied up with that task before you can help us go after your dragon?"

So she *was* going to help us go after our dragons! I was so relieved that it took me a moment to speak.

"I have fulfilled my task, but things didn't go according to plan."

As succinctly as possible, I described what had happened over the last few days, being sure to mention Saugdal and Imybram and how worried I was for all the dragons who had helped us. I hardly even noticed the effect I was having before I glanced at Ystren and saw his mouth wide open in astonishment.

"Dragons can speak to their riders?" he said in shock.

"A secret we prefer to keep among ourselves," Emla told him, her lips forming a hard line. "And up until now, it has only been purples with their riders. That Spara has managed to speak to other dragons ... this is a miracle all its own."

Krullmark was avoiding all our eyes, suddenly very concerned with the buttons on his coat.

"But that is hardly the most significant thing this girl has said. Tell me again, Spara. The Dominar has been overthrown? Enemies occupy the castle and sit upon the throne?"

There was a long line of worry between her brows.

"Yes," I said, letting a little of my own despair leak into my voice.

"Then now is not the time to be rescuing dragons," Emla said, turning to face Krullmark with a severe expression on her face.

"You promised me," Krullmark said, looking up just as fiercely from his buttons. "You gave me your word."

She shook her head irritably. "And I meant it, of course, but the situation has changed. If the Dominar is deposed but living, we must find him, secure his freedom, and give him the opportunity to claim his throne once more before he is killed or spirited so far away that he is beyond our reach."

As she was speaking, I'd taken a quick step forward to grab the man swaying hard and about to pass out, and when she was done, I cleared my throat.

"May I present," I said calmly, "Dominar Alexandrie of our good Dominion, Lord of Sky Cities and Sovereign over all these lands."

CHAPTER 10

EVERYONE FELL SUDDENLY SILENT. Ystren's jaw dropped even further. And I had to suppress a twitch of a smile. I liked surprising the Magika. He always seemed to think he knew everything and it was nice to show him that there were still surprises out there.

"Oh no!" Hasten groaned.

I'd forgotten that he'd been carrying the Dominar without knowing who he was. In fact, in my haste to keep Emla on our side, I'd forgotten about the students altogether. Hasten sank to the ground, covering his face and his dragon nuzzled him with a worried look in his eye.

You're fine, you're fine, I tried to tell Haxajael but I needed to speak to the humans before I could comfort him more.

"The Dominar's no longer poisoned," I said mildly as every eye — even the dragon's eyes — swiveled toward me. "But he is still suffering from the effects of the poison and possibly being influenced by some kind of magic that comes from an artifact given to his enemies by the Bright Continent. It steals the strength of his mind and spirit."

Alexandrie looked up with drifting eyes, barely clutching to consciousness. Would they believe me when he was hardly recognizable?

To my utter relief, Emla looked undaunted.

"Very well," she said firmly. "I see that this is who you say it is."

She did? It wasn't so obvious to me.

She stepped forward, trying to catch the Dominar's eye but he swayed, eyes closed and then collapsed.

Krullmark sprang forward just in time. He caught Alexandrie and lowered him to the ground with a concerned look on his face. And no wonder. He knew as well as I did that only the Dominar could get me out of the trouble I was in, posing to be a dragon rider when I was not, and condemned by the Dominar himself.

"I don't see it," Ystren said, tilting his head from side to side but he was not the one with authority here.

"There are five of us and three dragons," Dragon Rider Emla said, and then aside, "Yes, I'm sorry, Ceopkihn, eight of us. We will simply have to split up. I will take the Dominar somewhere safe where he can be hidden. The rest of you will fly with these trainees to rescue the dragons from where Krullmark thinks they are imprisoned. Yes, I know, you don't feel qualified to fly alone," she said to Shelbren as the girl opened her mouth. "Save your objections. You'll fly under the guidance of Spara Coldrock, *Dragon Rider*," her mouth twisted at the partial truth, but even in saying it aloud we both knew she was legitimizing my claim.

I felt my chest swell just a little and I wished Reshatharin were here with me. There was a hum of approval from the dragons listening and I thought I heard a whisper of *Clawsinger* from Haxajael.

Dragon Rider Emla was still speaking, "Your friend will fly under the guidance of Dragon Rider Krullmark of the Purple. That's sufficient supervision, I would think. One of you will carry the Magika, as well. Three riders are a lot to carry. Two are not even ideal. But you will carry them where they ask and stay with them until they have explored these warrens and ruled out the idea that dragons are hidden there, or — better yet — found and rescued their dragons. I will trust you will act as dragon riders despite your low rank, and that your dragons will prove disciplined and courageous."

Well, she'd struck the right chord. Both dragons and their trainees had their chests puffed out. Shelbren and Hasten shared a wondering look but I could tell they were nervous at this responsibility. Get used to it, was my advice. Once the people in charge started giving you tasks to do for them — no matter how impossible — they just kept handing them out.

"I'll try to send someone to you," Dragon Rider Emla said to Krullmark, looking worried all the while. "As soon as I can. You'll have to sneak through these hills without getting caught since *she*," she pointed at me, "has an arrest order in place. If you need anything and can find a purple dragon rider, you have only to send word to me and I will lend you aid."

I cleared my throat and Emla looked at me.

"The Dominar — Alexandrie." I paused when she turned pale at his name but then I pressed on. "He needs someone nearby he can trust. He has moments when he comes back to us. And moments when ... when he needs extra support. Whatever magic is in that artifact is fighting a war within him, I think. I'm not sure I should leave him."

"Are you saying you don't want to go after your dragon, girl?" Emla asked but I was shaking my head before she finished speaking.

"Of course not," I said with a helpless glance at Alexandrie. He'd come out of his swoon for long enough to have a pained expression on his face. Did he know what we were saying or was he really far away when he looked like that? "But what if he emerges and there's no one he recognizes?"

Emla looked at Ystren and he nodded. "I've read about this artifact, I think, though I don't recall much about it. It turns the heart and mind down a twisting inner path. Especially if they use it against just one person, then the hold is very strong. If they're forced to use it against more people, the effects might dilute."

"Enough that we can get him back?"

Ystren shrugged.

"He will be perfectly safe with me," Emla said firmly. "Go find your dragon."

It took a few moments to sort ourselves out but before I knew it, Ceopkhin was leaping into the air with Dragon Rider Emla and the Dominar on his back and Shelbren was gripping my hand kindly.

"It will be okay, Spara. He's in good hands."

"And we must make haste," Krullmark rumbled from his place up behind Hasten on Haxajael's back.

He gave me an odd look and I realized he'd been quiet the entire time that we'd been discussing the Dominar. Did he think I was abandoning my promises that we'd stick together because I was worried for Alexandrie? I hoped not.

"The entrance to the warrens is a little ways off," Krullmark said, "and we've wasted a lot of time talking here. We need to get to the entrance as quickly as we can — preferably before the relay race is over and our movements are hidden in the chaos of so many dragons moving around. Which means we need to leave immediately." He looked at Shelbren, avoiding my eyes, I thought. "Follow close on our tail and give a yell if there's a problem."

And then he nodded at Hasten and Haxajael leapt into the air, wobbling slightly with three riders, and Eyapty jumped after him.

I let the sensation of cool air rushing by and the feeling of a good dragon under us bring me a moment of relief. It would be fine. We would find Reshatharin. He would be well and happy to see me. And Emla Spinwell would take responsibility for the Dominar. Which was right and fitting. Even if it felt like I was abandoning a child I'd been set to watch.

"I'm sorry I thought you weren't a real Dragon Rider," Shelbren said to me. "We'll find your dragon, don't you worry. Isn't it great to be given such an important mission?"

I nodded, smiling, but I felt anything but excited.

I was worried.

Everything felt wrong and I couldn't even explain why, only that somehow I didn't think I should have left the Dominar.

Stop worrying, Eyapty said, joining his rider's sentiment. *And watch this.*

And then he executed a perfect barrel-roll and all I could think about was holding on.

CHAPTER 11

The entrance to these warrens was much further than Krullmark had made out. In fact, it was well around the edges of the hills we were in and close to where they'd set up a platform to announce the winners of the races and crown the victors.

We hopped and dodged close to the ground, keeping in the shelter of the hills and trees as we made our way to it. If the dragons competing above noticed our crab-like progress, none of them flew down to investigate, but I was still worried. That platform was ringed by gold dragons. And I knew what that meant now.

Traitors.

Possibly all of them.

You can't call all gold dragons traitors. It's rude, Eyapty scolded me and I didn't bother answering back. I hoped I was wrong and he was right.

Above us, the swirl of dragons still filled the sky as the relay race fielded multiple teams in three rounds. I watched them anxiously, listening for any dragon voice that might grow near and alert me to trouble.

"There are supposed to be three laps in total," Shelbren told me a little breathlessly after we hurried across an open area and ducked between the clawing trees again. "I think I've counted two completed."

We were a few jumps behind Haxajael who seemed to be enjoying himself despite the strain of possible discovery.

Well we are *green*, Eyapty said with a roll of his shoulders. *Our whole purpose is adventure and exploration.*

Then they were going to love what came next in these warrens.

They're dragon made, he told me proudly. *Run by dragon magic.*

Dragons had magic?

Of course. You have a lot to learn about dragonkind.

As we drew closer and closer to the platform, I could finally see the door tucked into the hill behind it.

In full view of anyone looking at the platform — which would be everyone. My heart sank.

It was a wide stone door set into the side of a shallow hill — not a mountain or anything even close — just a hill. But it was thick and blocky and if I hadn't been looking for it I wouldn't have noticed it there, for it blended in with the tumbled rocks of the hillside.

I looked from the door to the platform and froze. Gurenthal Hasclip was mounting the stage there, her dragon tucked in to one side of it. But terrifying as that evil dragon rider was, I was more afraid of what she was pointing at in the sky.

A knot of dragons were moving in a direct line from Dominion City. They flew over the competing dragons, high in the air, but even from here I could see the sun reflected off their scales. They were all silver dragons. And in their center rode a man who wore a crown.

Oh no.

"Hurry," I urged Shelbren and we plunged on, following Krullmark.

We still had to circumnavigate about a quarter of the arc around the race. We'd covered only half that when the "Dominar" descended with his silver dragons and took his place on the platform.

Faster, faster, the dragons chanted, but they were on foot, trying to squeeze between trees and scurry under their cover like mice.

Rude.

And we were still so far away!

"It's over," Shelbren said tensely, though there was still a note of pride when she said, "Our team won."

It was very green of her to notice that when we were in the middle of a covert slide through the woods. Her color was going to be proud of how she'd embraced them.

"Look," she whispered. "The Dominar is here to present the crowns. Are you absolutely sure that poor man who was traveling with you was the real Dominar?" She didn't sound sure at all. "Because that one they have looks very real."

I swallowed a lump in my throat. He did look very real.

And now all the dragons were gathering on the field before him, landing singly or in groups, landing with riders laughing or exhausted.

I had a creeping sensation running up my spine. Something wasn't right.

Something beyond this false Dominar and his false crown.

Stop worrying. We're getting close to the door, Eyapty said, but even that was fraught with danger.

We were coming up on the very edge of the forest. We'd have to cross that last section over rocky ground behind the stage. What if we were caught?

The "Dominar" moved to the edge of the platform, a magika on one side of him and a dark figure on the other. As they positioned themselves, the figure ripped a scarf from his face and I was not at all surprised to see it was Jhairen Que'Shal.

I clenched my jaw tightly and tried not to panic.

Ahead of us, Krullmark, Hasten, Ystren, and Haxajael had reached the tree line and stopped, waiting for us.

The Dominar began to speak, and I couldn't help it, I turned my head to watch. Beside him, Jheran Que'Shal lifted a glinting metal rod. My heart sped up so quickly that I could hardly catch my breath.

"Children of our vast Dominion," the man in the Dominar's mask said loudly. "We greet you."

He sounded uncertain. But perhaps it was only because I knew that behind that mask was Yulden, traitor and former friend of the Dominar.

"May our Dominion be great!"

He didn't sound like a Dominar at all. He sounded strange and stilted, and as I watched, the dragons and riders were murmuring to each other.

"Before I honor the winners of this Tournament of Dragons," he went on. The Magika with him must have been amplifying his voice for the crowd. "I must share with you grave news."

We caught up with Krullmark at that exact moment and he gestured for us to draw close. Eyapty put his head practically on top of Haxajael's while Krullmark whispered to us.

"We'll have to cross the open part quickly and hope everyone is focused on the Dominar."

Which meant they'd be looking in our exact direction.

"Maybe we should wait until he's done speaking," I whispered back.

"Our great Dominion has suffered a terrible treachery today!" The "Dominar" said and we all twisted to look at him. He was admitting that? "My very best friend has betrayed me."

My eyes went wide. Wait. Was that not Yulden under that mask?

"He tried to rip away the throne and authority from me and become my master." The Dominar paused. "And dragon riders have helped him."

A gasp went up and then, through the ranks of silver and gold dragons, a pair of guards — silver dragoons, by the look of them — dragged up two battered, filthy people.

I gasped, horrified. It was Emla and the true Dominar. I was nearly sure of it. And yet both had been terribly treated to the point that I wasn't sure anyone else knew who they were.

I lunged forward but a firm hand grabbed my arm, holding me back.

"Spara," Krullmark's voice was rough with emotion. "Spara, we can't."

I spun to look at him and whatever had been between us fell away. His face was torn with some deep emotion but laced all through it was compassion for me.

"Even if you ... care for him ..." he said, stumbling over his words. "You can't run to his rescue. Not like this with students on newly trained dragons. We need to keep going and get help — and particularly our dragons."

"But if everyone knew then they'd rise up and help us," I said, a little desperately. "The valley is full of dragons. I'll tell them all. They'll help us, Krullmark."

"Look!" Ystren exclaimed and we turned to follow his finger pointing at the field.

Shelbren let out a little cry and Hasten cursed. I wanted to cry out, too.

Jhairen Que'Shal was holding up the rod in his hand — the artifact the Dominar had warned against — and a dull light that almost seemed to make everything darker radiated out from it. It swelled out, hanging heavy over the dragons and the crowd and to my horror it seemed to sap the strength from them, causing dragons and humans alike to slow into the same kind of stupor that the Dominar had been in.

"Bow before the Dominar," Jhairen Que'Shal demanded. "Show your submission. All traitors will be punished and their evil driven from our lands."

Only a few dragons and riders seemed able to resist it. They launched into the air and I heard their dragons calling to one another in confusion.

"Now. In the confusion," Krullmark ordered, letting go of my arm and both dragons plunged forward.

For a moment, it took all my effort to grip the saddle but when I turned back to look at the valley I let out a cry of despair.

Yes, the dragons not caught had risen into the air, some with their riders, some without, some with riders hanging from a strap and desperately trying to climb aboard. But at the same time, surrounding the entire Dominion side of the field like a wide cup, Medusas were scrambling into the air by the hundreds.

A sound tore through the air that at first I thought was the earth itself ripping apart, but no ... worse ... it was hundreds of dragons crying out all at once. The very air seemed to be aflame as they spouted fire in outrage or panic or despair.

Calmly! Calm down! One authoritative voice cut through the chaos, but I couldn't make out who it was.

In my distraction, I'd nearly fallen from the saddle and Shelbren had to pull me up with an angry hiss.

"We're nearly there," she said tightly, as if she thought I was running out of strength rather than being distracted by many dragons.

I gritted my teeth and let her drag me as needed into the position she wanted.

Krullmark reached the door first, his dragon skidding to a stop. I followed his horrified gaze backward. Oh no.

Behind us, the dragons unaffected by the rod were engaged in an epic battle against the Medusas, flames spouting in every direction. As I watched, a dragon fell from the sky, four Medusas wrapped around him, their riders swarming over his back to grab his rider, cut the straps, and fling him from the back of his dragon.

The whole world seemed to stop for a moment and I think I screamed, but there was nothing anyone could do. The rider plunged to his death, his dragon, screaming that terrible ripping scream and spouting flame after flame, was dragged to the earth, crushing some of the stupefied riders below in the process, and then dispatched by the riders of the Medusas, no more able to defend himself than a trussed farm animal would be.

"No time! Focus!" Krullmark called, but his voice was lost over the clamor of the battle.

The dragons closest to us plunged out over the stage, uncaring that the black, silver, and gold dragons positioned there snapped and flamed at them. Our direction was the only hope of safety and they rushed toward us like a dragon-laden tide.

CHAPTER 12

THE "DOMINAR" on the stage, Que'Shal, and Gurenthal Hasclip scrambled for their mounts. I tried to track their movements, but Krullmark shouted over the chaos, "Spara!" and I whipped around to see him struggling with the stone door.

The door had scrapes along the edge of the frame and on the ground. Clearly that was from recent use, but there was no path leading to the door through the woods. The only people coming here were flying — mounted on dragons or those terrible Medusas.

Haxajael and Eyapty put their shoulders into it and helped Krullmark wrench the door open, stumbling a little under the pressure.

"Did you bring a lantern?" Ystren yelled, but no one had and there was no time to get one.

One glance behind me ripped an incoherent yell from my mouth. Krullmark followed my panicked gesture — the fleeing dragons were almost upon us and it was clear they planned to follow us into this narrow door.

Without another word, Krullmark leapt onto Haxajael's back.

"Forward, Hasten!" he ordered, and the poor Initiate leaned

forward over the neck of his dragon, speaking frantically to him.

No need for panic, Haxajael protested, but he was wrong. If there was ever a time to panic it was right now.

Ystren leaned over his shoulder, hand raised high. "I can make a light. Steady onward!"

From his palm a light flared, flooding the path before us and washing us all in the white glow. The cavern was two-dragons wide and taller than it was wide. We could only hope we could move quickly enough along it that we weren't overrun by the dragons pressing in from behind us.

"Stay mounted," Krullmark called back over his shoulder, his voice tight with stress. "There may be cliffs inside these caverns!"

And then Haxajael and his riders plunged forward and we plunged into the darkness after them. My good hand clutched at the saddle and Shelbren spoke to me in a way that sounded like her teeth were gritted the whole time.

"Do you know anything about these tunnels?"

"Only rumors," I gasped, risking a look behind us.

There was a roar and a flash of flame and if I wasn't mistaken there were already dragons diving into the darkness behind us.

"We have to go faster!" I called, but my voice was swallowed by the noise.

Faster! I echoed in my mind to the dragons, but though it spurred our dragons on faster, it also seemed to be obeyed by the dragons behind us. They surged forward with added vigor.

Haxajael seemed proud to have the answer to Shelbren's question, though I hardly cared as we scrambled over the rocks and Shelbren and I dodged rocky outcroppings in the darkness to keep from having out heads smashed.

It was said that in the days of the great Amel Leafbrought these underground tunnels moved people and supplies from far distances in a matter of hours, he said. *But even then these warrens were dangerous to navigate and after a series of enemies invaded them it was decided that they were no longer safe and most of the entrances were intentionally collapsed and the sites forgotten.*

But not this one. Thank goodness. Or we would have nowhere to flee.

Not this one, he agreed, as behind us a dragon flared far too close to Eyapty's haunches.

He jumped, nearly losing both Shelbren and me. I couldn't even see light from the entrance behind us. Too many bodies blocked the way.

These tunnels are more than that, though, Haxajael said. Who knew he was such a dragon scholar. *They are build by dragon magic, carved out by ancient dragons who came before us, and maintained by our efforts.*

They were?

All dragons know of them, though few use them these days. Much of the warrens collapsed during the difficulties of the past and our great dragon king Nasataa is only now turning his attention to restoring them.

I thought the dragons had a queen.

The Great Haz'Drazen, he agreed. *But there is also Nasataa.*

He said it like it was the most obvious thing in the world and now was not the time to question him.

It is the perfect place to hide things you don't want found. Especially something large. Like your missing friends.

Then I sure hoped we found them because the more bodies that pressed into the tunnel, the more I began to feel panic. What if there were nothing on the other end and we had to somehow turn around to get out? We would die in here in a press of bodies.

Do try not to panic so much, a voice from behind me said. *It's quite contagious.*

I tried to keep my thoughts to myself after that, though my

fingers grew more and more white-knuckled. As we moved further into the tunnel it widened, sloping steeply downhill. Our dragons loped along the ground faster than a horse could hope to run, and I held on for dear life as Ystren's ball of magic light bobbed with Haxajael's pace.

Many worries flooded my mind and not just the fear that we'd reach a dead end. What if this did lead somewhere? We were woefully unprepared for an adventure like this. Because Shelbren had been racing, she wasn't carrying food, water, or even a blanket. And who knew how long we would need to travel.

What if Reshatharin weren't down here and I lost both him and the Dominar — who it had been my duty to protect? Just thinking of the Dominar as I'd last seen him — beaten and trapped with Emla — made my stomach lurch. They must have been discovered almost immediately after they left us.

The light ahead vanished.

Eyapty gasped, and we dropped — falling what felt like a long way before his wings snapped out, catching the air, and gliding us back upward.

"Skies and Stars," Shelbren breathed a little unsteadily.

But now we could see.

Faint light filled what seemed to be an enormous cavern. It radiated out from a platform hanging high above. Protruding up from the platform stood a tall pillar decorated in glowing, dancing runes and it was from these runes that the light poured in.

I looked down, but I couldn't see the bottom of the cavern in the inky darkness. It could go all the way down to the very center of the earth and I would never know.

My stomach felt like it was full of bats at the thought. Very fitting.

I wish my stomach was full of bats, Eyapty said sadly. *Breakfast was far too long ago.*

How could he be so light-hearted in the middle of this crisis?

It's the best way to be! Eyapty declared as he sped upward toward the platform. Now that my eyes had adjusted to the faint light, I saw two things for certain — first, that our captured dragons were not here, but second, that even this huge dark cavern was quickly filling with dragons and every one of them was racing toward that pillar.

I bit my lip as we rose up toward it.

Haxajael was already crouched beside the jagged pillar, Ystren leaping from his back and rushing toward the glowing glyphs. The moment he touched the pillar, the runes grew brighter and the look on his face was pure ecstasy.

"I think the gateway is still open. We can go through!" He called to Krullmark, whose gaze was focused with concern on Eyapty until we landed beside him.

"I think this pillar links to other pillars in these warrens," Ystren said with glowing eyes, his fingers dancing from rune to rune. "I could possibly move us all from one to another without having to travel the distance between. Yes! Look! And this part of the pillar has no dust on it. Someone has touched this recently! It has to be the way to the dragons."

Tell him that the runes do exactly what he thinks they do and that he has to hurry.

"Ystren," I said as calmly as I could, "the dragons say it does do that and you have to hurry."

"Hurry?" he sounded affronted.

"Unless you think you can transport everyone," I said, tension in my voice.

And at that very moment feet hit the ground beside us and I gasped.

For the dragon that was joining us was not many of the fleeing dragons at all.

It was the gold dragon of Gurenthal Hasclip.

CHAPTER 13

SHE MOVED WITH SHOCKING SPEED. I had just been drawing back from her dragon when he leapt forward, flaming so hard that Ystren tripped backward and fell into Haxajael. But even as her dragon was leaping, Gurenthal stood up in her stirrups and leapt from his back, colliding square with my torso and sending both of us crashing off of Eyapty and onto the hard rocky island.

White stars flickered across my vision and I blinked wildly, trying to get my vision back as pain sliced through my head.

I still hadn't oriented myself when someone dragged me upward by the hair and the sharp bite of something against my neck told me to stay still.

"What do you want?" Krullmark's voice was laced with anxiety.

"Only the girl," Gurenthal said, a note of taunting in her voice.

"What use do you have for a single dragon rider?" he asked and I could hear his voice was moving as he spoke.

"Not one more step, growling bear," Gurenthal warned him as she dragged me backward one step and then another and another. We must be near the very edge of the platform. "Or do you value her so little that you'd watch her die by my hand? I thought not. And now, you'll do what I say, and every dragon in this room will do what *she says* — or was that stupid purple dragon lying when he said you could speak to dragons?"

'What purple dragon?" I gasped.

My vision was coming back slowly, but it was still blurry so that all I saw were glowing splashes of light instead of clear runes. I couldn't make out my friends as anything more than shadows.

"The one whose rider thought she could save her precious *Alexandrie.*"

I gasped.

"The one whose throat I slit like I'll slit yours."

Oh no! Ceopkihn.

Don't believe her! Eyapty said fiercely. *She's lying to hurt you!*

But what if she wasn't? And if he were dead, it was all my fault.

Don't talk like that.

"Now, tell me true, little broken girl. Can you talk to dragons?"

The knife bit deeper and I heard Krullmark hiss. My vision was getting clearer. I could see them now — three dragons crouched low on the platform. Ystren and Krullmark with hands up standing between me and the pillar. The two Initiates crouched low on their dragons, trying to make themselves small.

"Yes," I managed.

"Then tell them to listen to me," she murmured.

"Yes," I said again but the knife bit deeper.

"I don't think you're doing as you were told," Gurenthal said and her tone was almost playful if it hadn't been for the pain in my neck telling me her blade had nicked me more than once. "Let's try that again. Tell the dragons to listen."

Dragons! I called in my head.

Gurenthal's dragon's head whipped up, eyes wide with surprise, and both Eyapty and Haxajael straightened.

"That's better," Gurenthal said silkily. "It was a good try — escape, subversion, whatever you were trying to accomplish here. But it is over now. I will return you to the Dominar. You are, after all, his humble subjects."

And now finally my vision cleared enough that I could see the fear in the eyes of my friends and the distrust in the eyes of the dragons.

Krullmark mouthed the words, "I'm sorry."

But it was not he who was sorry, it was me. Because if Gurenthal took me back now then that would be the end for all these dragons. And it would be the end for Reshtharin who was counting on me to find him and free him. And it would be the end of Krullmark who had sworn to stick by me and of these Initiates who had done so much more for us than any student should ever be required to do.

And honestly, my life wasn't worth all of theirs.

And so I did the only thing I could think to do.

Dragons, I said with my mind. *Please listen. I'm going to need one of you ...*

And I hoped they'd listen. I hoped they'd care. I hoped one of them would be in just the right spot at the right time.

... to catch me.

And then with all my strength, I threw myself backward and took Gurenthal with me — right over the edge and into the blackness below.

And just at the edge of my hearing I heard the voice I'd been missing for all this time.

Spara?

It was Reshatharin.

DRAGON LEGACY

EPISODE SEVEN: SILVER NIGHT

CHAPTER 1

I FELL, arms windmilling through the air, the glow of the island far above disappearing far too quickly. Gurenthal grabbed at me in the air and I felt her hands claw my tunic, my leg, my foot and then she was gone, her panicked cries tumbling away from me.

Help! I called again, just hoping someone was close enough to catch me.

What's wrong? Are you in danger? Reshatharin called, and his voice was so sweet to me. He was alive — though he sounded far away and muffled like he was speaking to me from his sleep. *I'm captured, Spara, not dead.*

Everything is worth it if you're alive, I agreed. And it was. It didn't matter that I would die in a moment — though this drop was very long and I was still falling. And I was so, so icy scared inside.

Your voice sounds strange, he said. *Almost like a dragon voice.*

And then there was a sound like wind — or maybe like bats flying.

So complimentary, a voice in my head said wryly.

A strong dragon paw wrapped around me and caught my fall with a jerk against my ribs and I gasped.

Thank you, I breathed in relief. I blinked back tears of relief, clinging to the scaly paw like a life line. *Oh, thank you!*

What's going on? Who are you thanking? Reshatharin asked. He sounded agitated.

She's thanking me, a cranky sounding Ryfsmae said. *Because I'm the one who caught her when she leapt from that floating island. Again. You need to stop making such a habit of that, Spara. I'm not such a hatchling that I find it fun to catch falling humans at a moment's notice. It's hard work.*

I clutched at his paw, eyes closed, catching my racing breath. I didn't want to think about Gurenthal still falling in the dark.

"Spara?" Panza called down. "Are you unhurt?"

"I think so," I called back, a little unsteadily, feeling at my neck where Gurenthal's knife nicked me. It came away wet but it felt no wound there. The cut must be very small. "I think I'm fine. But Panza, my dragon is here somewhere! Reshatharin."

"Where?" she asked.

Where? Ryfsmae and I repeated together. I couldn't quite help that my heart was beating so quickly. After all, I thought I'd lost him. It felt too good to be true that he would be alive.

No faith, Reshatharin scolded. *Of course I wouldn't just die on you. Don't be so silly.*

But he had disappeared. Days ago.

I was captured. I'm ... on a floor, I think. With other dragons.

"I think they're on the floor," I called to Panza.

Ryfsmae descended, slowly. His wings fanned out to catch the air blocked my view of the light from the platform above.

"I think I have a lantern here somewhere," Panza muttered. Above me, things clinked and clattered as she looked. She must have recovered her huge equipment bags.

I'd forgotten how heavy those are, Ryfsmae said wryly.

Are you okay down there? Eyapty called from above. He

sounded panicked. *Only, the humans are very upset, and they can't hear you like we can. We're looking for a purple to tell them.*

I'm fine! I called back. And Reshatharin was right. My mental voice had changed to sound like a dragon's.

He was silent during this exchange — which was very odd for him.

Reshatharin? Are you still there.

Spara. He sounded a little upset. *Spara … are you talking to other dragons?*

Yes!

The silence spun out. Was he … upset about that?

She's the Clawsinger, Ryfsmae said smugly. *And stop being so uppity just because you have to share her now. Selfish much?*

Was that why he was upset?

Of course it is, Reshatharin said and he sounded … panicked?

Panza finally got her lantern alight and held it up. She was just in time. We had nearly reached the bottom of the cavern and as her light fell across it, I gasped. There, on the floor, were what had to be a hundred dragons, all asleep, laying one across the other like a heap of snakes. Only one had his head lifted. His sleepy eye found me and glittered in the reflected light of the lantern.

Spara. Sparrow. He sounded like he was sighing.

And I sighed, too, as Ryfsmae altered his angle just slightly, and then opened his paw so I could squirm out and drop onto the back of the nearest dragon and run to Reshatharin.

I threw my arms around his neck and let out an almost-sob, almost-sigh. He was here. At last.

I barely even heard Ryfsmae scolding Reshatharin. *Oh, don't look at me like that, you big lug. You owe me so much. I've saved her life twice now* and *helped her get her cure to that little Dominar of hers. You'll be paying in sheep for years to make up for this.*

Reshatharin's grumble sounded almost like a growl.

"Tell your dragon to behave," Panza said absently, slipping down from Ryfsmae's back to the heap of dragons and prodding the nearest one.

But I wasn't paying attention. I'd wrapped my arms around Reshatharin, breathing in his sulfury scent.

"It's you. It's really you."

Of course it's me, he said, sounding put out. *I am not the one who has been running around on adventures with other dragons while* you *were asleep.*

"You were asleep? For how long?" I asked.

A few hours? I do not know. I had been hunting. The deer were very tasty. And then a pair of gold dragons dropped out of nowhere and pinned me to the ground. It was very rude of them. And you sounded like you were in trouble and I began to grow concerned and then ... I woke up here.

"What in the world could make a dragon go to sleep ... and for so long?" I asked aloud.

"What indeed?" Panza asked, looking worried. She paused and stamped her foot hard on a dragon's back.

"I don't think you should be doing that," I said nervously. "It might hurt him."

Panza stopped, turned, looked at me and held her lantern higher. The lantern caught on all the edges of her rumpled dragon rider costume and her frizzled hair. She looked the exact opposite of who I knew her to be — a deadly clever and careful dragon rider who knew far better than I did what a dragon could or couldn't handle.

"Sorry," I said before she could scold me.

Panza nodded and went back to her examinations — rough as they were.

"How are they all still asleep," she wondered aloud, "when your dragon is awake?"

Incoming!

I looked up at the same time Ryfsmae and Reshatharin

looked with me. Shelbren and Eyapty dropped down beside us with a frazzled Krullmark riding behind her. He leapt from dragon-back and scrambled from dragon to dragon and to my utter surprise, he threw himself into my startled embrace me just as I'd jumped at Reshatharin when I'd discovered him.

I felt him press a kiss to my forehead as he breathed, "You're alive."

"Of course I'm alive," I said, a little stunned.

See? Reshatharin said. *It's weird when people act like that.*

"You're alive," he repeated.

"And Ursijek must be here somewhere," I told him gently. Because I hoped it was true.

Gurenthal must be here somewhere, too, I realized with a twist of my belly. Because she had not been rescued by Ryfsmae like I had ... which had to mean she was dead.

Her dragon is dead, Eyapty said with casual unconcern. *We saw to that.*

And it was only a short fall, Ryfsmae said uncertainly.

For a dragon. For a human it is a deadly fall, I reminded him.

I hugged Krullmark back a little awkwardly while Panza watched, straightened, and gave me a very long look.

"We have enemies above, likely pouring into a closed cavern. We have an army of stolen dragons under us who are asleep and we don't know why. We might have an injured and not quite dead deranged gold dragon rider down here with us and you're going to take your time playing kissy face?"

"No one kissed anyone," I said, my face hot, but Panza got what she wanted. We broke apart as if we couldn't get away from each other quickly enough and both retreated to looking through the piles of sleeping dragons.

I have a theory, Reshatharin said. *That the reason I woke was because Spara was near and screaming for me.*

My ears still hurt, Eyapty agreed.

It's a solid theory, a new voice said with a yawn and my head snapped around with the dragons all at once as we located the newcomer climbing up the mountain of sleepy dragons, his mouth wide and teeth on display as he yawned a second time.

"Ursijek," Krullmark said and it sounded like a sigh as he scrambled and climbed over to his dragon. The purple put his head on Krullmark's shoulder and I could almost feel their relief from where I was standing.

"Well, that's nice. You're all reunited," Panza said in a no-nonsense tone. "So now we can all get back to solving our problem, yes?"

CHAPTER 2

"THE OTHER DRAGONS show no sign of waking," Panza said urgently. "Which means we'll likely have to leave them here for now."

"We can't leave them," I protested.

"We can't wake them, and I don't know about you, but I can't fly carrying one on my back and neither can Ryfsmae, so your protests are just a waste of our time."

Is she always like this? Reshatharin asked.

Yes, I told him. *But without her I'd be dead and so would the Dominar, so it's best just to listen to her.*

"Krullmark," Panza ordered. "You can be lovey-dovey with your dragon another time. Fly up there and see about sealing off the entrance to the warrens. See if that magika you brought can help you."

Krullmark nodded and was already moving to Ursijek's back whispering gently to him before she was even done speaking. I felt my heart twinge just a little as he left. I'd been surprised by his embrace but now I didn't want to leave him.

Really? And what am I? A rock you found on a cavern floor?

Of course not! I set a hand on Reshatharin's nose and he hissed a cloud of irritated steam. *I. Do. Not. Like. Sharing.*

"Shabren," Panza said, "Fly back up to that pillar and join your student friends. Tell anyone waiting that we'll figure out the way through and they need to be patient."

"You want me to tell *full dragon riders* that?" she asked, sounding worried.

Panza gave her a long look and she squeaked, shaking Eyapty's reins to get him to leap into the air.

"You and I, Spara, are going to make a survey of what's here. I have a second lantern somewhere." Panza turned to her pack, rummaging around until she found another lantern, lit it, and offered it to me. "Give a yell if you see anything other than a pile of sleeping dragons. We'll fly a ring around them and meet back here."

I nodded and mounted Reshatharin.

Do you feel up for flying? I asked him uncertainly.

The day I can't fly is the day I die, he said boldly, but I saw how his wings shook as he leapt into the air and I knew he was just as nervous as I was.

We flew a path around the small mountain of sleeping dragons. They shifted very subtly in their sleep, their sides moving in and out as they breathed, but not a single one truly stirred as we circled them. We were about a third of the way through our circumnavigation when we found a gaping cavern.

"I wonder what's down there," I said aloud, but the lantern showed nothing but a reaching tunnel curving downward.

We flew on and found Gurenthal. I looked sharply away.

Dead, Reshatharin said bleakly. *But if she's the one who cut you with a knife then I'm not sorry.*

I was a little sorry. It was never a happy thing when someone died. Even someone who hated people you loved.

You have a sweet heart. Don't waste it on her.

I blinked back a tear. I'd missed him so much.

Reshatharin coughed and it shot out a small flame that lit the way ahead for a moment.

How long, exactly did you miss me for?

The entire time.

And that was?

Oh! I counted in my head *Five days perhaps?*

It was hard to keep track with all the running and hiding and being captured and imprisoned and getting free, but I thought that sounded right.

Reshatharin growled unhappily but there was nothing he could do. It simply was what it was. And we were together again, so surely we could face anything.

We'd almost reached the meeting point when a mental voice called down to us.

We're going to collapse the tunnel above. It might shake this whole place. Brace yourself. Pass the word.

Ryfsmae? I called.

I heard. Nearly to you. Hold on.

We met at the same time that the people and dragons above set off whatever they'd done to collapse the tunnel. The thought of it made me a little ill. What if we had to get out of here and the pillar didn't work and the passage didn't work?

We'll figure it out. Be calm. Have faith.

I had no calm and no faith.

Reshatharin barked a laugh but then the cave around us trembled for a moment and then nothing.

"Well, that was dramatic," Panza said as she rounded the corner.

"We found Gurenthal," I told her briefly. "And a cavern that might lead out of here."

We both froze. Beside us, a dragon twitched.

And then another.

And then a third.

All that talking nearby must be finally waking them.

"Up!" Panza shouted and our dragons barely managed to climb before the heap of dragons erupted with sleepy spouts of flame and such a mental tumult that I had to clamp my hands over my ears as we struggled to climb ahead of the pack.

What is happening?

Reshatharin and Ursijek hadn't woken like this. They'd been happy to see us. They'd been ... normal.

Our riders were there when we woke.

Oh.

Oh.

These dragons don't know where their riders are. And if they're anything like me, they don't know how long they've been asleep.

I could barely hear him over the overwhelming buzz of a thousand dragon voices.

And now we're really in trouble!

We burst up from the depths on a wave of wings. At the island platform Ystren and Krullmark were poised beside the pillar as if trying to get it to function, but their expressions were strained. As I watched, a group of twenty dragons standing on the platform within the glowing runes were suddenly gone.

"Get your dragons in position!" I heard Krullmark roar but such a surge of dragons and riders rushed forward that I didn't think they'd be able to fit. "Inside the runes or outside. Don't dare have a part of you sticking over!"

But no one was listening to him and this time when Ystren closed his eyes with a pained expression on his face, someone screamed.

When all the people and dragons vanished, half a tail was left behind, wriggling on the rock out past where the glowing runes covered.

CHAPTER 3

I FELT my face pale as the dragons surged forward again, and worse, the dragons underneath Panza and me were pushing us upward against our pleas. Soon we'd be pushed into that circle, too.

"Listen to me!" Krullmark roared, and if any human could be listened to, it would be him.

But even his voice was not enough, for half the dragons were riderless and even among the dragons I saw with riders, the riders were in no condition to direct their mounts. Sweaty, dirt-streaked, some with bloody wounds, some barely holding onto their dragon's backs they were battered and broken.

There were exceptions. I saw one dragon rider on a red dragon ordering the dragons around him — mostly red — who were forming up in an orderly way, and rider on a green dragon seemed to be holding back a whole knot of various colored dragons behind her.

There were very few purples. And the two I saw were carrying a third dragon across both their backs, their anxious riders trying to keep him from slipping off.

It was madness.

And unless someone could get these dragons to listen, more than one dragon was going to lose a tail. Or worse.

"Listen!" Krullmark roared as a third group vanished and the dragons surged forward.

I'd had enough. I straightened in the saddle and roared with my new dragon voice.

STOP.

And to my shocked relief, the dragons slowed.

Clawsinger, Clawsinger, Clawsinger, the murmur around me echoed.

If you do not listen to the purple dragon rider beside the pillar, I told them, broadcasting my mental voice. *None of you will get out.*

Our missing riders! One of the dragons from under me protested — or maybe many of them. It was hard to tell. They sounded on the edge of outburst.

Your missing riders will lose you forever and you will die in this cave if you do not listen, I told them severely. This was no time for dainty words.

The dragons pulled back a little.

"Ystren says he can handle twenty dragons at a time and that is it," Krullmark snapped into the sudden waiting silence. "You must be orderly. You must not push. The seal in the cavern will hold. Everyone will get out."

"And go where?" one rider called out the question.

"This pillar should deposit you just south of Questan City," Ystren said. "We will find help there."

And I didn't believe him anymore than they did. After all, if the enemy had taken the fields around Dominion City, could they not have taken Questan City, too? But I knew he was right that if they kept jamming forward, dragons and people were going to die.

"Injured first," he said, a little more calmly.

Injured dragons and dragons carrying injured riders first! I echoed and to my surprise, the dragons ahead seemed to pull to the sides to make space for the injured dragons to go through. The exhausted purples carrying their comrade went by and then a pair of greens with deep wounds on their side and a black who was carrying a rider who had three fallen humans slung around her saddle. She was biting her lip hard, her face etched with worry, but they all made it through.

The next round of twenty and the next went through, one on the heels of the next and I was beginning to feel hopeful, even if Ystren was beginning to look worn, and then I felt it ... a tremor of some sort in the air.

The island platform shook and a shower of rock dust fell from the pillar. Ystren gritted his teeth while Krullmark bellowed, "Next twenty forward!"

But the look they exchanged told me I wasn't imagining things. Something was wrong.

They're breaking through the barrier we made! a dragon at the back called. *We need to get out of here!*

And all at once the calm and order we'd produced became swirling dragons and bursts of nervous flame.

Stay calm! I called in my mind, and though I head the echo of *Clawsinger, Clawsinger,* it did nothing to calm the agitation. At least they hadn't charged the platform, and Krullmark and Ystren had gotten another forty dragons through.

I glanced over at them just in time to see Ystren collapse.

Krullmark let out a curse and ran toward him, but as I watched, the light of the runes and the pillar went out and the only light left in the cavern were the lanterns Panza and I were holding and the terrified spouts of flame from the trapped dragons.

Someone screamed. The rock shuddered again. And without letting myself second guess my choice, I called out aloud and in my mind, "*Follow me!*"

The cavern, I told Reshatharin. *We'll try that.*

It's a long shot ... Clawsinger, he replied and I could tell he was annoyed at that name, but he dove just as I'd asked and we shot down between the bodies of dragons below, back down into the depths where they had slept.

Panza says she'll take the rear since she has the other light, Ryfsmae called to me.

It was still hard to hear anyone through the babble of dragons all speaking over each other but I caught his words. I didn't like the idea of him vulnerable and in the rear, but I didn't even know if I were leading them to safety or just another trap, and maybe Ystren would recover and reactivate the pillar.

No. He might recover, but too much magic was pushed through that pillar and I think he was using his magika magic with the dragon magic, which made him able to perform all those transports in a row, but destroyed the transporter.

Did he know that was a possibility before Ystren burned it out?

We all knew. Ancient dragon lore. Why do you think there was so much pushing to get there first?

I swallowed, feeling awful that I had told some to wait when they all knew what might happen.

It was right for the wounded to go through first.

But there was no more time for recrimination. We'd reached the bottom of the long drop and the cavern entrance was right where we left it.

Reshatharin landed with a skid across the rocks, his feet spread out to take the impact. He slid right into the entrance and shook himself like a wet dog.

I'll be happy to get the stink of that place off my hide, I'll tell you that!

Behind us, other feet hit the ground and the din of dragon voices lifted as they remarked on my choice of exit. And then we were plunging forward into the darkness.

CHAPTER 4

THE CAVERN WAS large enough for a dragon to walk with someone riding on his back, but not comfortably and Reshatharin was ducked very low.

I held the lantern as high as I could, but so far the tunnel had plunged ever downward. I could not tell if it were part of the original structure of this place, or had been added later.

It's dragon made. Human made shows signs of toolwork and tends to be more angular. Dragon made has these melted patches and tends to more rounded structures.

So it could be very old, then.

Or it could be part of the efforts to rejuvenate the warrens. It's impossible to say.

I tried hard not to worry about the people behind us — about Krullmark and Ystren and Panza and Ryfsmae, but the press of dragons behind us was powerful, and Reshatharin was slithering as fast as he could while keeping his head from bumping the rock. It felt as if we were racing on our bellies with no knowledge of what might await.

It feels like that because it is that. Also ... while we're here, would you care to explain this "Clawsinger" name everyone is calling you?

Apparently there's some prophecy about someone who speaks to dragons.

Yes, but that can't be you.

Well, I said with a dry mental voice *that's a relief because here I thought I was the only girl going around speaking to dragons.*

I spoke to Alissi mind to mind, Reshatharin said, as if that proved anything. We both knew it wasn't the same, but I said nothing and a long time later he said, *I only just got you back. I don't think I should have to share.*

You aren't sharing, I said, pressing my cheek against his neck. *I can talk to them. Not be their best friend and rider.*

You could be my *rider,* a dragon from behind us said unhelpfully.

See? Reshatharin said grimly but he also twisted so that he could look behind us and he shot a burst of flame at the wall with a growl of, *Mine!*

Ouch! That hurt!

But though the skin on my face and hand stung from his flame, I was grateful. Jealousy meant he still thought of himself as my dragon. And now that I had him back, I wasn't giving him up for anything.

Good, he said, *because I think we have a problem.*

And then we burst out of the narrow cave and into a huge cavern and I gasped.

I have seen mountains and I have seen waterfalls and frankly, both are far more spectacular from the back of a dragon where their scale and beauty can be properly appreciated, but I have never seen them underground. More than that, this particular waterfall poured from a great height at the top of the cavern and glowed an almost magical faint aqua color while on either side of it grew some kind of moss or lichen that glowed the same aqua only more brightly.

It was so bright, in fact, that it lit the entire cavern. Juts of rock formed layers along the sides that made it appear to be made of and underground mountainside and more shocking even than that were the strings of lights along the rock suggesting there were humans here — a lot of humans.

I was just straining my eyes looking for them when Reshatharin sucked in a huge breath and I saw something far worse than simply humans.

The walls of this underground cavern were covered with creatures, and as we fell into the great underground bowl, they detached themselves from the wall and dropped into the air.

Medusas. Hundreds of them. And we had no idea which way was out.

Fly! Fly! Fly! Reshatharin cried urgently. He was already picking up speed, his mighty wings pushing against the air while behind us a steady stream of dragons poured from the cavern we'd just been in.

I felt frozen, uncertain what to do or say when the problem looming before us was so great. Only so many dragons could squeeze through that cavern at a time. Which meant we were arriving in ones and twos — steady, yes, but not a lot at once — and the Medusas were minutes from reaching us.

Frantically I scanned the walls for a way out. There had to be a way out, right?

Unless the way that we just came in through the way out, Reshatharin said.

Scatter! I ordered. *Look for a way out of here!*

What's happening? Came from further back the line and even the dragons who arrived with us seemed confused.

Medusas, I said and I couldn't be sure that my voice wasn't shaking.

What are medusas?

Enemies! Raolcan roared and then their forces clashed with ours, and the cavern was lit with flames and screaming humans shooting arrows as the medusas closed with us.

Forget looking for a way out, Reshatharin said. *We need to form a wall so dragons can slip through into this basin without being shot to pieces. Form up! Make a ring around the opening.*

I kept my mouth shut but I didn't see how we could hold them off. Even as I thought that an arrow sliced through the air past my ear.

Reshatharin leapt forward, grabbed one of the Medusas by a leg, and shook it like a dog with a rat.

I lost track of anything else after that as we dove and struck and flamed. All I caught were edges.

Someone fill this gap!

Red dragons — attack!

With the action came a steady stream of dragon exclamations and curses. But with no saddle and a very enthusiastic dragon attacking the enemy, it was all I could do to hold on and not throw up as we dodged and wove wildly, Reshatharin attacking and harrying and leaping into danger.

Once I bit back a cry as something struck my bad arm — I couldn't tell if it was a arrow or a wall or something else. By the time I turned to look, we'd dropped down, plummeting toward the ground, snatched up a medusa and lit him on fire with the fury of Reshatharin's breath. His riders fell, screaming.

I hoped someone could catch them. I hoped I didn't fall, too.

Don't be such a wet blanket. This is exactly what I needed! It shakes out the cobwebs.

"Spara!" I heard my name. With relief, I turned my head, nearly falling in my attempt to find the source of Krullmark's voice.

"Krullmark!" I called back.

"I think there's something behind the waterfall. We'll watch your back if you can check!"

He just wants all the fun to himself, Reshatharin grumbled, but I didn't care who wanted what fun. I was just grateful to be able to think and see straight for a moment as my dragon straightened and dove toward the waterfall, shooting flames as he went to ward off any headlong attack. The smell of sulphur washed over me and I clung to his neck, nearly vomiting again at the combination of airsickness and that terrible smell.

You need to get better at flying, he chided as though we hadn't been attacked and just trying to stay alive.

"Actually," I murmured, fighting a rebellious surge of nausea, "I think you're the one who needs to get better at flying so I don't feel like I've been shaken up and thrown down a waterfall."

He didn't reply to that which was fine by me. My head was spinning too hard to manage much conversation.

I apologize Spara, Reshatharin said, sounding actually contrite, but before I could answer we dove straight into the waterfall.

A deluge of frigid water poured over me, soaking me to the skin, plastering my hair across my face, and making it even harder to hold on. For a moment, I panicked, but his voice brought me back.

Easy. Easy, Sparrow. I'll keep you on my back. It's easy to forget how vulnerable humans are when you've been apart.

Krullmark was right. My eyes widened as they adjusted to the dark behind the waterfall, and to my delight, five different gaping holes were there behind the water and each one was surrounded by a carved frame as if to indicate it was a proper door to somewhere.

"Can you read the writing around them?" I asked, awed.

No, but it's dragon, I think. Deep dragon. Ancient.

Deep dragon, deep dragon. The dragons behind us had heard our words and were echoing them.

"I don't know why," I murmured, "but this one feels like it would lead to Dragon School."

Reshatharin seemed to consider that. *If it feels like that …*

maybe it does? The old dragons spoke differently than we do today. They spoke one heart to another.

Whatever language this spoke, that particular door with a flat bottom and domed top made me think of freshly baked bread, a warm blanket, and my mother's smile. What would be happening to her right now with all those dragons and riders in the thrall of Yulden and Jhairen Que'Shal? I tried to push the thought aside. My mother was a capable woman. If anyone could survive what was happening up on the surface, it was her.

Let's tell the others, I said to Reshatharin and he spun, flying straight through the waterfall again and soaking me to the skin,

There's no other way, he said with a grunt. *Which is probably why the doors remained hidden.*

And they were hidden. There was no sign of anyone coming or going — no prints on the bioluminescent coating that made the rock behind the waterfall glow, nothing at all to indicate anyone passing through them.

We pushed through the falls and back out to the cavern and my heart froze in my chest.

All through the massive cavern, dragons fought medusas, and we were terribly overwhelmed. My eyes shot to the entrance into the caves just in time to see Ryfsmae dart from the darkness with Panza on his back. She was looking behind her and as she broke free, a gold dragon leapt out behind her. It took me a moment before I realized that the gold dragon wasn't one we'd freed or one who had escaped. Not at all. This gold dragon was ridden by Jhairen Que'Shal, and behind him came a surge of silver dragons.

CHAPTER 5

"OH NO," I whispered.

Oh no, Reshatharin echoed.

But there was no time to panic, even if my body was definitely panicking, my breath coming too quickly and my hands shaking. I was the only one who could help right now.

DRAGONS, I shouted with my mind. *ATTEND. WE ARE OUTNUMBERED BUT THERE IS HOPE. FIVE CAVERNS ARE BEHIND THE WATERFALL. SPLIT UP. FLEE FOR YOUR LIVES. THOSE WHO SURVIVE WILL MEET AT DRAGON SCHOOL.*

I wasn't sure why I picked the school, only that I was certain — in a way that I couldn't explain — that one of these caverns led to it and it was my home.

They were moving before I'd finished my speech.

The first to move was a grim-faced Panza, riding Ryfsmae at his full speed toward the falls. The little dragon bobbed and huffed, clearly already exhausted from his flight. Just looking at him made my stomach clench.

I'm fine. I'm fine. I'm fine, he chanted.

Right on her heels were a pair of red dragons — which I hadn't expected. Reds loved to fight, but these two were helping in a different way. They were loaded down with a wounded white dragon slung across them and on their back I saw the white rider working feverishly over another man who was bristling with arrows. Whites were healers, but this white would be a hero if he could save a man so injured.

I bit my lip, turning to find Krullmark, but Ursijek's voice sliced into my mind.

Spara. Krullmark begs me tell you not to wait. Go quickly. He'll meet you at Dragon School.

But I couldn't abandon my friend. Not after everything.

Yes we can. Come on! Reshatharin was already turning, his color distorting in the aqua of the falls and the orange blaze of spitting dragon fire.

"You can't leave them," I said aloud, trying to tug at his neck, but it was no use. He would do exactly as he pleased and never mind that I felt like I was abandoning a friend who had never abandoned me.

Stop it. I'm doing what needs to be done. What will these dragons do when they get to Dragon School? They need you to speak to them all and rally them. You're the go-between for the humans and dragons when so many don't have riders. You're too important to lose here.

"Please," I whispered, but I was ignored, and it was with tears in my eyes that he flew us under the deluge again — this time in a host of fleeing dragons — and then darted straight into the doorway I was sure led to Dragon School.

We weren't the only ones. I could see footprints on the floor of the tunnel now, but any dragons before us were lost to sight as the passage turned and twisted. My lantern bobbed. It might be running out of fuel. And then just as I thought that, it winked out, and I was left in the dark clinging to my dragon and frustrated that decisions were being made for me against my will and against my duty.

I thought you were getting sick of the responsibility of having to do everything. He kept his tone light but I could hear that our journey was taking its toll on him, too. *Maybe you can take this as a chance to rest a bit.*

Is that what you did when someone grabbed you and dragged you away against your will? Rested? Took it as a sign to relax?

He didn't answer me and now I felt guilty about that, too. Because I'd thought he was lost forever and dead and now that I had him back I should just be grateful instead of fighting with him. Shouldn't I?

You should.

I wish he'd stop listening to my thoughts.

I was frustrated. I had responsibilities. I had people who were relying on me. And I'd left them to face Jhairen Que'Shal on their own with hundreds of medusas and silver dragoons at his back. I hated that I'd run.

And I hated worse that I'd had no choice.

I wasn't a child anymore and both Reshatharin and Krullmark should stop treating me like one. I had the right to make my own decisions and if Reshatharin didn't agree with them, then we should talk about them rather than him just getting to make the choice for both of us because he was bigger and I was riding on his back.

We had scrambled maybe an hour through the darkness — it was hard to judge time here — before we heard a sound ahead.

I tensed, unsure what I was hearing.

There it was again. A sawing sound.

Reshatharin slowed to a creep, clearly as nervous about the sound as I was, and then he stopped abruptly.

Are you ... hurt? he asked and I was sure he was speaking to another dragon.

Just exhausted, Ryfsmae's voice said in my head and I breathed a sigh of relief. We'd caught up to friends.

"Panza?" I hissed in the darkness.

"Spara," she sounded both tense and relieved, too. That was

the problem with this darkness. It was impossible to tell friend from foe.

"Can we help?" I asked and realized with a sudden stomach-turning understanding that I was about to do what Reshatharin just did to me. Because I couldn't carry Ryfsmae's big bags and I couldn't carry Panza. So if we were going to help, it would be him doing the helping and yet I'd just offered help without asking him.

Exactly. And I appreciate your kindheartedness, but this is how a partnership works. Sometimes one person steers. Sometimes the other. We have to have faith and confidence in each other's choices. You should not be angry that I made you leave a deadly battle to seek safety even if we could have helped if we hung back. Not all those dragons had riders with them, and you are worth ten of any rider to me.

I swallowed.

Press your offer. I will carry the big woman and her big bags if it helps.

"Reshatharin could carry your bags," I suggested, not even pretending I thought Ryfsmae might allow a different dragon to carry Panza. They were all protective creatures these dragons of ours.

We switched the bags over with some difficulty as we had to do it all by feel.

"No, the other buckle," Panza grumbled when I tried to pass her the wrong one. I couldn't tell the difference in the darkness. "They say you didn't go through Dragon School before becoming a dragon rider or properly go through the ranks and it's showing. You should be able to saddle a dragon in the dark."

Which was what we were doing. There was no way Reshatharin could carry all the gear without a saddle to sling it to, so we were saddling him.

She did not go through the school because she was busy saving my life, Reshatharin said huffily. *Besides, the school had poor judg-*

ment. They wouldn't take the greatest dragon rider of her generation. How is that a sign of their worthiness? Whatever she needs to know, I will teach her.

I wasn't sure how much of that was passed from Ryfsmae to Panza, but the other dragon rider sniffed.

"Has a mind of his own, I see."

And in the darkness I flushed because that's what I'd just been complaining about.

I think you'd better take both riders, Ryfsmae said reluctantly to Reshatharin. *I've been flying day and night for three days with hardly a break, and multiple riders, and I just don't think I can take much more.*

And then to my surprise, Panza clambered up into the saddle with a warning to Reshatharin as she climbed.

"No saucy tricks from you. And you'll stick with my dragon so we don't lose each other in this darkness or it will never work."

"Yes, Panza," I said meekly and she snorted, practically in my ear as she settled herself in the saddle.

"Spara? Is that you?" someone whispered from behind us.

"Shelbren?" Surely there was some limit to how many times I could feel relieved, but I hadn't reached it yet. I'd been so worried about her and Eyapty. She was only a student and not meant to be in this mess.

"It's me and Hasten both," she hissed.

"Good," Panza announced in her carrying voice. "All you student dragon riders are to stick close to me. You should never have been in this position in the first place, but now that you're under my wing, I plan to get you through. Is anyone injured?"

It felt good to have Panza take over.

So much for your independence.

Ouch.

Panza hastily bandaged a wound on Hasten's leg, checked my injured arm by feel and declared it to be only bruised and maybe abraded but not bleeding anymore, ran a hand over Haxajael's foreleg and declared that while it was badly burned there wasn't much to be done for it yet and he should try to fly as much as possible and avoid bumping into it if he could help it. Between us, there was half a skin of water and just a few tiny oatcakes she'd had with her. She passed those around briskly.

"Fine then. It's the four of us. No one else has caught up and fortunately there have been no enemies yet either, so stick with me. Ryfsmae will lead since he's in front already. Haxajael will take the rear, since he's there all ready. Both of you be on the alert, and everyone else stay as quiet as you can. We'll find our way out of this worm hole."

Hey! Reshatharin objected and Haxajael let out a snort of dragon laughter.

"Quiet!" Panza reminded them, and then we were moving again, but I felt less alone and less afraid than I had when it was just Reshatharin and me.

Besides, despite Panza's warning, she was the one who wasn't quiet as we slid through the tunnels.

"In events where a student and rider are separated from supervision your best option will always be to trust your dragon, take care of yourselves, help anyone in need, and return to Dragon School as soon as possible. You don't yet know where your color keeps their safe houses and supply stashes, but other dragon riders will help you if they can."

"We have supply caches?" Shabren asked in awe.

"Of course," Panza said. "Each color has their own and they are secret, so I can't tell you where the Greens keep theirs."

"I think it's safe to say that we should avoid the Silver ones," I said grimly.

"Silvers operate on their own rules," Panza agreed. "But yes. I think it's safe to say that right now they can't be trusted."

And we were all silent for a long time after that.

Time stretches out when you're in the dark and can't judge

how much of it has passed. We human were tense and worried and the dragons were working hard. All that could be heard much of the time was our breathing. I couldn't even hear the sounds of pursuit.

"Do you think they are following us?" Shabren asked Panza.

"Very likely."

"Then how are we staying ahead?" Hasten whispered.

"A dragon can only move so quickly down a passage like this. It limits all of us the same way," Panza said confidently. But I noticed she hadn't said anything about medusas and I wondered how fast they could swim up these tunnels and if they were in pursuit even now.

It was maybe an hour later when Ryfsmae — in the lead — froze and we collided into his tail.

Quiet! he said, and Panza hissed a shushing noise at us.

What is it? Reshatharin asked.

I hear something ... ahead.

We started to creep forward again, this time even more carefully but as we went the sounds got louder until we humans could hear them, too. The passage began to show just a hint of diffuse light until soon I could see Reshatharin's head, and then Ryfsmae's, and then we were awash in light and sound as we emerged into another huge cavern.

Oh no.

CHAPTER 6

I HAD THOUGHT we'd been moving quickly, but whether we were slow or a different passage was just faster, we came out into a battle between dragons and medusas and their riders and it was obvious immediately that our side was losing.

Two dragons lay slumped on a central island where a dark pillar stood — one just like the one Ystren had used to transport people before it went dark, too. I couldn't tell if those dragons were dead or terribly injured, but they didn't so much as flick a wing.

Four more dragons fought in a knot around the island — three without riders and one — oh! It was Ursijek with Krullmark and Ystren on his back! The magika was still in a swoon, draped over the purple dragon's back just ahead of where Krullmark was sitting.

Ursijek!

He might have glanced over at me, but I could be sure. He was flaming and flaming over and over and I was sure his throat must be sore. A dragon couldn't flame like that forever could he?

Certainly not, Reshatharin said grimly, but though he lunged forward with a new burst of speed, I was worried.

There were at least a dozen medusas attacking the dragons — three red dragons and Ursijek — and on their backs I counted twenty-five men with spears and arrows. It was all the dragons could do to dodge the constant barrage of arrows, so much so that I saw little offensive action beyond the spouting flames.

I wasn't sure how much we could help. Reshatharin was tired — I could feel it in his movements — and he was carrying Panza, me, and all the gear. Ryfsmae, though no longer loaded down, looked like he was barely hanging on. His head drooped and his wing movements were spare as if he were conserving energy. The two other dragons were with student riders.

"Get me to the platform," Panza urged Reshatharin. "There's a trick in those bags of mine."

I wasn't sure a trick — of any kind — would be enough and I said so, my voice sounding far more nervous than I wanted to be.

We were seconds from closing with the medusas. They hadn't seen us yet, distracted as they were by the fight with the other dragons, but they'd notice us in a moment.

Umm, excuse me if you don't mind, Haxajael said and I was surprised for he'd been very quiet this whole time. *Not to interfere, as I'm sure the large human has an excellent plan and the means to accomplish it.*

Just tell us what you have to say! I urged. One of the medusa's riders had noticed us and he was yelling to the others. Before I could blink, three of them had swung around and launched a barrage of arrows at us.

It's only that I know how to operate the pillar, Haxajael said, dodging an arrow that nicked along the length of his wing, leaving little spots of dark dragon blood across the green scales.

Reshatharin dodged down suddenly and I held my breath, clinging to the saddle while Panza grunted behind me. He lunged forward suddenly, grabbing the Medusa around the neck and shaking so hard that his two riders went flying from his back, their arrows and bows scattering as they fell into the darkness.

I gasped, horror and fear fighting in my chest as a second medusa sailed toward us.

If we can all get onto that platform and maybe drag those injured dragons within the ring, then I can use it to get us to ... you said Dragon School, yes? Haxajael said.

Yes!

Something hit me from the side and for a moment all I saw were stars. My fingers slid from their grip and for one bad moment I was falling and then thick arms grabbed me and Panza pulled me to her chest, cursing violently.

"Hasten's dragon can work the pillar," I told her breathlessly.

"It's dark," she objected. "Broken."

Simply needs to be activated, he said coolly. *I've seen it done before I agreed to go to Dragon School.*

Then we'd better hurry!

"Get everyone to the platform!" I yelled aloud and in my mind, too. We'd just have to trust that Haxajael really did know.

Well, I wouldn't say I could if I couldn't. Really. I think a little trust ...

This time when Reshatharin was hit, I saw the hit. Two medusas flew at him, one from each side and as he tried to dodge one, the other bumped him in the armpit under the wing, causing him to tilt wildly — throwing both Panza and I from his back with the sharpness of the jolt. Panza had the rider belts buckled and she dangled precariously from the straps, but I was thrown wide of Reshatharin's wing and flew straight toward a medusa decked with three humans.

I think I screamed. It was hard to tell.

Everything was happening at once.

The pounding of my heart and roar of fear in my mind

drowned out everything else. The world spun and then I crashed — hard — against one of the humans and slid down into the medusa's basket.

The scent hit me first — like a slap in the face. The medusa smelled of dead fish. I nearly vomited and only just recovered enough to keep my wits about me.

Spara! Reshatharin screamed in my mind, a little late. The ragged man I'd struck teetered wildly as I fell to the floor of the basket. His bow and spear went flying as he pawed at the man beside him, dragging him backward. The lip of the basket caught them, but they crumpled against it together.

That still left one human. He reached into his coat and when his hand came out it had a gleaming knife in it.

Clawsinger. Clawsinger, I heard in the back of my mind, but I couldn't let it distract me.

With all my might I grabbed the edge of the basket and hauled myself to my feet. The knife flashed, slashing toward me and I thought it would be too late. I winced.

And then the medusa flipped over and around me screams filled the air as we all fell, spaced out, but one in this terrible moment of rushing air, frantic screams, and clawing, useless limbs.

Something caught me so suddenly that it knocked my breath out of me. And as I struggled to breathe against the pain in my chest, the humans I'd been falling with kept plunging down through the darkness.

A red scaly neck shot out from over me, grabbed the medusa in its jaws, crunched down hard, and then opened wide, wide, wide and swallowed both the wriggling medusa and the basket all in one gulp.

I barely bit back a scream.

My gaze followed the red dragon's head and the huge bulge that went slowly down his neck. I should be worried about everyone else and grateful I was alive. Instead, I couldn't stop shaking.

I asked with a small mental voice, *Won't that hurt your stomach when it gets there?*

No. Never has before, the dragons said, sounding quite pleased with himself.

And he said nothing else, just flew up silently and gently set me beside the two fallen dragons slung across the rock island and when I finally recovered myself enough to look, I saw that there were no more medusas attacking my people.

But I also couldn't see Haxajael or Eyapty anymore.

I opened my mouth, distress making me uncertain what to say as Reshatharin set down on the rock beside me.

Ursijek and Ryfsmae followed him, and one of the other reds. I felt a tear start and streak down my dusty face and my lower lip trembled and then just when I was about to sob, a head rose over the lip of the island.

Haxajael and the other red dragon — scorched, streaked with blood, wings tattered a little from arrows — rose up side by side and laying over top of them was a limp Eyapty, his eyes shut and a sobbing Shabren on his back.

"Hurry," she said through her tears. "I think he needs help."

CHAPTER 7

He did need help, it turned out. And so did the dragons who I checked on the platform. They were all still breathing, but their breath was thready and faint.

Spara, Reshatharin said, as I checked the other dragons' condition. *Sparrow. I'm sorry, I'm so sorry.*

He had nothing to apologize for.

I shouldn't have let him hit me like that.

I looked at him wide-eyed. *And how would you have prevented it? You were attacked on both sides!*

I should have been the one to catch you.

But that didn't matter, because *someone* had. Actually, I had forgotten to get that dragon's name.

Laepsio, the red dragon said. He shuffled over to beside me and began to help push his fellows closer to the pillar where Panza, Ryfsmae, and Haxajael were examining it. Panza's hands ran over the sides of the stone as if looking for something to pull or press.

Leave it to me, Haxajael said, but of course she couldn't hear him.

It should not have been this red dragon who caught you.

Reshatharin stomped an irritated foot and I froze, turning to look at him.

My eyes widened. *Are you still jealous, Reshatharin? This is going to become a problem between us. It has been affecting everything since you work up. Would you have preferred I fell to my death?*

Beside me, Laepsio snorted a laugh. His amusement was not making Reshatharin any calmer.

Of course not, but I would have preferred to be the one to catch you.

I'll see what I can arrange next time, I said dryly. *This time, I was just trying to stay alive.*

He looked away sheepishly, but he was having a hard time with how I could speak to other dragons and I didn't think he'd settled it in his mind yet and if my near death was not enough to help him face it, then I wasn't sure how we'd get past this.

He wasn't the only one with a sudden need to scold me. While I was still working to move unconscious dragons, Krullmark descended from Ursijek's back and strode toward me, running a worried hand over his head like he often did when I was nearby.

This is hilarious, my new friend Laepsio said. *I want to stick around you, funny human.*

"Are you hurt?" Krullmark asked gruffly.

"I'm fine," I started to say, which was partly a lie since everything hurt and I was bruised, but I wasn't hurt enough to be complaining. He pulled me into a rough hug and murmured into my hair.

"I'm sorry."

"Everyone needs to stop apologizing," I said, but my voice was muffled against his chest and honestly, I really did need the hug. The last few minutes had been terrifying and try as I might, my hands were still shaking and my knees didn't seem quite happy to be holding me up.

"I promised to keep you safe," he said, his voice still pitched for just us. "I shouldn't have let you go through the tunnels without me. I should have been there."

But I didn't see how that would have helped, or how he was going to practically manage that when we were in the middle of a situation that looked like it was becoming a war.

"You have nothing to be sorry for," I said, pulling back from the hug. "And you can't always keep me safe. That's not your job and you'll just feel guilty when you can't." He looked uncomfortable, so I kept talking. "And I'm glad you're safe, too. I didn't like leaving you back there. It was Reshatharin's fault."

My dragon stood a little taller at that like he was proud of it, and Krullmark gave him a thankful nod. Rude. They were conspiring against me.

"How is Ystren?"

Krullmark cleared his throat, looking glad to have been steered away from more emotional talk. "I can't tell. I think using all that magic drained him. His eyes flicker open now and then but I can't tell what he's saying when he tries to speak, and any attempt at movement is only a twitch."

"He must need to rest then," I said, but I was watching the direction we came from anxiously. There would be more creatures in pursuit of us. And since we both got to this pillar by different tunnels, who knew how many medusas might follow us here. "He won't be safe until we all are far away from here."

Krullmark grunted and from over by the pillar Panza said, "They've clearly been using that place as a hiding spot for a while. That was a lot of dragons to have captured and kept in one cave, only to have a linked underground fortress. With care, I think they could have supplied them from the surface, but I don't think they've been using these pillars to travel."

"Why not?" I asked, moving over to Ystren on Ursijek's back to check on him. I didn't know what I was looking for, but he did just seem worn out like Krullmark said. He was breathing. He moaned a little when I thumbed an eyelid open.

"Because they were so concentrated in one place," Panza said. "If they could dash all around then they'd be able to afford to have their forces more scattered."

I wasn't so sure.

Got it! Haxajael announced suddenly at the same moment that the lights in the pillar flared and bright dancing runes formed a circle on the ground all around it. *Everyone inside?*

And when we agreed that we were inside, he ducked low so his head was almost to the ground and I thought I heard the edge of a dragon murmur of *Dragon School* and then there was a flash of light and we were standing beside a different pillar on a different island. This one had a crack in the stone above it and bright daylight streamed through, flooding the cavern.

Was that a way out?

I don't think so, Reshatharin said, blinking rapidly in the sudden light. *But a way out must be close.*

Haxajael flapped his wings a little proudly, preening himself — and well he should. We had made it through — well and whole from what I could see — and none of our enemies had come with us.

I bit my lip all the same. What would happen to the rest of the dragons and riders back there? The ones who didn't have Haxajael and his knowledge to guide them through.

They will make it. Somehow. We can only do our very best and hope that they will do theirs, Reshatharin said. *We cannot live their lives or fight their battles for them.*

That seemed sensible.

It is imminently sensible, my sparrow. We have enough of a task before us to keep us occupied without worrying further for them.

When I looked up, I could see he was right.

"We'll have to crowd as many humans as we can on the smaller dragons," Panza was saying. "That means Ryfsmae and

Ursijek will have to take three humans each plus gear so that you bigger dragons can carry the three who are in trouble."

I thought I heard Ryfsmae sigh and I could feel Reshatharin radiating jealousy, even though he said nothing.

"I don't want to leave Eyapty," Shelbren said tearfully.

We'll have to take them in shifts anyway, Reshatharin said seriously. *There's no way each of us can carry another dragon on our own.*

So it was decided. Our new friend Laepsio would stay and keep watch over the two unconscious red dragons while the rest of us found a way out and a place to put the injured dragons and then we'd come back and ferry the other two out in turns.

It wasn't far out to the surface, it turned out, and with no one chasing us and no terrible magic making everything urgent, the journey was not nearly so fraught as the way *into* the warrens had been.

We emerged on a forested hillside beside a lake and far, far in the distance I spotted the dramatic cliffs of Dragon School.

Home.

It rang in my heart like a bell and kept me smiling as we set up what we could for a camp and brought all the injured to rest there. It was too far to fly them to Dragon School easily and the sun was close to setting, so we made camp for the night and hoped to find a more hospitable place in Dragon School tomorrow. There would be blankets there, and hot food, proper medical supplies, and cotes for the dragons. I could hardly wait. There might even be a bath.

I was still gathering wood for a fire and daydreaming about a hot bath while Panza was crawling all over Eyapty stitching and complaining to Shabren that she really wasn't the best one for this job, when I saw a flash of light from the cliffs of Dragon School. And then another. And another.

"Panza?" I asked, straightening. "What's that coming from the cliffs of Dragon School?"

Panza froze, watching and then her face turned grim. "That's a distress signal."

CHAPTER 8

*W*E CAN'T SPEND *the night here without knowing what's happening at the school,* Reshatharin said, shifting uncomfortably.

Whether to go to the school tonight or wait for the morning had been debated for almost an hour and I felt caught in the middle. Like Reshatharin, I was worried for my family and friends there and I thought that if there was a distress signal being sent, then they might need help right now and the morning would be too late.

But Panza, Krullmark, and Ryfsmae were also right. The two students were exhausted, Eyapty badly injured, Haxajael drained from using the dragon magic. Ystren was still unconscious. Ryfsmae was exhausted to the point where he'd simply collapsed by the fire, shut his eyes, and gone to sleep the moment he emerged from the tunnels the last time. The two red dragons we'd carried here remained slumped in a heap beside Ryfsmae and Panza said she couldn't go another moment without a rest.

Which left Reshatharin and Laepsio as the only ones demanding that we go right now.

"Morning will be soon enough," Krullmark said from his place beside the fire when he saw me place a hand on

Reshatharin's snout once again. "Tell him to stop fretting and let his human sleep."

And to be honest, I was swaying on my feet, suddenly exhausted now that I wasn't fleeing for my life.

I could tell by how Krullmark watched me that he wished he could hug me again, but he remained stationed by the fire, keeping the high-spirited dragons in check.

"Go to sleep, Spara. I'll take first watch," he said in a low burr. Panza was already asleep and snoring loudly enough to be heard all through the camp.

I curled up beside Reshatharin and hoped he'd sleep, too. Whatever we found at Dragon School tomorrow was going to take all of us to handle and I needed my dragon at full strength.

I'll try, he promised as I cuddled closer and closed my eyes. *And Spara?*

Yes?

Thank you for not giving up on me. For refusing to quit when anyone else would have thought me dead.

I'd never give up on you, I told him.

I ... I have been jealous of your affections, he admitted.

I hadn't noticed.

I felt the humor in his voice. *Can you forgive me for loving you too much?*

I can forgive you for expressing in it in such annoying ways, but the love I will keep, I said and he made a satisfied sound beside me.

It was good to have him back. More than good. It made me feel whole again. That was my last thought before sleep claimed me.

I was shaken awake by Krullmark to take the last watch — he had let me sleep most of the night while he sat up and I felt sick thinking about how tired he must be. He did too much for me. He was too kind. It made me frown for this was surely more than friendship, this attentiveness and protectiveness and yes, he'd indicated as much by saying he'd decided not to leave me and by wanting to hold me every time he thought I'd died and then it turned out I'd survived by a whisker of luck.

I needed to sort out how I felt about him. He made me feel warm and safe. He made me feel accepted in a way no other human did. Was I ... could I want to be more than a friend to him, too?

I sat in the darkness before the dawn with my back against my warm dragon and my feet in front of the embers of the fire and I watched Dragon School and mulled over this strange feeling that I had to make a decision about Krullmark.

I'd come a long way since I left just a few weeks ago. It felt like I was a whole new Spara. One so much more vulnerable than the old Spara, but so much braver. One who had lost friends and family but gained others — so many others, and most of them dragons. One who had realized the world was so much more broken than she'd thought but realized now that she was loved more than she could imagine.

And I was just *grateful.* Grateful for the friends and family and even the strangers who had helped me and my beloved dragon get this far. And if we couldn't find peace again, if we didn't succeed against our enemies ... if all the world was lost, then we still had this love that had stitched us together and held us together still. And I could never regret that.

I sniffed, close to tears from the emotion of the thought, and then a whisper cut through the darkness and made me straighten, eyes wide.

"Alissi? Is that you?"

"Who's there?" I whispered back, and from the darkness of the trees a figure limped into our camp, holding himself upright on a makeshift crutch.

"Stars and skies, it is you!" he said, relief flooding his dirty face.

I scrambled to my feet, my breath snatched away. "Wawrin Tanglefoot?"

He nodded wearily.

"But where are the rest of your riders?" I asked, worry tinging my voice.

"Lost," he said, his face falling. "I lost them all."

"Dead?" I asked, my voice stricken.

"Who is dead?" Panza threw a pair of logs on the fire and a spray of sparks puffed up. Her eyes were sleepy and her hair even more messy than usual but her face was set and grim, and more distrustful than I'd ever seen it. I looked back and forth between her and the red dragon rider, suddenly wondering if I should be worried.

"No one is dead," Wawrin said, but the lines on his face deepened and a dark shadow fell across his face. I shivered. "At least, I hope not. But my dragon and all those with me were snatched away weeks ago and taken to Dragon School and I have been living here in these woods hoping to find someone — anyone — who can help set them free from the traitors who guard them there."

"Sit down and take it from the beginning," Panza said, though I noted that she stayed standing.

Wawrin Tanglefoot nodded, sitting with difficulty on a log near the fire. His leg didn't bend and I frowned watching it. He had been the strongest, most martial and authoritative dragon rider I'd met. Now, whatever way he'd been hurt looked permanent. And where was his dragon?

"When I last I saw Alissi, I was commanding a wing of the Red."

He nodded at me, but while Panza's eyebrows went up at the name "Alissi" she didn't stop his story. I flushed hard at being caught in my lie — pretending to be my cousin when first I inherited Reshatharin.

"We had determined to break into groups to try to escape

some magic that had us penned in, shooting arrows at us. One group went with a gold rider — Gurenthal Hasclip."

Panza hissed in a breath and Wawrin shot her a bewildered look. "You know the name, purple rider?"

"When last I saw Gurenthal," Panza said, "She was dead — having betrayed us all."

Wawrin grunted. "Then that explains why those sent with her were found in cages on the backs of strange creatures. We found them a few days later, having circled several times, lost in the mist and unable to get free. We weren't far from Dragon School when we found them and of course we engaged the enemy, trying to free our friends. Those who had captured our compatriots rode strange animals — like some many-legged creatures of the sea that swim through the air. On their backs are baskets filled with archers."

"Medusas," I said grimly.

"But the land-crawling ones are worse," he said, nodding at me in acknowledgment. "They put one in mind of a great turtle with a cage on its back. And in the cages, we found our friends. Wounded. Ill. Some of them dying. And all prisoners. We fought and we lost." His gaze turned inward. "I do not know how we lost or who was ..." He shook himself liek he couldn't quite bring himself to admit that some of those under his command were likely dead. "I was injured and thrown from my dragon. When I regained consciousness I was alone. I could not find my friends. I could not find my dragon. But we were close to Dragon School. I tried to go there for help and found our enemy there, occupying the school."

"We saw a distress signal from them last night," Panza said. "Why would they do that?"

Wawrin Tanglefoot shook his head. "They have been doing that since they arrived and I have watched helplessly while dragons and their riders hurry to help and never leave again."

I sucked in a breath. That was terrible!

Wawrin nodded as if he could read my thoughts.

"It gets worse," he said grimly. "Yesterday a wing of dragons arrived. I thought this was our chance to free them. I signaled them from the ground, and they set down waiting for me. In my delight, I hurried out to them with no thought to treachery. They were Silvers. The Dominar's own guard. One of them shot an arrow at me the moment I cleared the tree line and then another flamed in my direction. I ran as best as I could and hid under a pile of leaves until they left and you arrived. If I hadn't recognized you, Alissi Coldrock, I am not sure that I would have had the courage to try again." His expression turned earnest. "But somewhere in the school is my dragon. And dozens more. And if they live, then we must rescue them."

"We?" Panza asked. "Look around. There are only a few of us and half are injured."

He opened his mouth, frustration and despair already on his face, but I raised a hand to stop him.

"There are only a few of us for now," I said. "But there are more coming. Who knows. They may even come quickly."

Wawrin looked at me squarely. "Pray that they do. For if Dragon School has fallen, then Dominion City and the Dominar are next."

"Well that's the thing," Panza said, sucking her teeth to punctuate her next words. "They already have."

CHAPTER 9

THE NEWS we brought would have shocked anyone, but Wawrin Tanglefoot had been waiting and hoping for help for so long that it was worse for him. He seemed to almost collapse in on himself.

"Make tea," Panza told me briskly. "I will talk to him." She handed me a cloth bag full of leaves from some inner pocket. "There's a creek just through those trees. I found it last night. Follow the sound of the water to fill the kettle and water skin. I keep the kettle in Ryfsmae's left saddle bag."

I followed her instructions, almost glad to make my escape. With both the capital and Dominar fallen and now Dragon School, what were we to do? I had hoped that a leader of the fighting color of dragons — Red — would know the answer to that question but one glance told me now was not the time to ask him. He was huddled over himself, face in his hands while Panza spoke quietly but urgently to him.

I made my way to the creek, passing Shabren as she nursed the injured dragons. She spoke quietly and didn't look up and I left her feeling sick. Now what? What if the dragons we freed didn't make it out of the warrens? What if the ones left back at

Dominion City in thrall to the artifact turned on those of us left? Could any part of the Dominion stay standing?

I hadn't meant to cry, but the tears started to flow anyway. This was all too much for us. Too much for me. I didn't know what to do.

In a wild impulse I fussed with my belt pouch and pulled out the little book Raolcan had given me. I'd hardly looked at it in all this time. But he'd said his old friend — one of the last of the great Lightbringers — had told him that the prophecies weren't just for Amel Leafbrought's time. That they had the power to stretch across time and mean something now. Could it be possible that there was something in here that could help us now?

I read a few lines in the front of the book.

"No man owns peace. No man may hold it tightly and forbid its theft. We may only respond when war is brought to our gates and pray we respond right for truth is often mocked and lies win hearts faster than flames consume a forest. Who can stand when men give way on every side to the force of their desires twisted against them?"

Well, I didn't know if it was helpful but it was definitely true. We could only respond and I had been responding the only way I knew how all this time.

That was my *home* over there beset by enemies. If any of the staff were still in Dragon School — prisoners or forced to serve the people there — well, those were my family. Literally in some cases and because they helped raise me and grew up with me, in others. I wasn't going to turn my back on them now.

I scrubbed my tears aside furiously and hurried to finish filling the kettle and bringing it to the embers of the fire to brew tea. By the time I returned, Krullmark was awake and rubbing tired eyes, and the uninjured dragons were all up and huddled around as he fed the fire and gave the students what reassurances he could.

"Spara, is it?" Wawrin asked me with a twist of his mouth as I settled the kettle on a rock beside the fire.

"Yes," I said, jutting out my chin. Behind him, Reshatharin let out a burst of steam from his huge nostril, his eyes on the red dragon rider. Wawrin looked behind him, took a wary step away from my purple dragon and turned to me again.

"He doesn't seem to like me much."

"He's a loyal dragon," I said tersely. "To the Dominion. To Dragon School. To me."

Wawrin paused, seeming to think for a moment, and I could tell he didn't like it at all that I had been staff and he had been tricked, that he was now at the mercy of a purple dragon who was glaring at him ... and at my mercy, too.

"And I think I know a way to get into Dragon School and to retrieve your friends," I said carefully.

That brought everyone's heads up.

Krullmark was frowning, clearly worried. Panza cocked her head to one side as if she'd like to be convinced, and both students watched me with worried expressions. I felt for all of them. The last time I'd led them somewhere, we'd ended up in a cavern full of medusas and enemies and we'd barely escaped with the skins on our backs.

I flashed a guilty look at the injured dragons still sleeping in a pile, but Wawrin had a dragon out there somewhere, too, and his dragon needed help, too.

"Tell us more," Wawrin Tanglefoot said quietly and I knew he wouldn't bring up that I had been staff again.

"Dragon School has all kinds of ways in," I said, telling them something everyone knew. "The whole face of it is accessible by dragons, obviously, who can fly right to their cotes and the river flows right up to the edge of Dragon School and people can climb the ladders from its banks or go up the ladders. And, of course, if you're on top of the butte you can climb down to Dragon School. But there are entrances for supplies, too. Entrances you might not think about if you had taken over the school and were trying to defend it."

"I'm sure they'd put a guard at any door," Panza said practically. "And Ryfsmae says that when he squints he can see dragons patrolling in front of the open cliff face, so that's out."

I nodded. But it wasn't any door that I was thinking about.

"In the spring," I said carefully, "when the waters swell, they ship down butter and cheese in big barrels from the north. They float them down the river while the water level is high and float them right into this one door that is mostly flooded when the water is high, but is far back from the bank the rest of the time. One spring, I was sent with some others to clear away the bushes around it before the river swelled so they wouldn't get in the way. They grow up very quickly. So quickly, in fact, that if you didn't know the door was there you'd never see it."

"Well, they'd still see the door on the inside, wouldn't they?" Panza said. She wasn't being rude, only sensible, but Wawrin and Krullmark had frozen, their eyes glazing over as they los themselves to thought.

"Perhaps not," I suggested diffidently. "The entrance is only used for butter, cheese, cream and other supplies like that. It goes right up into the buttery through a long tunnel and a series of narrow staircases. It's a pain to navigate and very narrow — far too narrow for a dragon. Even my mother said it pressed against her hips too much. It's a relic from the old days when people were smaller and the school wasn't a school at all but an old castle."

"I've never heard of this entrance," Shabren said, frowning. "And I went into the buttery once to ..." she flushed. "Well we were looking for extra cheese after curfew."

I smiled, but I didn't let her distract me — even if the cheese thing was an obvious lie. She had either been pulling a prank or meeting up with an admirer, and I thought that of the two, the Butterly was more likely to be a place for a prank.

"They stack the butter and cheese so deep that it hides the entrance. You only really notice it's there when the butter runs out and the new shipment comes. Which would have been last month. It should be stacked full right now and no one would notice the door."

The kettle started to boil and I drew it from the fire and added Panza's leaves before returning the little satchel to her. Everyone was silent.

"You'd have to be small to wriggle in then," Krullmark said, biting his lower lip. "And even getting to the lower entrance would be difficult. You'd have to float down the river, I think, and maybe cross the path from it to the door at night. And hope the barrels and crates blocking the door weren't so many that they were impossible to push aside. Which means no dragon can go."

"Dragon!" Panza scoffed. "You can't go, you bear of a man. And neither can Wawrin. And neither can I." She looked down at her girth. "I built this body to house the world's most ingenious brain, not for squeezing through holes like a mouse."

No wonder she got along with dragons. She practically thought like one. Reshatharin snickered at my thought.

"No laughing, you big lug," Panza said, slapping him roughly on the snout, but a human cuff didn't hurt someone with scales, and Reshatharin only snickered harder, sucking in a breath too sharply, and then coughing on it, his little tuft of coughed flame nearly lighting a worried Shabren on fire.

She squeaked and leapt to the side, wringing her hands.

"You don't … I can't …" Shabren started to say, but Panza was already cutting her off and making shooing motions.

"No one is asking you to leave your injured dragon. In fact, we need someone to stay with them and nurse them. Not that dragons need much, mind, but fresh water and a fire banked nearby can't hurt and if we don't come back, there should be someone left to fly for help."

"Fly where?" Shabren asked miserably. Her expression had been relieved, and then hopeful, but now she looked from face to face anxiously as if we'd all already died and left her with the burden of telling someone about it.

"Fly to Raolcan and the banner of the Dragon," a muffled voice said thickly and then a disoriented Ystren stumbled into the ring around the fire and sat down hard beside Wawrin Tanglefoot.

"Ystren Cartrender!" The older dragon rider said, grabbing Ystren by the shoulder and shaking him affectionately. I thought I saw him blink away a tear. The man must have suffered a great deal out in these woods. "You survived."

"I did," the Magika said wanly, as I passed out tea and put a mug in his hands. "And I have ears so I heard you all. I think Spara has a solid plan." He motioned at me. "And the ones to go are obviously her and me. Her dragon can float us down the river at night and then we'll go in and set any prisoners free and you all can wait close by for our signal. And before I go, I'll give Shabren directions to go for help if everything falls apart."

None of us looked at her dragon. I didn't think any of us thought he'd be ready to fly anywhere soon, but we didn't want to admit it — especially me, because Eyapty had done a lot to help me and the fact he was injured was my fault.

Not your fault. None of this is. We've been pressed hard by the enemy and there will be those who are injured and killed. You must not take it to heart. We are warriors.

I *did* take it to heart and I was going to just keep on doing that, thank you.

"It's a half-baked plan," Krullmark grumbled. "You're barely standing. And you expect us to let you and Spara go in there by yourselves when you don't know what you'll be facing? And what? The big plan is for us to watch and see if you wave to us to fly on in?"

"Do you have a better plan?" Ystren asked, but no one did.

This plan — as faulty as it was — was the only one that had us get in without being detected, and flying straight there wasn't going to work, so we'd have to sneak. We didn't have to like it. We just had to do it.

"We sit tight all day, sleep if we can, hope some other dragons might find their way to join us, and then when it gets dark Spara and I will sneak into Dragon School with her dragon," Ystren said, finishing his tea. "And when we call, you'd better answer. Come in hot and ready to fight. Trust us. If we put pour faith in each other and no one gets cold feet, this is very possible."

But no matter how much he said the same thing again in different ways, I was afraid it might be wishful thinking disguising the fact that we had very little chance.

CHAPTER 10

I'M STARTING to be an expert at floating down rivers on dragon back, I told Reshatharin later that night as he crept on his belly through the forest to where we could slip into the water.

Throughout the day as we rested, there had been several dragons who had made their way to Dragon School and been collected by us before they could be caught by the Silver Dragons. They were all from our underground escape and all currently riderless. And while I was sure it was nicer to have more numbers, their stories made me feel ill with guilt. Each one had a harrowing tale of hours caught in meandering tunnels in the darkness, harried and chased by the enemy, watching friends fall, only to break free and find themselves with us and up against an overwhelming force again.

This is not your fault, Reshatharin had assured me. *Without you, we would all still be prisoners. Besides,* he said and I didn't find this part reassuring. *They might have killed us all once they had the Dominar and the riders above secure. You've saved them as much as anyone can. And we are in a war now. This is only the beginning.*

I didn't want to be in a war.

No one ever does.

I wanted a warm bed and food in my belly, my friends and family safe and no more trouble.

Everyone wants that.

Well, if everyone wanted that then why were we here?

Correction ... most people want that and then the ones who want power and control ruin it for the rest.

And that was why we were here floating down the river. But at least Krullmark and Panza had a few more dragons to help as they prepared to fly in and fight once we gave the signal.

Behind me, Ystren clung to my back wheezing slightly in the cold. I hoped he wouldn't die on me. He seemed to be constantly on the brink of collapse and to care about his health less than anyone I'd ever known.

That's magikas for you — always sacrificing their health for their goals.

It made me uncomfortable.

You're telling me.

Twice, we had to hunker down and wait while flights of silver dragons flew overhead, their shadows darkening the forest around us, but eventually the way was clear and we slipped into the cold river.

Oh yuck, I hate the cold, Reshatharin complained.

I had to bite my lip the cold water edged upward to my waist and then my chest, snatching away my breath.

"I hope you are right about this secret way in," Ystren whispered in my ear. It was the first doubt he had voiced and I understood his concern. If we washed up on the banks like this — cold, soaking wet, and without shelter — the cold alone might kill us before the patrols even knew we were there, but even so I bridled.

"It's not secret, it's just that it's only used by the staff. For a purpose. Because we do the work."

His snort of laughter was nearly silent. "I trust you, Spara.

Or I wouldn't be here. Haven't I proven that again and again. Now. Trust me."

Good advice, Reshatharin said, shivering a little. *Trust me, too. All you have to do is call and I will return for you.*

Trust, I told myself as we eventually slipped from Reshatharin's back and slid through the shadows up the river bank to where the door was hidden by willows.

Trust, I told myself as I ripped back the willows and opened the creaking door.

Trust, I said as we went inside and Ystren made a faint ball of light appear over his hand.

Trust, Reshatharin reminded me as I closed the door behind us, and my heart closed tight like a fist at the thought of being separated from my dragon when the last time that had happened I'd nearly lost him forever.

Trust, I demanded of myself as we squeezed into the passage — barely wide enough for me — and up the steep, damp stairs.

The stairs seemed to go on and on and I wondered if Ystren was doubting me even as I heard his occasional half-there whisper of trust. And then we were both out of breath and Ystren had paused before a heavy oaken door.

"Hold onto your courage," he whispered and he pushed the door open —- just enough for a very thin person to be able to almost squeeze through. To my surprise, he wriggled through the gap, his very narrow hips pushing through a slot that mine could not have possibly breached. The smell of cheese filled the damp passage, and then the door tugged open a little more and I spilled into the buttery and the warm, dry, safe scent of my childhood.

I'd hidden in here once playing hide and seek with my cousins — hidden until I'd become to scared to stay and wait to be found — and it had smelled just like this. I searched for Ystren between the wobbling stacks of cheese and butter and found him with a chunk of cheese in one hand, the magic light in the other, and a mouth so full he couldn't speak.

I gave him a long look.

He swallowed and whispered, "What? I'm younger than I look and I get hungry."

And with that not-properly-serious comment we pushed deeper into Dragon School.

The next rooms up from the buttery were the meat locker where the dried sausages and hams hung and the root vegetable cellar. Ystren ate as we went as if he hadn't eaten in weeks.

Even I stole a dried sausage, trying to keep from gulping the way he had — and then belatedly, tucked a few into my pockets for Krullmark and Panza. I took a few more when I realized everyone would want one. We were going to get found just because we smelled like smoked meat, I knew it.

It was when we emerged from the vegetable cellars into the kitchen that I froze. The kitchens had always been a place I was welcome. A place that was warm, bright, and full of the most delicious smells.

No longer.

A vat of soup sat on the fire and someone leaned over the spot stirring it, but it was not Cook Garlin or any of my friends or the other staff, it was a man dressed in rags like the riders of the medusas. I couldn't say what got into me — maybe just the wrongness of seeing someone else in these kitchens — someone who shouldn't be there — but I crept forward, grabbed a huge ladle, and before I even really admitted to myself what I was doing, I hit the man hard on the back of the head.

He didn't fall over like they do in the stories. He hissed, his hand going to the back of his skull, turned, and drew a wicked blade from his belt. I had just enough time to get the ladle up and suck in a breath of panic, when he fell to his knees and then to the floor in a slump. I turned to look over my shoulder. Ystren had a hand flung up and his little magic light was gone.

"You stick to guiding. I'll deal with the enemy," he told me with an annoyed look on his face.

Fair enough.

Dragon School was meant to be an outdoor sort of place. Dragons are outdoors by nature — even in their own cities and homes they don't like to be confined and most things are open to the air — or so I've been told. And dragon riders, in turn, tend to prefer to be outdoors with their dragons. The very bookish or those not hardy enough to withstand blistering cold or terrible heat on the back of a dragon generally didn't choose this life, or were weeded out for other roles during the training. Actually, they were a lot more suited to be magikas. I glanced out the side of my eyes at Ystren's sickly complexion.

Because of that, Dragon School was built to be open to the air as much as possible and the students, staff, and teachers almost solely used the outdoor ladders to move up from one level to the next. Every level of the school was built into the side of the cliffs and every level was open to that side so that dragons and their riders could come and go as needed. Even the dorms and sick rooms had huge open windows — large enough for a dragon to land and slide within them, if needed.

The storerooms, kitchens, and staff housing were on the lowest level, and the dragon cotes were on the highest level before the actual surface above. Everything else was in between.

We slid out from the kitchen to look up at the other levels and froze. We could see the levels without issue, but from this close, the occupiers were also clearer than ever.

Silver dragons and their riders dashed in and out of the upper levels and medusas clung to the walls, sleeping in the darkness.

Great.

We wouldn't be able to use the outside levels at all.

"Where would they keep prisoners?" Ystren asked in a whisper.

"The dorms?" I asked.

"They'll need those to house the silver riders and these medusa riders," Ystren said with a frown.

"Infirmary?" I asked.

He made a sound like a maybe in the back of his throat.

"Staff housing?"

"Where is that?"

"It's on this level," I whispered, "that way."

"We'll try there first," he said and then followed me as we crept through the inner passageways.

Despite the man we'd found in the kitchens, the time of day meant there wasn't anyone else bustling around in there and the passages that were usually full of cheerful, hurrying staff were empty and echoing.

I grimaced, almost physically hurting at the lack of people but when we reached the staff housing, we had to pull back. A full silver dragon was curled around himself in the passage and a pair of silver riders were playing cards at a low table as they guarded the passage.

"This will be them," Ystren whispered to me as we retreated back around the corner. "They wouldn't be here guarding this spot for nothing."

"It may be only the staff that they captured," I whispered back.

"Then why a full dragon to guard?" Ystren raised an eyebrow. "No, Spara. This is what we're here for. But now what? Two riders, I could deal with."

I admired his confidence. Silver dragoons — the riders of the silver dragons who guarded the Dominar — were the best trained warriors of our nation.

"But what will I do with that dragon?" Ystren asked, frowning.

I swallowed, nervous, but there was only one way forward and behind these guards might lie my friends or even my family. We couldn't just walk away from this.

I drew up as tall as I could and straightened my shoulders. "I think you'd better leave the dragon to me."

CHAPTER 11

Our plan was simple — which isn't the same as easy. Ystren would distract— and hopefully immobilize — the guards while I dealt with the dragon.

"I can't immobilize the dragon," Ystren had whispered. "Too big. And I need to go light with the guards or I'll be too tired to be much good. I can probably make one fall asleep and distract the other, but you'll have to manage the dragon."

I wasn't sure of my plan of attack. Should I reason with him? Plead with him to release those he was guarding? The idea of either made my palms sweat, but Ystren had left this to me.

"I have absolute confidence in you," had been his parting whisper. Which — well, I liked not being treated like a child and being trusted with something important, but I wished it wasn't something quite *this* important.

In the end, I chose neither pleading nor reason, and when Ystren made a strange sound with magic and the guards abandoned their cards, one to chase after the sound and the other to succumb to magic sleep just like the guard in the kitchen had, I made my move.

I thought Silver dragons were supposed to be the best there were, I said, still hiding around the corner.

The silver dragon's head came up suddenly. He hadn't seemed too interested in one of his human friends running off and the other falling asleep but he hadn't left his place guarding the door behind him.

Who is talking to me? A mouse? he sounded young, to my surprise.

I thought that silvers were meant to be the wisest of all dragons, and that was why they were chosen to serve only the Dominar.

We are. He straightened as much as he could in the small corridor, puffing out his chest.

That can't be right. You're in a hallway guarding things with no claws or flame and not guarding the Dominar at all.

The dragon blew out an irritated burst of flame. *Kova says this is how we serve now.*

And where is Kova? I pressed.

He is with me. He is my rider and I would never leave him. He is simply ... tired. The dragon looked around and snorted at the sight of his rider asleep, slumped across the card table. *Who are you, anyway, to question me?*

I swallowed, nervous, but I needed to say something to convince him and this was the only thing I had.

I am here on behalf of the Banner of the Dragon — sent by Raolcan, head of that order.

There was a long pause and for a moment, I thought all was lost. He didn't believe me and the second he saw me he would flame me.

Command me, he said reverently. The tone of his thoughts had changed. *I am Kergemad, dragon to Kova of the Silvers. I am loyal to the Dominar and to the Flame. What would you have me do?*

To start, you could stop keeping those loyal to the Dominar locked up behind you, I said.

We only keep the rebels confined, he said confidently.

You're the rebels, I said wryly. *I saw with my own eyes as Jhairen Que'Shal, the commander of those medusas who are here with you, took the Dominar captive. He was beaten and barely able to stand. The Dominar. Who you are sworn to protect.*

There was a roar and Kergemad was on his feet in an instant. He snatched his rider up in a paw, shaking him.

Wake up, wake up, you stupid human!

Wait! You're going to hurt him!

Have you proof of this that you tell me? Kergemad asked me.

Outside there are dragons waiting for me to return. They all saw it, too. You can ask them.

His head swiveled toward the open wall beside him and I saw that he was about to leap out there and ask them but I forestalled him.

Wait. Do you trust me?

When he spoke, he sounded distraught. *You know that Raolcan the Purple lives and that he leads the secret Banner of the Dragon which all Silvers revere. I have seen him when I was guarding the Dominar who is his friend. If you are here under his authority, then I must believe you, and this explains why Kova has been so cagey. Why he has not told me aloud what we are doing when usually he has the courtesy to at least say our orders out loud for me to hear. Why his friends have acted like all of this is a secret. Why they ... why they bound other riders and did not explain ... oh no.*

Oh no, what? I was worried enough that I stepped out from cover and we were face to face — him with his eyes huge and worried. Me, a tiny human standing before him. He looked down at the slumped human in his forepaw and a gust of steam leapt from his nostrils.

What have you done, Kova? I gave you my life.

Uh oh. He was far more upset than I'd anticipated. I thought that maybe I could taunt him into leaving the door vulnerable or even reason him into opening it for us. I hadn't expected that he'd immediately leap to the conclusion that his rider had betrayed him but the grief and misery in his voice was undeniable.

May I pass? I asked cautiously. *I am under orders to release those you are guarding so we may free the dragons unjustly imprisoned and return this place to the authority of the Dominar.*

He groaned, a miserable groan of someone who had just realized they were in so much trouble.

You'd better do it, he told me, *and quickly. Before I'm in even worse trouble than I already am. They must think we are traitors!*

Who?

The Dominar and those loyal to him!

He sounded panicked.

I am panicked. I am not a traitor!

Then let's get these prisoners free, I said, sliding past him.

I felt terrible that he had been tricked and awful that he felt so guilty, but it didn't mean I didn't feel a little sick with worry as I crept around his huge silver tail to get to the door behind him. If he changed his mind, he could crush me in an instant.

I am no traitor, he echoed sadly, staring at the human in his forepaws with the saddest eyes I'd ever seen.

I cleared my throat, trying not to tear up.

"Spara?" I heard a whisper down the hall. Ystren had returned.

"That is Ystren Cartrender," I said aloud to Kergemad. "He's here to help."

The dragon didn't even look up.

"Over here, Ystren," I hissed back. "Hurry."

I didn't wait for him — there was too little time. I opened the door with a strong tug and as the light spilled into the common room of the staff housing wing, I gasped.

CHAPTER 12

Knowing that dozens of dragon riders had been captured was one thing, but seeing them all there was something else. I stood stunned in the doorway for a heartbeat as my eyes took in the sheer number of people stuffed into the staff common room.

I'd grown up in this room — played in it as a small child, celebrated festivals with the other staff here when we were done clearing up for parties above, walked through it every day on my way to my family's rooms beyond. Seeing it now, like this, felt like I was walking through a dream.

Ystren appeared beside me, out of breath and looking nervously over his shoulder, but I had no time for him. Not when my eyes looked greedily past the captured dragon riders to the staff.

From one corner, someone said, "Spara? Is that you? Oh, Spara, your poor mother thought you were dead!"

And then my old friend Corana pushed through the crowd, shoving full dragon riders in their rider blacks out of the way, and gathered me into a huge hug. I couldn't help the tears smarting my eyes. I hadn't expected to feel like this — hadn't let myself admit how scared I was for everyone here. But I saw them over her shoulder — old Kendall who carried charcoal to all the braziers. Christif and Jorel who handled waste. Yevel who did most of the mucking. Sadie and Sweda who did all the laundry — and dozens more. People I grew up with. Friends. Family, practically.

They gathered around me, fighting to be the next one to hug me as we tried to whisper and keep our voices down.

Ystren coughed pointedly as he tried to get control over a suddenly chaotic situation.

"Who ranks highest here?" Ystren said, just loud enough to be heard, but hopefully quietly enough not to attract attention.

"I'm Flenna of the Red," a dragon rider told him from somewhere near the back. "I have seniority. But they took our dragons — those that survived."

There were far fewer dragon riders than there were staff, and of those that were here, most were injured or wounded.

"We need to take back the school," Ystren told them. "We don't have the option of just escaping. We'll be hunted down one by one if we do that."

Flenna looked grim, but she pressed through the crowd toward him. "There are twelve of us still fighting fit — mostly. We'll have to leave the staff here where they are safe, obviously."

"No," I spoke up.

"No?" She lifted an eyebrow at me.

"Everyone has the right to fight for their own fate. Their own future. Their own lands. And no one has the right to tell them to step back and let someone else take that honor."

There was a murmur of agreement from the staff around me and Flenna grew flushed with annoyance.

"These people aren't trained. They'll be killed."

"They'll be your guides," I said, unmoved. "There are secret places all through Dragon School and they will show you how to get around."

"It's a good plan," Ystren agreed. "From what I can tell, the bulk of the enemy seem concentrated on the central levels."

"The dining hall and the dormitories," Kendall said in a low voice. "That's where they were concentrated before they locked the staff down here. We served them at first — the silver dragon riders — but when they started to capture anyone who came here, well, we couldn't be party to that, you understand."

"I understand," Ystren said as if he had the right to make judgments and find they were innocent. They *were* innocent and even honorable, but I didn't think they should be looking to him to confirm it. That got my back up. "We'll split into four groups, led by whichever staff feel they want to help," Ystren continued in a mollifying voice. "Surprise is to our advantage and when we're ready to pounce, Spara will give word to the dragons waiting for us and they will cause a distraction outside."

"Spara?" Flenna asked, looking a question at me.

"She's a purple rider," Ystren said by way of explanation. "It's my understanding that they speak to their mounts."

Heads nodded in agreement and the staff around me watched with huge eyes whispering to each other, "Our Spara?" And "Just like Alissi. It's in the blood!"

I felt my face color.

"I should go to the dragon cotes," I whispered. "I can speak to the dragons there. Free those I can. Maybe explain to more of the silver dragons what has occurred. Kergemad might not be the only one to find what they are siding with appalling."

"Kergemad?" Flenna mouthed the name, frowning at me, but I didn't bother to tell her that I could speak to all dragons or that I could likely speak to hers. Leave that for another time when we weren't in a hurry.

"We should leave immediately," Ystren reminded us. "Someone will notice the guards are down."

There were no objections and to my surprise, the staff and

riders sorted themselves very quickly into groups — one group that would remain here to tend the young, the old, and the injured, four groups to split up like Ystren wanted, and one group to go with me to find the dragons.

"We'll be in position by the time you get up to the cotes," Ystren told me with a confidence that I didn't share. After all, there was no way to know what he might face along the way. We thought that the hidden servant passageways were a secret — but it was possible they'd been found. "As soon as you get in place, signal the dragons outside to attack. This is the best chance we'll have."

CHAPTER 13

PERHAPS YSTREN WAS right to be confident after all, because we reached the cotes without anyone finding us. My group was comprised entirely of staff — friends, really.

"You'll be breaking chains and freeing dragons. It shouldn't be a fight," Ystren had said, but I could tell he was only saying it to bolster the spirits of those with us. We didn't have enough trained fighters for everything we needed to do and we were going to have to rely on anyone willing to try. And that meant staff.

I'd passed Kergemad on the way.

What will you do? I had asked him. *You could wait here and keep your rider safe. Or you could make a run for it. I fear the dragons coming will consider you an enemy and they might flame before asking questions.*

I have much to atone for, he'd said sadly. *Foolish Kova has made our paws very dirty with his choices. I think I'll choose a different path.*

And what path is that? I asked, but he seemed no more certain than I was of what he could do and I'd had to abandon him in the hurry to get up to the cotes.

Now, we were here, hovering just outside the hidden door to the hallway where we'd be able to sneak past the guards.

"I'll talk to all the dragons I can ahead of time," I told Yeval and Sweda who were with me. "Just follow me and when I point to a dragon try to get them untethered. If anyone sees you — run and hide."

"You said we could fight," Yeval said a little hopefully. He was older than me by about ten years and very strong from his work.

"It's not up to me what you do," I hissed. "Make your own choices."

But he was looking at me and I sighed. "Fight if you want to. Just try to be safe, alright?"

But I was already feeling sick at the idea of leading them into danger. Maybe that was why Flenna had been so reluctant.

I took a deep breath and called to my dragon.

Reshatharin? Can you hear me?

Yes! The answer was faint but there.

It's time! I called, and then I burst into the cotes and right past the stunned face of medusa rider who had been walking down the passageway with no expectation of facing running opponents suddenly right there. I heard him grunt behind me. Yeval must have hit him.

Up dragons, up! Up! The Dominion needs you! I called, and the moment I burst into a cote, the dragon there leapt up, shaking himself like a dog.

He was a huge red dragon. Their color was usually sleek and smooth of scale, but this one was gnarled and old, his skin and wings ripped in places and barely healed. He must have put up quite the fight when they captured him. His head was held in a metal harness linked on either side to the wall.

Do not flame us! I warned him as Yevel and I struggled to unhook the chains and rip them from where they held him.

In the doorway, Sweda watched for anyone coming.

"Hurry!" she whisper-yelled. "Hurry!"

What is this? the red asked in my mind.

We're freeing whoever we can. There are dragons coming to help. We must take back Dragon School!

Yesssss! he roared in my mind at the same time that he also roared aloud, and just in time the chains broke and we leapt back from his roar and hurried to the next cote.

In this cote, a green dragon was already standing, clawing at the ground, clearly worked up.

Calmly now! Calmly! I told him. *Or we won't be able to get close to free you!*

He calmed immediately and I left Sweda to rip his chains free while Yevel and I raced onward to the next cote where another red waited, this one already flaming wildly out the cote door.

Hurry, hurry, hurry, he chanted at us.

I motioned to Yevel to free him, too, while I hurried down to the next cote, but when I stumbled inside the red dragon there was pinned to the ground by a silver dragon with a rider on his back.

The silver flamed at me and I barely danced backward in time to avoid a terrible burn. From his back, his rider hissed, his face contorted with concentration, and then two more silver dragoon burst into the room. Before I could dodge, one grabbed me and threw me.

I hit the wall, my head thwacking the stone so hard that I saw stars. My vision was dark but I felt it when he dragged me up and pinned me against the wall. He was saying something I couldn't quite make out. Something about traitors and death.

And then something bright shot across my vision, blinding me again, and the hand released me to slump to my knees on the ground.

To my surprise, I heard a voice in my head, speaking with authority.

Silver dragons. Hear me now. I am Kergemad your friend and ally and I bear terrible tidings. We have been lied to. We have been deceived. By those we trusted most dearly. Halt in your passion! Cease your flames! These other dragons are our friends, for it is the humans who have betrayed us.

I blinked again and my vision began to clear as another set of hands helped me up. I blinked into the determined face of Sweda. The other girl was sweating and streaked with soot, a burn mark scorched the hem of her dress, but her face was set with determination.

My mouth fell open at her incredible courage.

"Spara," she gasped, trembling all over. "Are you hurt?"

Behind her, Kergemad perched on top of the other silver dragon, one forepaw gripping his neck, and one forepaw gripping the red dragon's neck as if he alone were keeping them apart. Head flung back, he was still speaking, urging the silvers to listen. On the ground in front of me, the two Silver Dragoons who had attacked me lay burnt to a crisp.

I gasped, trying desperately to catch my breath, while Sweda said, "Come on, there are more!"

She was already moving to untruss the red dragon — then if Kergemad ever let him up he'd be free then.

I had to trust that Kergemad knew what he was doing and that he'd convince the silver dragons. Because there would be no time for me to try to reason with them. Not with the sound of battle coming from every direction.

I hurried to the next cote and found it empty, but the emptiness gave me a chance to look out and try to assess what was happening. From below, the shouts and clashes of humans fighting filled the air and when I looked down, I saw a man wrapped in rags tossed out the window, screaming as he plummeted toward the ground.

Heart in my throat, I looked down the line of dragon cotes at the dragons in every entrance chained and fighting against their restraints. And then to the skies, where the fighting was so intense that it was hard to keep track of who was fighting whom. Silver dragons were everywhere, their fire spewing into the clouds. In the middle of them, in small knots, dragons of other colors fought in twos and threes. I needed to get more dragons free to help. I didn't have time to wait.

I turned, planning to run to the next cote, but my way was blocked by two men in rags and as I watched, a medusa squeezed — literally squeezed its body — through the human-sized door and the men began to laugh.

"Here to cause trouble?" one of them asked, and I think I'd been expecting an accent or something to mark him as foreign. I think I'd been expecting them just to advance in terrifying silence.

What I hadn't expected was that they would sound just like me. What I hadn't expected was that one of them would pull down the rags around his face and I'd recognize him.

"Janzen?" I asked, horrified.

Because I knew exactly who this was. Janzen. A boy who had failed Dragon School and become one of the staff. He'd disappeared last year and everyone had assumed he went to make a life somewhere better — though no one thought there actually was a place better than Dragon School. Janzen hadn't like the work. Or the submissive attitude of the staff. Or what we ate. Or a lot of things. Did he like it better as the bandaged rider of a medusa? What would they eat?

"Janzen," he echoed, his smile growing. "Who would have thought they'd let crippled Spara become a dragon rider?"

He was taunting me.

"I don't like that word," I said boldly, even though they outnumbered me. Even though the men were moving up on either side of the wall while the medusa blocked the exit. I backed up a step, and then another, but there wasn't much room before I'd reach the edge. "And it's not true, either."

"We'll use whatever words we want," Janzen said, his smile growing more wicked. "We're masters of this place now and we will form it in the way we want and people will bow to us now. I think you should start. Bow to me, Spara."

"I don't think so," I said, backing up again. I could feel the wind on my back. I cold feel that my heel was over the edge.

"Bow to me ... or fall."

They were closer now, and Janzen drew a wicked knife from his belt.

"No," I said in a small voice.

"There is no one who can protect you now," Janzen said.

And he was right. I was all on my own. I was out of options. And this time I didn't think there would be a dragon who could catch me when I fell.

"Then you will die," Janzen said and lunged forward.

I closed my eyes, braced myself, and then suddenly my hair was whipping in the air and I opened my eyes in time to see that I'd been snatched from the edge by a purple dragon paw. Flames filled the space where I'd been standing before and Janzen screamed, pinwheeling over the edge, his friend with him, their bandages licking with bright flames.

I gasped, horrified and in my mind I heard, *You first, little bug.*

And I looked up into the glowing eye of Reshatharin.

You might want to close your eyes for this part, Sparrow, he said, and before I could obey, he took one leap forward and closed his jaws around the medusa with a loud *crunch.*

I'm developing a taste for these, he said, pausing as he chewed to notice I was looking pale. *Sorry about the humans, though. I was late and then it was you or them, and I pick you. Every time, I pick you. Forever.*

DRAGON LEGACY

EPISODE EIGHT: PIT OF DREAD

CHAPTER 1

I SEE two more just over that ridge! Reshatharin said and then he dove in a way that made my stomach buck.

I clung to him as he roared, scattering a flock of birds and making my ears ache, but I shared his elation and triumph.

Behind me, Panza was collecting Shabren and the dragons who had waited with her for the battle to be won or lost. I stole a brief glance at them. They'd be relieved. Just as I was.

And because I was looking over at them I got to see the moment that Wawrin Tanglefoot's dragon descended like a red streak from the sky.

It warms the heart.

I could only imagine the kind of tearful reunion that would be.

Please, don't. I was having fun.

We'd found him chained in a dragon cote, burned and wounded and missing one eye.

Yuck. I told you, don't remember! Better to move on!

The second we'd taken his chains off he'd roared just like Reshatharin was doing now and leapt from the cote, sinking his teeth into the neck of one of the silver dragons and then spinning to gobble down a medusa in three wrenching bites.

It seemed Reshatharin was not the only one who liked eating them or the only one who thought nothing of shaking the humans from their back to do it. It made me feel ill.

Once you get past the fishy taste they have a nice chew, Reshatharin told me as we swam through the air over the ridge and the two medusas we were chasing came into sight. *Toothsome.*

But they were living things! Just like him. Just like all the dragons I was quickly becoming attached to. Maybe the riders in the medusa's basket had been attached to them. Maybe they were friends.

Friends is going a bit far. If they are attached, it is only as one would be attached to a farm animal. The medusas do not think as dragons do, nor as humans do, he conceded as if humans were enough lower than dragons that I might be insulted.

But I wasn't sure I wouldn't feel any less sympathy if these were chickens or sheep.

Exactly. But you still eat the chicken. I've seen you do it. And these chickens are a lot of trouble and come with riders who hurt dragons. So. Leave me to my feeding.

I closed my eyes when we came up on the next one and just held onto the saddle as we wrenched this way and that in the air. Something was crunching. Oh gross. Make it stop!

Chicken. Mmmm.

I only opened my eyes when someone human cried out.

She was falling through the air, eyes panicked, bandages wrapped around her face so it was hard to tell anything else but on instinct I reached out and caught her, clawing at her with my one good arms while my knees squeezed into Reshatharin's sides. The impact of hugging her close sent me hard into the saddle and Reshatharin turned from where he was shredding the medusa and looked at me, shook his head, and went back to it.

Save whoever you want, but you know she's trouble. It would be better to eat her.

Eat a human?!

Well ... of course not. I didn't mean that. Medusas are easier.

Dragons had a very straightforward approach to friends and enemies. I wasn't quite so heartless. But despite his seeming indifference, he adjusted so that the woman I'd caught could fall into the saddle in front of me a little better. She sat very still, knuckles white where she gripped the saddle, breath sawing in and out at an incredible rate.

"Umm, you're my prisoner now," I told her because I wasn't sure what else to say.

She spat curses in a language I did not know but I was taking that as acknowledgment of the situation.

Only one of the medusas had been being ridden. Reshatharin snatched the other one on the wing and didn't eat it, just dispatched it and let it fall. If there were riders, I did not see them, but I was shaking now — and moreso with a woman in my arms who had almost died falling to her death. Victory was not sweet at all.

You're telling me. I cannot shake this fish taste.

Was it possible that the horror of it brought out a gallows humor in him? The forest around Dragon School was going to be a mess of littered bodies. Most of them deserved their fate ... but they were humans. Just like me.

I swallowed roughly. I could not take death as easily as the dragons did. People had died. And for all I knew, they thought their cause was justified.

They took out a dragon's eye. And hurt him. And these are the people you have compassion for?

I swallowed, feeling ill for everyone at once.

"Who are you?" I asked my prisoner, trying to think of anything else but what we'd done and had done to our friends.

With a trembling hand, she reached up and ripped the bandages from her face and head.

She was a girl about my age with short, uneven black hair and a very determined, worried look in her eyes.

"You're young!" I said surprised.

"We're all young," she said and there was a tremble in her voice.

I thought about Janzen and the terrible way he'd fallen from the cliff, lit on fire when Reshatharin saved me and I shuddered.

"You speak like you're from the Dominion," I said, too stunned to express what was troubling me — that these people had taken the capital and killed dragons and riders and they were ... from our own lands?

"I *am* from the Dominion," she said and there were tears in her eyes alongside the venom. "Are you going to kill me? Get it over with."

"I don't think so," I said but the confusion I felt made me sound very uncertain.

I told you — better to kill her before she causes more trouble, Reshatharin said.

And I told you ... she's a person.

He was winging his way back to Dragon School now and in the distance I saw that the fighting there had slowed, silver dragons and their riders had been corralled on the flat plateau that was the roof of Dragon School, and all the dragons and riders that had chased after fleeing enemies were headed back in, too.

What were we going to do with our prisoners? And what if they were all like this girl?

"I'm Spara Coldrock," I told her. "And this is my dragon, Reshatharin. We are taking back Dragons School."

But the girl did not offer her name in return. She just looked paler and greener the closer we got to Dragon School and when we finally set down on the cliff edge there, I realized there were very few of her ragged band of insurgents still alive.

"I serve Jhairen Que'Shal of the House of Shadows of the Ethereal Lands," she said fiercely just before we landed. "And the Dominion will be ours, no matter how many have to die to see it happen."

"I don't think I'd be saying that to anyone else right now," I told her grimly.

Or they'll be the ones to kill her.

I felt my cheeks grow hot, but it was one thing to fight for your life and another thing to kill someone just because they might be trouble later or inconvenient right now. I would not allow murder.

"Come on," I said instead. "Let's find out how many of your friends survived."

But though I said it to the other girl, I was worried about it for myself, too. The fighting had been hot and intense and I had a terrible feeling that people who mattered to me might have died.

Let us not be fearful when we do not know, Reshatharin said but all I could manage in response was a pat on his neck.

CHAPTER 2

WAWRIN TANGLEFOOT and Panza Boldbrewer had just landed as we arrived and from the air I saw them striding boldly to where Ystren Cartrender was pointing and gesturing. I let out a relieved sigh. It was good to have competent people in charge. People who weren't me.

I had enough on my conscience without having to think about what to do next.

But someone was missing. I scanned the plateau but there was no growling bear of a man anywhere on it. A spike of worry shot through me. Where was Krullmark?

He'll be there somewhere. Probably Ursijek is having fun harrying Silvers out of their hidey-holes.

I didn't like the sound of any of that. If he was fighting through the chambers of Dragon School there were many places where he could be ambushed or hurt. He would do everything he could to save the defenseless.

Reshatharin landed, skidding across the ground and a sudden buck from the girl in front of me reminded me I had a prisoner to deal with before anything else.

"I think you'd better give me your name," I told her as we slid to a halt. "And tell me if you have an injuries that need tending."

Reshatharin had landed right under the tree where Alissi and I had met before the fateful night of our flight and I felt a sudden pang at the memory. I had envied her so much back then. If only I'd realized how much she needed my support and love. She'd been scared that night — and with good reason. Because medusa riders had chased her down and shot her through with arrows. Just like this one I had taken prisoner.

My stomach twisted at the thought.

"I serve the House of Shadows of the Ethereal Lands," she said through gritted teeth. "I will not give my name, my mission or the names of anyone else here and no torture will drag that information from me."

"No one wants to torture you," I said with a sigh as I looked over to where Ystren had the dragons lined up on one side and their riders under guard on the other.

Are you sure about that? Reshatharin asked.

I was sure no one *would* be doing any torturing. Not if I heard about it.

Christif and Jorel were standing facing the prisoners, swords in hand and looking nervous. They were staff, just as I had been. Others might think they were out of their element but I'd risen to meet the challenge and I knew they could, too.

They were overseen by Flenna of the Red who I'd met imprisoned below and more dragon riders were climbing the ladder with prisoners or without and taking their places around the men and women huddled there. Everyone was breathing hard — some with wounds, others dirty and rumpled. The fighting had not been easy for any of us.

Hostages, Reshatharin told me, grimly. *They are being kept apart to ensure their dragons' good behavior.*

And would that work?

We'll quickly find out, I fear.

There were no captured sentinels with them.

All eaten.

I tried not to think about that, but there were a handful of ragged people set right along the edge of the cliff with two dragons guarding them. One was Ryfsmae, and the other — to my surprise, was Kergemad, his unconscious rider had been tied to his back with ropes and he looked extremely agitated as I hurried over with my prisoner.

Is all well? I asked them with my mind.

I'm unharmed, Ryfsmae told me as he sat on his haunches and scratched an ear with a back foot. *If these give trouble we can flick them off the cliff.*

Mmm, Reshatharin agreed.

Enough you two! You are so bloodthirsty! They horrified me with their casual talk of death. *There will be no flinging people off cliffs. There will be no torture. There will be no eating people.*

It was only a joke, Ryfsmae said but Reshatharin was laughing like it wasn't.

I am also well, Kergemad said nervously. *Will you speak for Kova when he wakes? I fear for what will be done to him.*

"Of course," I said aloud, laying a hand on his neck and peering worriedly at Kova. There was little that could be done before he woke.

I left my prisoner with the others, feeling sick as I did it. I didn't like any of this.

Tell her that. This is her fault and those others. We did not bring war and violence to them. They brought it to us.

The prisoner shot me one last glance as I was leaving and said, "The Dusk Covenant never really left. And we are back now from the Ethereal Lands. Tell your leader."

"What?" I asked, my eyes growing large.

"Tell him," she said and then sunk into the group of others wrapped in rags leaving me blinking and suddenly feeling like I couldn't quite catch a breath.

Do you know who the Dusk Covenant was?

Of course I knew who the Dusk Covenant was. You'd have to really not be paying attention to have missed hearing of them. A hundred years ago they nearly ruined what there was of the Dominion. They were the ones whose symbols were all over Jhairen's artifact. And if they were back and behind all this … well, Raolcan might need to call on his Lightbringer friends — such as there were — as soon as possible.

Do you think it's true? I asked Reshatharin.

I always think everything terrible is true, Reshatharin replied. *That's why I'm still here.*

Sometimes I thought he just liked saying things that made him sound dashing, but he made a good point. We would have to assume that this horrible news was true until we could disprove it. And that meant telling Ystren.

Don't worry, Sparrow. As soon as you've done your duty, we'll go find your angry bear.

I felt my cheeks heat. Perhaps I had not been subtle in my worry.

Promise? I asked, hopefully.

Absolutely, Ursijek bet me he could eat more medusas than me and I ate five. I think he'll be paying up. Reshatharin preened as we moved toward Ystren, Panza, and the others.

How do dragons pay? I asked him.

In reputation, he said. *But only if beds made of gold coins aren't available.*

They aren't.

Then it will be paid in reputation. Watch while your dragon becomes the most feared in all the Dominion.

CHAPTER 3

If I thought I could just talk to Ystren and then do as I pleased, I was quickly shown that was not to be.

"Ah, Spara, you're here," he said seeming relieved.

Uh oh, Reshatharin said.

Exactly my thoughts. The last thing I wanted was someone needing me right now.

"We need you to speak to these silver dragons for us and explain the situation. Panza's dragon already grabbed the one you spoke to below and has him over there out of trouble and with something to keep him busy."

I felt my eyes widen at that. He was calling guarding our most important prisoners something to "keep him out of trouble"? That seemed a dangerous attitude to take.

"He risked everything to help us," I said, trying to keep my voice calm.

"As he should have," Ystren agreed.

"I want that taken into account," I said, pausing and letting that sit until he opened his mouth. "For both Kergemad and his rider — Kova."

"He fought against us." Ystren seemed unconvinced.

"The dragon did not."

Ystren looked at me a long time before scowling. "Fine. Yes. It will be taken into account."

"Weren't the medusa riders here first and then the silvers arrived later?" I said, turning the conversation back to his original request. "So weren't they the ones in charge here? Shouldn't they be the ones we speak to first?"

"Yes," Wawrin Tanglefoot said adamantly, his face red. The way that Ystren drew physically back from his as he spoke suggested they'd been fighting about this very thing.

"Have we found the ringleader for the medusa riders yet?" I pressed.

"Immaterial," Ystren dismissed my thoughts with a wave of his hand and Wawrin made a furious sound in the back of his throat. "They're vagabonds and refuse. Hardly worth sniffing out. The silvers, on the other hand, betrayed the Dominar, glory to his name, and took up Dragon School as a fortress. We need information from them but their riders refuse to say a word."

"The silvers wouldn't have rebelled except that they supported Yulden's bid for the Dominar's throne — or possibly were tricked into believing he was the real Dominar giving them orders," I said quietly.

Panza coughed and finished my thought for me. "They may very well be innocent of wrong in their own minds if that is the case. And Yulden would not have acted without the prompting of Jhairen Que'Shal who started this mess. That makes the House of Shadows of the Ethereal Lands a dangerous foe."

"As you know," I reminded him, "for you were nearly killed by them twice."

"The House of Shadows of the Ethereal Lands?" Ystren repeated, raising one eyebrow and totally glossing over his near escapes. "You are certain?"

"That's the closest I've found to a name for them," I said,

but then added, “Though the prisoner I took claimed the Dusk Covenant has returned.”

Wawrin hissed through his teeth and Panza spat on the ground as if to ward off a great evil. Even Ystren looked upset at that. He bit his lip and I wondered if he knew more than he was saying. After all, Jhairen Que’Shal had said he had worked with him and had tortured him looking for information about something missing. What was he keeping from us?

“I know far more about Jhairen Que’Shal than you can know in just a few tiny interactions, and I’m telling you that the people he sent here are not our main concern,” Ystren said, trying to seize control once more.

He might even be right, but it couldn’t be a good idea to treat any enemy as lesser. Not when they’d caused so much hurt.

Ystren cleared his throat to draw back my attention. “What we need from you is to speak to these silver dragons. Find out for us who they are and what they were doing here. Just because their riders won’t talk doesn’t mean the dragons won’t.”

“Can she really do that?” Flenna of the Red asked in a low voice from where she stood guard.

“Spara,” Ystren said a little imperiously. Did that go over well with his magika friends or did he tone it down with them?

I doubt he tones this down for anyone. It’s right in his bones.

“*Spara*, if you would,” he pushing me with his tone of voice.

I shot him an annoyed look.

I didn’t like being ordered around, but I clambered down from Reshatharin’s back and arranged myself in front of the silver riders. They stood or sat or moved around without looking at us or acknowledging us in any way, as if we were not even in the same world. I couldn’t tell the rank of one from another, but they all had the same furious grimace on their faces.

"Will you speak to me," I asked them. "Will you tell us if you still serve the Dominar?"

One of them spat and the rest turned away from me. I was getting very sick of all this spitting.

And not even fire. You'd think humans would give up on spitting when they realize they can't breathe fire.

With a sigh, I turned to face their dragons.

Some of the dragons looked defeated. Some injured. Others affronted. There were a dozen overall which made my stomach flip as I was sure there had been many more when we started fighting them. A quick count of their riders gave me thirty-five and I felt suddenly dizzy.

Easy now. Easy.

We'd killed dragons. By this count, we'd killed many dragons. I wanted to cry.

But you won't. You'll do it later after the task Ystren assigned for you. We cannot all be heroes, Spara, but we can all do our part to act heroically.

And speaking to these dragons is acting heroically? I asked.

It is if you are their only voice.

I glanced back at the riders, swallowing hard at the tell-tale signs. Some of them were already coughing. And I knew those who had lost their dragons would not survive for long without them. We had killed them, too. Even if we hadn't meant it that way.

I cleared my throat.

Silver dragons, I began, a little awkwardly. *Do you have a leader among you?*

There was no response.

Do you know what you were doing here?

Serving the Dominar, glory to his name, the one closest to me said with a stomp of a forepaw. He was so sleek in appearance that I could nearly see my own face in his scales. *A thing you should have considered before you flew in here and attacked us, rebels!*

Don't threaten my rider, Reshatharin growled into our minds, surging forward at the insult. I stopped him with a hand and he let me.

How were you serving the Dominar here? I asked.

We were defending Dragon School.

How? I pressed. But no one answered that. *By imprisoning any dragon who came near? By locking up the staff?*

Well, I wasn't getting anywhere with these accusations. All the dragons were either too ashamed to look at me or overly defensive like this nearby dragon, staring me in the eye and snorting fire.

Hear this, I told them, *Whatever your riders have told you, you are not serving the Dominar, but rather the man who overthrew him, Yulden Peaceholder, a gold dragon rider. You are not fending off rebels but rather capturing and killing truly loyal and noble dragons.* The ones who looked guilty hung their heads even more but most of them glared at me, mistrustful. *Now, you are offered a choice. Work with us to return the true Dominar to the throne. Tell us everything you know about the plans against him and fight with us side by side.*

Or? The belligerent dragon asked, snorting a long black trail of smoke.

Or find out what it means to defy us, I said, though I had no idea what that might mean.

Ystren had been watching us, his gaze flicking back and forth between us. He seemed to have caught the conversation by our body language.

"They do not want to work with us?" he asked me.

"Not yet," I said.

"Then tell them we'll throw their riders from the cliff one at a time until they do."

The nearest dragon reared back at that, roaring, and several other dragons did the same, their dismay written all over their faces, though to my surprise, they did not burn us where we stood, or even burn Reshatharin who had thrown himself between us and them.

I turned to Ystren in horror. "I will not be part of murder."

"It will not be your call," he returned, flushing hot.

"What are you becoming?" I asked in horror.

He looked like he was in agony. "I am becoming what I must."

"You are becoming the monster you claim to fight," I told him, barely holding back tears of horror.

Wawrin Tanglefoot grabbed Ystren by the collar before I had to say more an roared in his face. A literal roar. Like a dragon.

"No."

Good for Wawrin.

Beside him, his dragon trembled with obvious rage and I took a wary step back, clinging to Reshatharin.

"I am taking charge of the dragon rider prisoners," Wawrin Tanglefoot said, quivering with fury. "I will speak to them. And as ranking dragon rider here, I will determine their fates. And as the highest ranking red dragon rider here I am declaring it an emergency situation and conscripting all dragons present under my command. No dragon will be ordered about except by my leave. No rider will be commanded. No prisoner treated with anything but the utmost of respect. Get yourself from their sight, magika."

To my shock, Ystren strode away, fists clenched at his sides.

Wawrin Tanglefoot turned to the dragon riders. "No one is being thrown from cliffs. I am Wawrin Tanglefoot of the Red. By the laws and ordinances of the Dominion of Sky People, you are my certified prisoners and will be afforded every right of a prisoner, including the right to remain silent if you will not cooperate. If you choose to speak, I will hear your words. If you choose not to, you will be held here at Dragon School until such a time as the Dominar agrees to release you."

I chased after Ystren, leaving the dragons and prisoners in Wawrin Tanglefoot's capable hands.

What are you planning? Reshatharin asked.

I didn't know. I just knew Ystren looked like trouble.

I don't like you descending without me!

He spoke anxiously — which was fair enough. After all, he'd just saved me from nearly being killed down there, but Ystren was fast — already halfway down the ladder to the next level by the time I was at the top of it. I had a bad feeling he was up to trouble.

I have to go, I told Reshatharin. *I have to make sure ... Krullmark is still down there somewhere and Ystren is furious and ... and I don't know, I just think my place is there.*

Fine, he said, *But please, Spara, stay out of trouble. Ystren Cartrender will turn this Dominion upside down to get the Dominar back on the throne and he will use you to do it.*

I know.

I can't come with you. There's no room for me to fit, he said anxiously.

I know, I agreed.

I'll just be up here watching the prisoners. Should I keep a special eye on that scrap of a human you grabbed?

That would probably be a good idea. She'd seemed like she knew something.

I stole a last glance at Reshatharin huffing as he flopped down beside Ryfsmae. The smaller purple dragon stuck his tongue out the side of his mouth, panting happily while my dragon glowered, but I noticed Panza was also missing. Maybe she would catch Ystren if I wasn't fast enough.

Be fast enough, Reshatharin warned. *And keep talking to me. I don't want to be alone.*

Agreed.

And with that assurance, I grabbed hold of the ladder and began my descent.

CHAPTER 4

I DIDN'T USE the ladders at Dragon School very often. I usually used the lifts, because ladders are hard to manage with just one working hand, but the lifts hung limply now from cut cables and they'd need expert repair to be functional again. My only option was to grit my teeth and go as quickly as was safe with my capabilities.

The first level down was the dragon cotes and so was the second and by the time I got that far I was puffing and gasping from having to work twice as hard as most people.

It wrenched my heart to look down the lines of cotes and see the dragons injured with their riders desperately trying to tend them. Other dragons slumped in heaps that I knew meant they were dead.

Twice, I had to pause, my head too light to climb, blinking back stars and darkness at the thought of the poor dragons.

I was so distracted that I nearly missed Ystren arguing with Panza on the third level.

I slid from the ladder, grateful to hold a wall as I hurried up to them.

"Hand it over," he was saying, pointing to a courier bag she was holding.

"This is purple rider business, Ystren Cartrender," Panza huffed, "Which makes it none of yours."

It was only now that I was closer that I saw another small purple dragon in the cote behind them, his sides heaving as he tried to breathe, his rider slumped against him with his eyes closed.

"What's happening?" I asked, worried as I hurried past them to check the pair.

The dragon didn't seem injured, just exhausted. Quickly, I began to work the handle of the pump in the corner to draw up water to the stone trough there. He drank thirstily as the water rushed up and filled the trough.

Are you hurt? I asked him.

No. Tired. Flew a long way. Three days. Two nights. No sleep.

I put a hand on his muzzle. *Rest now. I will see to your rider.*

And then I was moving again, over to the slumped rider as Panza addressed me.

"He came in just now with urgent dispatches. Had no idea that Dragon School was occupied. Didn't arrive until we were cleaning up stragglers. That makes this Dragon Rider business," she said, giving Ystren a pointed look but then turning back to me. "Purple business to be exact. We do not open messages. We ensure they are delivered properly." She frowned, anxiety filling her eyes as she looked at the rider. "He looks rough."

"His dragon says they flew day and night for three days."

They both looked stunned at that.

"Read the messages," Ystren demanded, his whole body practically twitching.

"I must not," Panza protested. "It goes directly against our code. People need to trust us or they will not send messages to us at all."

Ystren gritted his teeth and made an annoyed sound in the back of his throat. "The Dominion has fallen. The Dominar is likely dead. Just look through the messages and give me any that relate to the school or him or *me.* Is that to much to ask?"

I left them to it and focused on the real problem right in front of me.

Was this dragon rider ... going to live? I patted the dragon rider's cheek but he didn't so much as flinch. He was in a swoon against his dragon. Carefully, I checked him for wounds or injuries, trying to shift him so his limbs were more comfortable as the magika and dragon rider argued. He seemed unhurt.

He's simply exhausted. He needs rest, his dragon told me, already closing his own eyes and motionless on the ground.

In the end, all I could do was wet a cloth for his rider to suck in a little water and then loosen his scarf and wrap a blanket around him. He probably wouldn't want to be parted from his dragon anyhow. I knew I wouldn't. They were both asleep by the time I was done.

"This one is addressed generically," Panza admitted as I stood again. "'To He Who Holds the Reins at Dragon School,'" she lifted an eyebrow before cracking the message open.

"That would be me," Ysten protested. "I am in charge here."

"Wawrin Tanglefoot might dispute that," I said in an undertone as I looked for a second blanket.

But Panza spoke right over us.

"The Banner of the Dominar, glory to his name, has fallen and Raolcan the Purple is slain."

Our silent shock was almost something you could feel. I paused mid step, staring at her.

"Go on," Ystren said hoarsely.

Panza kept reading. "This missive is addressed to anyone still loyal to the Dominar. Every sky city south of the Dominion City and Sky City has fallen. The Lands of Haz'drazen are under assault and we must expect no help from them." She paused looking up. "It does not say fallen to whom, but we can assume it is our color changing medusa friends."

"Or the Bright Continent," Ystren said. Did he know something I did not?

I lifted an eyebrow at Ystren over that but he didn't look at me.

Are the prisoners still secure? I asked Reshatharin.

Yes.

Now, more than ever, that was vital.

"The missive begs that whoever is holding Dragon School while the Grandis are away practices all caution as it surely must be a target of the enemy."

"A bit late for that," Ystren said with a bitter tone to his voice.

But for my part, I felt a gaping hole in my heart. I had immediately liked the old purple dragon. I couldn't believe he was gone. Absently, I patted the book in my pocket. The book he'd given me about hope in hard times.

I hadn't even realized I was crying until Ystren began to read and I had to wipe my eyes to see him properly.

"This one is for me," he said a little grudgingly but he told us what it said as he read it. "Magika House has fallen. Our people are scattered. I am to gather any I can find and reinstate the Lightbringers, the ancient order of those who would defend truth and the Dominion."

"Who sent that," Panza asked quietly.

And of course I knew why. Whoever sent that was the leader of those of us who would resist. Especially if he were reinstating the Lightbringers.

"I must not tell you," Ystren said, but for once I didn't think he was holding this over us just because he could. I had a sense that keeping this secret was important. He cleared his throat. "You must consider me their representative holding all their authority — on behalf of the Dominion, the magikas and the Lightbringers."

He must love that, Raolcan said in my mind as I passed on

Ystren's words, but strange as it might seem, I did not think he did. He looked a little green.

Panza made a face but she must have come to the same conclusion. "Very well. Consider me a Lightbringer."

"That would put you under my authority," Ystren said coolly.

I snorted and Panza made an even worse face but she didn't take back her declaration. Instead, she went back to her work sorting through the missives in the pouch. I doubted any of them would be as important as the ones we'd already read.

What could be more significant than the loss of half our country and the death of our greatest hero?

"You know I am a Lightbringer, too," I said hesitantly and was surprised by Ystren's terse nod. He looked almost fragile. Like he was surprised by this sudden responsibility that had thrust him into this position. Now that he had the authority he kept demanding, it seemed he wasn't so pleased after all.

"This one was for Grandis Childra," Panza said a moment later in a dark voice. "From someone who seems to be an informant in Dominion City. It says that by order of the Dominar, his best friend, the traitor Yulden, will be executed before a public assembly at the end of the Month of Flowering." She looked up. "That's twenty-eight days from now."

"That makes no sense," I said.

"It will be the Dominar," Panza said, looking sick. "If his friend has taken his place, he will be pretending that the true Domineer is him. And with this act, he will take his place forever."

I swallowed. And beside me, Ystren looked sick, too.

This was terrible news.

It meant that not only did we need to take back half the kingdom, we'd have to do it in twenty-eight days. And with only the barest of forces of men and dragons.

I stumbled to the edge of the dragon cote, and without ceremony I vomited up everything I'd eaten in the pantries.

CHAPTER 5

I LEFT Ystren and Panza to panic together. I'd never really considered Panza one to panic, but the news was grim enough that I supposed anyone might.

I needed to find Krullmark and I couldn't wait any longer.

Easy. Easy now. The fate of all the world does not rest on you. Share a little of it with us.

It took me longer than I expected to find Krullmark. First, I found the infirmary where dragon riders and staff wounded in the engagement were being tended. My friend Corana was taking the lead in helping the others, her eyes tight with worry but when I asked her if they needed more help she just shook her head.

"If you find any surviving white riders ..." she'd said, and then her voice had trailed off.

The silence between whimpers and moans was almost too much to bear. I was ashamed of how relieved I felt as I hurried away.

I had not seen a single white dragon rider since the battle and that made me worried for another reason. The whites had always been close allies of the golds, and the way that the golds had recently kidnapped other dragons made me worried. What if they'd turned on the whites first?

I found the remaining staff huddled in the dining hall.

"What are we to do?" Old Kendall asked me, looking a little helpless. I was glad to see he'd survived, but his head was bandaged, and the others looked just as banged up.

"We should start by helping anyone hurt to hungry," I told him. "That will keep us busy for a while."

"We ... Tage went to check the kitchens and he hasn't returned," he said in a fearful voice.

I frowned, biting my lip.

I told you, no danger!

"I'll go down there now and bring a few of you with me. If it's safe, you can start making food for everyone. If it's not, you can run while I call for a dragon."

Wait. No! Spara!

They laughed at that, though it wasn't a joke.

I'm coming!

It would be fine. Probably Tage was just busy dealing with the man we'd killed there earlier.

I don't want you finding that out. Just wait!

I did not wait. And I was right. He was still working his way down to me when I found Tage.

"It should be clear to work the kitchens now," he said grimly. He had a rag in hand and bucket of dirty water and neither of us had to say what he'd been doing. I left the staff with him when they seemed to have it under control but I wasn't willing to wait with them.

I was beginning to worry. I'd expected to see Krullmark by now.

In the end, I found him in the rooms where the staff and riders had been held.

A knot of medusa riders were pressed to one side with

Ursijek crouched low and threatening in front of them. There were burn marks splashed across the wall in front of him.

Two dead medusas lay in a heap on the other side of the room and I felt more than a little ill looking at them.

Refusing to be intimidated, I pressed between the dragon and the dead medusas, avoiding his thrashing tail — the sign of an upset dragon. I could ask him what was going on, but now that I was so close, I needed to see Krullmark for myself. I needed to touch him and know he was alive.

I pushed into the rooms in the back, separated by a tattered curtains. It was eerily silent.

And there, across the entire length of the hallway Laepsio stretched, dead medusas in piles on either side of his prone body.

I gasped.

Somehow, as we'd fought to take Dragon School back, the enemy must have slipped in here to kill the wounded. The enemy back there being guarded by Ursijek. No wonder he was so furious.

A sinking sensation filled me.

Where was Krullmark?

If he was still fighting, it would have to be loud, surely. And there was nothing here but silence.

I laid a hand on Laepsio's tail.

It was warm, but his sides did not heave as a living dragon's did and he did not so much as twitch at my touch. Hot tears flooded my eyes and I blinked them furiously.

Heart in my throat, I clambered over his fallen form, glancing into the rooms to either side of the hall as I passed. The wounded were in their beds — alive, I thought, some slumped in unconsciousness, others watching me with wide-eyed terror, dead medusas in their doorways. Some of those who had stayed behind with them were huddled back in the corners of the rooms, terror filling their faces.

And no wonder. It seemed as if the fighting had only just ended.

If I'd come here first, maybe this wouldn't have ended like this. If I'd brought help. If I'd only been here.

I was fighting back tears, stumbling down the hall with my heart aching.

Laepsio had saved my life. And told jokes doing it. He was the best of dragons. He'd wanted to come and fight so badly.

This time, I am coming. Reshatharin's voice was firm.

I was shaking all over when I reached the end of the hall and found Krullmark there.

The last room was empty — no one was watching him here. He was safe — if only for a moment — to let his guard down entirely, and he had.

Krullmark sat on the ground, slumped against Laepsio's still snout, face in his hands, heaving with silent sobs.

I'd never really known what to do when people were hurting. I had always felt so terribly useless. But I did the thing that came naturally.

I sank down beside him, put my back to the wall just like he did, and slid my hand up to grab his hand. He tightened his fist around it like it was a lifeline, never taking it from his face. And so I felt his tears on the back of one hand and my own on the other. We sat like that for a very long time, sharing sorrow.

Eventually he shook himself.

"I'm sorry," he said gruffly.

"Why would you be sorry?" I made myself sound angry. Because someone should be angry at him for apologizing for being human.

"I shouldn't be so weak," he said with a shudder.

"You shouldn't be anything else," I whispered. "You shouldn't be the kind of person who could see this and not be upset." He choked and I pressed the back of my hand to his cheek. "You shouldn't be the kind of person who wouldn't care about those lost."

He nodded, as if he didn't quite trust his voice. He pulled me to my feet, though he turned for a moment and rested his forehead against the wall so he could sob a bit more. And he did not let go of my hand and I didn't want him to.

I stayed with him until he'd dried his swollen eyes and then I put my hand gently on Laepsio's snout in my own goodbye.

Everything in me squeezed painfully. He'd never found his rider again. He'd given his life for all these wounded people while still waiting for his own wound to heal. It was too much. I didn't dare think about it.

We made our way slowly back to where the medusa riders were held.

Ursijek avoided my eye. I thought maybe he was trying not to think too hard about it, too.

"Did you find their leader?" I asked Krullmark softly.

"Yes," he pointed to where a man lay dead among the medusas, a knife plunged through his heart. Krullmark's knife.

"It will be hard to question him like that," I said grimly.

Krullmark only shrugged, but by the set of his mouth I could tell he was embarrassed.

Had it been revenge, then, and not something that happened in the heat of the moment? I shot him a worried glance but he gave nothing away.

Not revenge, Ursijek told me and I breathed a sigh of relief.

"Who is the leader here now?" I asked the prisoners.

No one replied.

"I know you are of the Dominion and that you can understand me perfectly well," I said, and Ursijek flamed as if to emphasize my words, setting the prisoners shrieking, though no one was burned.

One of them began to answer in a tongue I did not know and I sighed. Maybe they weren't all from the Dominion.

"I'll have to take them up to where we're holding the others," I told Krullmark gently. I was reluctant to let go of his hand.

"I must remain with Ursijek," he said in a thick voice. "To honor the dead and see to the wounded."

"I'll send someone to help," I told Krullmark.

Which left the prisoners all to me.

I bit my lip and thought about trying to get them up through nine more levels of Dragon School with the injured and exhausted everywhere without losing a single one.

Impossible.

Reshatharin? I called.

His response was immediate. *Almost there. I should never have let you go down there without me.*

But I didn't have the heart to reply. Instead, when he rounded the corner, I threw myself against his neck and buried my face into his scales.

Easy now, Sparrow. Easy. We've taken back Dragon School. There will be no more death today.

CHAPTER 6

It was not until the next morning that I saw Krullmark again.

I'd ended up falling asleep, exhausted, next to Reshatharin. We'd spent the day rounding up and tending the prisoners of the House of Shadows of the Ethereal Lands and then we'd stood guard while the others each dealt with their own work.

Some had tended the injured. Others had been busy at burial. We didn't have near enough dragons for everything that needed to be done, though slowly as the day progressed tiny knots of dragons joined us from those who had escaped the warrens and come to Dragon School.

By the time I woke, there were enough new dragons here that the undercurrent of *Clawsinger, Clawsinger* was everywhere.

I don't enjoy their attention on you, Reshatharin said possessively and I agreed. It was unsettling. But it had also been incredibly useful in saving lives.

He couldn't argue that. I cuddled closer to him. His reassuring bulk was helping me with the terrible uprooted feeling I had seeing my home destroyed and my family missing from it. They must have all gone to the Tournament of Dragons. I could only hope they had made it through the madness there.

Reshatharin was still shrugging when an exhausted Krullmark led Panza, Wawrin, and Ystren to me.

"Tell her yourself," he said, running a weary hand over his face.

"I've decided that with all dragons able to listen to you, you are ideal to lead an expedition northward," Ystren said.

He looked imperiously in that direction, the rising sun lighting one half of his face while the other half remained in shadows — an apt metaphor for him, I thought.

"Northward?" I said, uncertainly. "Surely our enemies lie to the south. Where they have taken the sky cities. And the Dominar, glory to his name, and threatened the dragon lands."

Ystren sighed and once again I could feel that under his veneer of arrogance, he was actually nervous in his new role.

"Wawrin Tanglefoot is senior here," he said briskly.

The red dragon rider nodded sharply to me as one military man to another but he softened the nod with a slight smile. He was looking saner. Stronger. His dragon had survived — wounded and in need of rest, but alive. There was a lot a dragon rider could stand if it meant being reunited with their dragon.

"Wawrin will be taking over the defense of Dragon School against the enemy with as many riders and their dragons as we can keep here or train here."

"Train?" I asked.

"The staff," Wawrin said with a tired smile. "I plan to train the staff to help me hold this place. It is, after all, their home."

My heart soared at that. What I wouldn't have given to have been made that offer when I was staff. I smiled encouragingly and he looked away, blinking away a glimmer in his eyes.

"I'll need you to speak one last time to the silver dragons before you go, if you please," he said a little gruffly. "I would like to see if there are any fit to serve with us rather than remaining prisoners. We have already lost some of the riders whose dragons died in the fighting. It would be a shame to lose anyone else."

I nodded, opening my mouth to protest that I hadn't agreed to go anywhere yet but Ystren cut me off, "Panza Boldbrewer is needed to set up the network of Lightbringers. She's been a purple rider for long enough that she knows every communication network and hidden spot. She knows the Castelan families. She knows the hidden caches and where other dragon riders might flee. This task is best suited to her. We'll try to rig her communication contraptions so that if she succeeds we can send messages quickly."

My eyebrows rose. No wonder Panza was looking so smug. She winked at me when I glanced at her and Ryfsmae was practically preening. The sheer necessity of communication was going to launch her invention into use.

Ystren cleared his throat to draw my eyes back to him. "But someone needs to fly north and carry a message to Baojang. They are nearest to here and most likely to be able to help. We need allies. We need them now."

"Will you be coming with me? To speak with them?" I asked him and he snorted.

"Absolutely not. It is my duty to plan the campaign."

"Campaign?" I asked, wide-eyed.

"To take back the Dominion," he said as if that was obvious.

I just stared at him, looked around us and then back to him again as Reshatharin laughed inside my mind.

"What about your ... superior. The one who wrote to you?"

He didn't answer.

"Did he give you this role? It seems like a lot to ask when you have no real forces and no real —"

"Forget what I'm doing," Ystren said impatiently. "The last thing I need is to be second guessed by a girl who is barely a dragon rider."

Rude.

I lifted an eyebrow at that, too. Ystren was barely older than me, and while he might be a spy and a Magika both, I had done a few things with Reshatharin that had proved our worth. It wasn't fair to disregard us now.

Which made me wonder. Was he only hiding insecurity at his new role, or was there another secret?

Either way, his plan is sound for us. We do need allies.

Ystren couldn't hear Reshatharin persuading me so he tried himself. "We need you to leave. Immediately. Before we lose anymore time."

I paused and swallowed. "I think I should bring one of the prisoners with me," I said. "Proof of what I'm talking about. Proof of what is happening here."

"Absolutely not," Ystren said at the same time Wawrin said, "It's a solid idea."

"The one I took myself," I said, before they could argue *again.* "She's from the Dominion. Maybe, with time, she can be persuaded to return to us. It will serve two purposes — both that and to convince Baojang that we really do have people invading our land."

"She might escape on the way," Ystren said, annoyed now. "It's just a distraction and a possible hurdle to completing the task I'm setting for you. Why must you be so difficult?"

"She could bring another rider with her," Wawrin said, smiling at me from over Ystren's shoulder.

I thought that he'd forgiven me for lying to him now that he had his dragon back and knew I'd helped with that. He certainly seemed keen to take my side of things. Or maybe it was just because we were both dragon riders and so we saw the world the same way.

"We're already stretched thin," Ystren snapped. "No need to stretch thinner. You'll go on your own, Spara Coldrock and I won't hear any objections. If you want to bring the prisoner, then bring her, but I'll hear no more about stealing able-bodied dragons and riders from us here to fuel your own ambitions."

I gritted my teeth, annoyed. What exactly was he hiding behind this bluster? He was useful and even noble when he was hurt or sick or weak, but give him one drop of power and he threw all kindness out the window.

"Translate for Wawrin quickly," he ordered. "I want you gone by nightfall. I'll pen a letter for you to take to Baojang. Give it to the first government official you can find and then get back here right quick. We need every bottom in a saddle that we can find."

There was a cough from behind me.

I turned to find Krullmark there — grave, sober, one might even say grim-looking. I wanted to reach out and squeeze his arm. He looked so terribly unhappy. Watching our dragon friend die had brought him to the edge of despair, but he seemed even more upset than he'd been when I last saw him.

I opened my mouth to ask if he was okay, but Ursijek was in my mind, urgently shushing me.

Don't interrupt him, the dragon begged. *This is important. He needs to speak these words himself.*

I snapped my mouth shut and took a step back as Krullmark stalked right past me, grabbed Ystren by the shoulder, and pinned him agains the dragon who had been standing behind him — Wawrin Tanglefoot's red.

Oh, I say! the poor dragon said, but he looked more bemused than upset.

"I was there when they took the Dominar, Ystren Cartrender," Krullmark murmured to him, and though his voice was low, it put a shiver of dread down my spine.

I shared a startled look with Wawrin and Panza. It was only us three with these two. Everyone else was too busy for this meeting and I was glad for that.

"You know I was there, because I was carrying you. And it's

not that I'm not grateful to you for springing Spara and me loose, but you are just one man in the middle of these terrible times. One man who has decided he's going to take the reins up himself. Well, maybe I don't object to that in general. But I do object to you taking my reins. And Spara's."

"I'm only asking her to take a message," Ystren said coolly, but he was flushed and I knew he was afraid of Krullmark. "It's what purple riders do, after all."

"It is," Krullmark said, but he didn't sound friendly. "And so I'll be joining her. If she agrees to go?" He looked at me and I nodded immediately, worried about what would happen if I hesitated.

"I need —" Ystren started to say but Krullmark cut him off.

"You need to go write your letter because we're leaving soon," he reminded the magika. "And you need to remember that we aren't pawns in your game. None of us are. We are people who have the right to make our own decisions. And my decision is to go north with Spara. Are we clear on that?"

"Yes," Ystren said, straightening the front of his clothing as Krullmark finally released him. "If you say so."

But he didn't look happy. This was going to be a problem later.

"I'll round up supplies for a long trip north while you're busy translating," Krullmark told me in an undertone. "Take all the time that you need."

He didn't meet my eyes and while I longed to reach out and touch him, to reassure him, everything — even his dragon! — told me now was not the time so I just smiled and thanked him and then followed Wawrin to translate before I left.

And you? I asked Reshatharin as I hurried to help. *What do you think? Do you want to go north to deliver this message?*

There was a long silence and then Reshatharin said, *Anything that will get us away from your Clawsinger cult. Do you know I've had five dragons ask to be part of my wing just this morning?*

Your wing? I asked, surprised.

There was a long pause and then he said, *They want to be your dragons, too. They want you to lead all of them.*

Oh. Well, that explained why he felt so sulky.

I was so distracted I nearly walked into Wawrin's back but I turned to look back at Reshatharin so he could see my eyes when I told him, *It's only you, you silly purple bat. I'm not taking on any other dragons.*

And the relief I heard in my mind as he echoed, *Bat?!* made me smile.

Don't act so surprised, I told him. *You have a lot of similarities to a bat. Winged. Surprising. Enjoys the night.*

Scares humans?

In your dreams.

Flies in a pack? and I could tell he was still testing me.

Never, I told him. *You're the only dragon I'll ever be rider to. You're the one who picked me when no one else did. And I'll keep picking you forever.*

CHAPTER 7

WE SET OUT BEFORE DARK. It seemed like a silly time to be leaving on a long trip, but honestly, I didn't trust Ystren not to make things more difficult or to snatch someone away — Krull-mark, probably — if we waited.

Before we left, Panza yanked me aside and whispered to me behind her dragon's flank — as if all the dragons couldn't hear her powerful whispers anyway, but I supposed she was trying to hide them from the humans.

"My contact in Baojang was Ahvad Ahkahnah, Regent of the Seventh Province. When the Dominar, sent me with a message north, it was to him. Whatever Ystren thinks, you cannot just dump a message on anyone there and hope it finds its mark. Bring it to Ahvad. He's in Hex Plajoram City. He'll welcome you and feed the dragons."

"Thank you," I'd said, squeezing her hand, and then there had only been the painful goodbyes to all the dragons and my friends, worried looks ,and trying to figure out what to do with the nameless, bitter girl I was dragging north with me.

"Best to let me carry her in a paw," Reshatharin said wryly. "Though likely she bites and I'll have human tooth marks in my scales."

"She'd break her teeth," I'd said, laughing. "And I doubt she'd do it more than once. But I won't make you carry her."

In the end, I'd found a litter for carrying the sick and we'd bound the prisoner tightly and tied her in it. She'd refused to say so much as a word — not to us and not to her companions — and she was going to be very awkward to drag around like this but I was undaunted.

These people were Dominion citizens. And while they had committed treason and betrayed us all, I refused to believe they were past hope.What this girl needed was someone to talk sense into her. And besides, when she saw Baojang and our allies there, she'd have to realize that Jhairen Que'Shal's people couldn't win against us forever. Surely Baojang would put a stop to it. Or Ko'Torenth. Or someone.

She just needed to see it for herself.

A little voice in my heart reminded me that nobody had stopped anything so far, and the Dominar, glory to his name, was lost to us, and so were the Banner of the Dragon, and Ystren — Ystren! — was the Dominion's last hope, but I told it to be quiet. I'd need to be brave to fly far north to another country to speak to foreign officials and beg them for help, and I refused to start a journey like that with doubts.

Fortunately, I had Krullmark with me. Krullmark who was steady in all things. Krullmark who refused to leave me. Even now when he was reeling from the blow of losing Laepsio.

I took comfort in that as we flew. First, just by stealing glances at him from afar, more and more as the moon rose and I thought he couldn't see me doing it. Did he know how confused he made me feel? I still didn't know why he was so loyal and such a good friend. I still couldn't figure out how anyone could be that noble and good. And I found I wanted to know him better and find out all his reasons and all the things that made him who he was.

It was a few hours after dark that the girl spoke to me and I was so surprised that I startled.

"Can you speak to the man with your mind, too? Or just the dragons?" she asked.

My gaze whipped over to her and I didn't know what to say. I didn't even realize she knew I could speak to dragons.

"It's just that you've been staring at him for so long that I wondered if you were talking to him."

I blinked.

In my mind, Reshatharin snickered very rudely.

Well, she does have a point.

"Or maybe you're just in l—"

I cut her off. "If you won't give me your name then I'll have to name you so that I have something to call you."

She glowered at me.

"Perhaps Violet," I said, trying to hide my smile while Reshatharin snickered even more loudly, and to my absolute horror, Ursijek joined him.

"Oh, look, he's looking right at you," Violet said and I glanced toward Krullmark without meaning to.

Our eyes met in the moonlight and I felt like I wanted to fall right off Reshatharin and die. He'd seen me watching him. I wrenched my gaze away and back to Violet.

"I don't know what you're talking about."

This time she laughed — a very mocking, cruel laugh.

"But if we are going to talk," I said with as much dignity as possible, "then I think you should tell me all you can about the House of Shadows and the Ethereal Lands."

She closed her mouth with great deliberation.

"No?" I said, "Then let me tell you about the Dominion. And why living free with the support and kindness of our dragon friends is worth all the loyalty and hard work we could ever give."

Exactly, Reshatharin said.

I told her for most of the next three hours while she remained silent and glowering. Only when the moon was high did Ursijek interrupt.

Krullmark says we should land and pitch camp for the night, he said.

I think we should keep flying, I returned. Despite hours of lectures my cheeks still felt hot.

He says to please impress on you that he is very much in earnest, Ursijek said.

I sighed.

I think that means he'll get foul tempered if we refuse him, Reshatharin prompted.

He said to remind you that some people haven't had any sleep in a long time.

And that was fair.

In the end we found a clearing on top of a hill. We didn't dare light a fire — not when last time we'd flown this far north it had been crawling with medusas — and we didn't dare untie the prisoner. Violet. So we spent the night leaning against the dragons for warmth, huddled in the blankets Krullmark had brought and eating a little of the cheese and dried meat he'd found in Dragon School.

"Does she say if there are more of them in this direction?" Krullmark asked me quietly, drawing me away from the others.

"She doesn't."

"Keep an eye on her," he said grimly. "I'm not saying it was a mistake to bring her but ... just keep an eye on her."

And then he'd patted my shoulder awkwardly and practically run back to Ursijek as if *I* was the one acting oddly and I was left with the distinct impression that everyone but me had gone crazy.

Are you sure you aren't crazy, too? Reshatharin had teased as I curled up beside him. But I was too tired to reply and I fell asleep before my eyes were even all the way shut.

CHAPTER 8

"SPARA," the whisper woke me. "Spara, are you awake?"

I blinked up at Krullmark and he set a finger over his lips, taking one of my hands and drawing me to the side and down the hill a little ways from where the dragons and our prisoner were still sleeping.

As soon as he paused I whispered, "Did you see enemies? I know they must be out here somewhere. They were everywhere before they took Dragon School."

He shook his head.

"It's strange really, that we haven't seen them," I said, looking around as if they might pop out right now from behind a bush.

"I haven't seen any enemies," he said, clearing his throat quietly.

"Then we should fill our water skins and get moving," I whispered back. "Baojang is still a long way off and we have to get Ystren's message to them."

"I wanted to say something," he said, running a hand over his hair awkwardly and looking over his shoulder.

"If you're mad that I brought the prisoner, I still think she'll help, Krullmark. I really do," I said urgently. "I know it's more work to bring her along and I know she could betray us, but I just have a feeling that she needs to be on this journey with us."

He nodded but he looked troubled and he still hadn't spoken, just swallowed.

"And Panza gave me the name of her contact in Baojang and that should certainly make delivering our message easier," I pressed, tapping the message holder on my chest bandolier where Ystren's message was tucked in safetey. "So you needn't worry that we'll be caught up with this task for too long."

Krullmark nodded again, still silent but his eyes were so intense it was like he was trying to tell me something without words.

"And I can't read minds no matter what the prisoner says. I really can't," I said, not even knowing why I was trying to reassure him.

"Of course you can't," he agreed.

I waited, but still he didn't tell me what he wanted, just looked away awkwardly, and I just couldn't leave things alone. I had to reassure him. I had to do something about those hungry eyes.

"You don't always have to come with me when I go places," I said in a small voice. "You don't have to feel like you need to protect me."

"You seem to protect yourself just fine," he said, but the look was still there.

"And you don't have to protect others from me. I'm not dangerous. I've found my way to being a responsible dragon rider," I pled. "Even if I'm not really one. Not officially. I've been responsible. I've been self sacrificing."

"Yes," he said earnestly. "You absolutely have been."

I shook my head, confused. I didn't know what he wanted.

"I'm sorry," he said suddenly. "I'm sorry for being so hard on you when you lost Alissi. I'm sorry for chasing after you and refusing to trust you and acting like you didn't know what you were doing."

"I *didn't* know," I confessed, wrapping my arms around myself.

His voice rose a little, like his emotions were rising with it. "I'm sorry for following you and not asking if you wanted that."

"But I did want it," I said awkwardly, worried now. Was he going to leave?

"I'm going to tell you something," he said. About time. He'd certainly drawn it out for long enough. "And you don't need to do anything about it. Or say anything. Or ... anything. It's just a thing that is. It doesn't need to make you feel, or do, or say ..."

His words trailed off but his gaze still held mine so I said. "Just tell me. It will be fine. I won't be upset."

He swallowed again, looked away, cleared his throat, and he still didn't look at me as he said, "I've fallen in love with you. You're going to have quite the hard time getting rid of me. Because I can't help but want all the good things for you and none of the bad things. And that made me order you to leave when things got bad in the caves. And it made me insist on going with you on this journey. But I hope you know I'd never demand anything from you like loving me back. Or giving me anything more than the chance to lay down my life for yours."

I swallowed. My mouth fell open in surprise. He *loved* me? I knew he cared about me. I knew I cared about him, but this ...

He swallowed, his face twisting with emotion. "I just wanted you to know why I was doing these things so that you wouldn't be confused."

He cleared his throat again, nodded sharply and then he was gone, striding back to the dragons and leaving me there blinking at his back.

He was crazy. That's what he was.

Who would fall in love with me? And who would tell me that and then just ... run? Crazy.

All you humans are crazy, Reshtaharin said lazily from on top of the hill. I saw his tail flick into the air as he rose and stretched. *Besides, I don't know why he had to say it. Everyone already knew he was in love with you.*

Everyone? That seemed like an exaggeration.

Well, you had to have known.

I didn't know!

She didn't know? Ursijek asked, sounding horrified.

She says she didn't know.

That makes no sense.

"*How would I have known?*" I protested.

We could all smell it, Reshatharin said smugly. *Practically from the moment I claimed you as my dragon and he found us together. We thought you knew.*

"*I didn't know!*"

Well, it should have been obvious, Ursijek said flippantly.

"*I. Didn't. Know.*"

Well now you do, Reshatharin said. *So maybe you should think about what you're going to do about it.*

Oh, Ursijek said, *And don't break his heart or I'll burn you to a cinder.* There was a long pause and then he added. *Just joking, of course.*

You'd better be. Or we'll see who is the cinder, Reshatharin said with a growl and up on the hillside there was a flare of fire and Krullmark called down to me.

"Spara! Come do something about this oaf you call a dragon!"

CHAPTER 9

WE FLEW ALL that day on separate dragons and I was busy enough flying over ground I'd never seen before and trying to get our prisoner to talk to me that I didn't have time to think about Krullmark's words to me.

"The Great One will see you all gone and every last dragon on this earth shattered and put into the ground from whence they have come. This will all come to pass when the door has opened and the new world pours out," Violet told me.

"What an unpleasant thought," I said, giving her a very long look. She'd finally begun to talk but it had all been like this. It was not helping matters. Although it was definitely freaking me out.

"He needs no dragons in his world," she said, her eyes glowing with fervor.

I shivered.

She was still tied by the hands, but for today I hadn't tied her feet or tied her into the basket beyond a safety harness. It didn't seem kind to truss her up like a hog and I was hardly going to win her confidence with cruelty.

I think she's a lost cause, Reshatharin said. *And so does Ursijek. When we get to Baojang, you should leave her with them.*

I wasn't sure he was wrong. Violet still hadn't given me her real name and everything she'd said today had been nothing but this same awful stuff.

But at least he wasn't still talking about eating her.

Only because the time to joke has passed, he said soberly. If Reshatharin were being sober then things were very grim indeed.

"For generations the Great One has waited, but now the sins of the Dominion will be punished. You have consorted with dragons and made friends of the evil nations to the north."

"Baojang?" I said with a raised eyebrow. "I doubt they're more evil than any other nation."

"And Ko'Torenth," the girl said with a sober look in my direction.

"And that's what the Great One doesn't like?" I lifted an eyebrow.

But whatever she was going to say was lost to a sudden roar from Ursijek.

I didn't see him flame, but he must have, because suddenly the trees just below us were engulfed in flames. They were conifers and when they lit, they were wreathed immediately in sickly yellow smoke, curving up in fitful coughs into the sky.

Reshatharin leapt, climbing high so quickly that there was a feeling like strain under his wings, and then to my stunned horror, something *leapt* from the woods into the air — something that I could have sworn was made of fire.

Eefrit! Reshatharin screamed into my mind.

But that couldn't be right. I'd heard of Ifrits — giant air elementals that clawed at the land and destroyed dragons, but they were not made of fire.

Only this one was. It was easily twice the height of the highest tree and as it swirled up in roiling flame, I distinctly saw two flaming eyes in the center of what might have been a head and then a flaming hand reached up from the flame and clawed at us.

Reshatharin rolled to the side so quickly that both Violet and I were flung out and hung by our safety straps alone, whipping and snapping in the wind.

I heard her scream and bit off my own cry of fear, catching the saddle with my good hand just in time to use it to lever me back into place as Reshatharin finished the roll and ended right side up again.

Violet hung from her safety straps, screaming, as the fiery fist reached toward her, and then suddenly Reshatharin was shoved forward and we fell into a long, lightning-fast dive.

For just a moment my heart was in my throat and I was sure we were about to die.

Not dying, not dying, he chanted as the fall turned into a swoop and just as his feet dragged against the grassy turf, ripping up tiny shreds of it, we were in the air again and shooting up into the clouds.

We climbed and climbed until the air was cold and it was hard to draw in a breath and when I finally recovered myself enough to look behind us, I saw Ursijek was on our heels doing exactly the same thing.

To my horror, Violet — still swinging from her safety straps — was laughing and no amount of effort from me could drag her back up again as she fought against my efforts.

"He's come for me," she said. "I knew he would. The Great One."

Beneath us, a surge of scalding heat struck, banishing the cold and as I gritted my teeth against it, the fire rushed up directly from underneath us, clawed at us, and for a moment, I felt like we were being dragged downward and then with a feeling like a snap, we were bobbing back upward and I could catch my breath again.

I looked down.

The safety strap holding Violet was broken and she was nowhere to be seen.

CHAPTER 10

"VIOLET!" I called, reaching down.

Flame shot up toward me and Reshatharin grunted, putting his touch underbelly between me and the flames but his grunt brought me back to reality. She was gone. Fallen to her death, or burned up along the way — either way, she was gone. My belly lurched at the thought. I had been so sure we could change her mind. And now what?

Now we'd better run! Reshatharin said, climbing again. *And please ... I need to concentrate.*

I gritted my teeth, clutched his saddle, and tried not to have loud thoughts as he ducked and wove and spun away from gouts of flame. Ursijek flew parallel to us, doing the same thing, but when I glanced over at him to see if Krullmark was alright it just made my stomach sick. We were moving too erratically and too quickly to do more than keep my own seat.

My skin felt tight and tingly from the heat. The smell of burned hair told me that I'd been singed a little. And my leathers squeaked like they were dry. Beneath me, Reshatharin was steaming a little and I was growing very worried when — suddenly — the flames retreated and we shot out from over a forest to a rocky outcropping that was clear of trees or bushes.

Both dragons plunged toward it as if it were a fortress we could flee to.

It practically is.

And I finally risked a glance behind me.

There was nothing but forest.

But shouldn't that forest be on fire after all the flames that had chased us?

Absolutely. Those could not have been normal flames, Reshatharin said.

Eefrit, Ursijek said miserably. *And he will be back.*

Well, we don't know for sure that—

He will be.

He might have other things to do.

There was a long pause and when I glanced at Ursijek his eye had narrowed and he was staring at Reshatharin.

Fine. He'll be back.

And there was no way to fight him. How did you fight a fire? How did you stop it?

Neither dragon said anything about that. Which must have meant they agreed and they couldn't think of a way to stop them, either. I didn't even realize I was trembling until my fingers began to hurt and I looked down to see they were clutching Reshatharin's saddle too hard.

Brace yourself.

I was trying to *un*brace myself.

There are others here.

And then we were landing on the rocks and I was trying to peer past his head and when I finally did, I gasped.

There *were* others there. Lots of others.

And they were ringed around the top of the rock formation like it was a castle and they were the guardians and in the center of the group the rock moved and I gasped.

It's not the rock ... it's a dragon.

A huge dragon. Maybe three or four times the size of our

dragons. And he matched the rock precisely, the exact same shade of greyish-brown. I gasped.

He was magnificent.

Cough.

Did Reshatharin just *say* cough?

She is a very old dragon. And she appears to be injured.

She?

Surely after Drazena you are not so foolish as to think that female dragons are not real?

But Drazena was just like any other dragon. And this dragon is not.

No, she is not. Respect, I think, is in order.

She wasn't even a color. Just grey and brown.

You do know that female dragons can change color, right?

Drazena had usually been purple.

Which was a lovely sentiment seeing as she was traveling with us — but she could have been any color she wanted to be. Much like this dragon. And now, you are being rude. Please, try not to embarrass me.

Embarrass him? My eyes went wide. Rude! When had I ever done that?

You're doing it right now. You're. Oh. No.

I swallowed a little awkwardly. We landed inside the circle, Ursijek tucked in tight beside us, and the dragons immediately bowed low and Krullmark leapt from his saddle so he could bow from a place on the ground, too, and that only left me.

Down! Get down off my back and bow!

And so I scrambled down as fast as I could and bowed, too, my heart racing in my chest as the people who had ringed the rocks all drew long, curved swords and one of them peeled off from the rest and strode toward us.

Uh oh. This could not be good.

These people were dressed in loose but well-made clothing, their heads covered from the sun with conical helmets. A single point drove up through the top of the helmet and the base was wound with cloth. Their clothing was rich with color and pattern and trimmed with lush fur. I knew them even before they began to speak.

They were from Baojang.

The man who must be their leader strode to the front and made some sort of demand, harsh and urgent. I looked to Krullmark, but he shook his head. He didn't know their language anymore than I did.

I tried ours. "I have a message for the government of Baojang — your Prince of Princes."

The man barked at us again.

Behind him, the dragon yawned, and then I heard her in my head and she sounded so ... different.

What manner of creatures are ... you?

Behind me, Reshatharin drew back and I tried not to look at Ursijek doing the exact same thing.

You're sooooo colorful. Like poisonous frogs. I ate one of those once and breathed purple flame for three dawns.

I saw Ursijek exchange a glance with Reshatharin. They both looked surprised and ... concerned.

Of course we're concerned. She's ... she's ... she's...

She's not from the Lands of Haz'Drazen, Ursijek said calmly and I saw Krullmark startle like he'd spoken to him at the same time.

She's not a dragon like us. Reshatharin sounded so stunned I thought I would have to pick his jaw up off the ground.

The human ... prince? from Baojang barked at us again, this time gesturing at the message cylinder I had taken out to show him. They had many princes in Baojang. They were in charge of cities and armies just like our Castellans.

I should say not, the female dragon said, shaking herself off and unfurling her wings up and over the warriors of Baojang. Her movements startled them, leaving a ripple of little cries and quiet curses and the *shing* of more swords being suddenly drawn — but not against her — against us.

The prince — I was sure he must be a prince — bounded forward and raised his sword as if to place it to Krullmark's neck. To my surprise, my friend grabbed the prince's forearm and spun him around, using his greater strength to pin the prince to his chest, the blade now at the other man's throat.

Krullmark grunted explosively and the prince's eyes met mine, black and surprised. His long dark hair spilled out from his helm around his sweaty face. He looked younger, suddenly. He was maybe thirty years old. And though he was well built he was nothing on Krullmark's bulk and he seemed to realize it. He held up a hand, speaking quickly and the men with him lowered their swords.

I, the female dragon said a little fastidiously, moving her forepaws back from where the warriors were backing up and into her, *am Anyrwen Caohten Eeotjoy of the Ethereal Lands and I will have your allegiance.*

And as if to punctuate her point, she opened her mouth and blew.

I had just enough time to get an arm up to cover my face. A blast of ice hit me so hard that I fell back, smacking my bottom hard on the ground with a sound like shattering glass as an entire finger-width layer of ice that had coated the front of me fell off and smashed to a thousand pieces.

CHAPTER 11

Both dragons roared, Krullmark leapt forward to grab at Ursijek's head, losing his hold on the Baojang prince, and I had just enough time to yell, "*NO!*" before both dragons charged.

She is not of Haz'Drazen! Reshatharin roared.

She's still a dragon, I said, urging him not to fight her.

Is she? Is she? Ursijek stomped a foot. *With breath like ice? Saying we are too colorful? She's not one of us.*

Well, obviously not. She was from Baojang.

She's not from Baojang. She's from the Ethereal Lands where Jhairen Que'Shal also claims residence.

Que'Shal? Anyrwen Caohten Eeotjoy asked, arching her neck back and narrowing her eyes.

I gave up on Reshatharin and sprinted to a pace midway between the two dragons, my good hand held up.

"*Please!*" I said. "*Will you listen? We don't need to fight.*"

She's an enemy, Reshatharin roared.

Enemy, Ursijek agreed.

Anyrwen Caohten Eeotjoy spat. And then looked at me.

And who are you? she asked me. *That you can speak to me as a dragon does? I can only speak to Prince Allomar.*

Prince who?

Anyrwen Caohten Eeotjoy nodded toward the prince Krullmark had held against his chest. The man straightened his clothing, barking orders to those with him.

Him.

"I'm the —"

Don't! Ursijek interjected but it was too late. I was already thinking it.

"Clawsinger."

Clawsinger, the female dragon thought. *Clawsinger. Here? Now?*

She seemed confused and then she stomped a foot, and around her the warriors of Baojang roared.

Peace, she said. *There will be peace. There will be no Clawsinger stirring up the peace.*

And to my surprise the furious looking Prince Allomar strode up to her and laid a hand against her neck, looking worried.

He says they will kill you for me, Anyrwen Caohten Eeotjoy said casually.

Reshatharin growled low in his throat.

But, of course, I won't allow that, the female dragon said easily. *Not when your timing is so perfect. You're puny things to call yourselves dragons. But you'll have to do.*

"Do what?" I asked.

Come with us to the Ethereal Lands, of course, she said airily. *And close the open door. It never should have been opened in the first place.*

She said it all as if it were obvious. And we just stared at her until she sighed.

Make peace with them, Allomar, she demanded, and then to my surprise Prince Allomar turned to us and spoke the tongue of the Dominion — heavily accented, but still intelligible.

"Have tea with us," he invited, offering a smile. But I couldn't tell if he were trying to be friendly, or if the bared teeth were a warning to stay well back from him. Either way, I found it unsettling.

You'll get used to him, Anyrwen Caohten Eeotjoy said coolly.

And that's how we found ourselves seated in a ring of warriors of Baojang, their leader trying to tempt us with fresh-brewed tea, and their dragon matching ours in a long staring contest.

"We were entrusted with a message to your people," I tried to tell Prince Allomar, gesturing to the missive he'd taken from me. "We need your help."

The look of despair on his face left me so unsettled that I had to look behind me to make sure he was looking at me and not some monster — maybe even that fire monster.

"The same is true for me. I am to find your Dominar and ask him on the behalf of our Prince of Princes to come to the aid of Baojang."

I swallowed as a stab of pain shot through me. Uh oh. This was not good.

"The Dominar is ... he cannot help you," I said in a low voice, ashamed to even admit it because it had been my job to save the Dominar and it was my responsibility now to undo what had been done. "Perhaps, if the Prince of Princes ..."

"He cannot help you," Prince Allomar said harshly. "It is he who needs ..."

Just tell her, Anyrwen Caohten Eeotjoy said, stomping a forepaw again. *Just tell her.*

And then the prince let out a dark curse and when he looked at me again he was trembling.

"He's been taken. And the capital city has fallen, our forces scattered. The Dominion was our only hope."

Beside me, Krullmark stiffened and Reshatharin let out a snort of smoke.

"Fallen?" I asked, as my heart sank.

The prince made a chopping motion through the air. "Your

letter has nowhere to go. Your people have no one to call on for help if you are looking to Baojang. We are the last."

"There are only twenty of you," I said, appalled.

"Thirty-two," he said grimly. "Including our new ally, the dragon."

Anyrwen Caohten Eeotjoy. The female dragon reminded us of her name in a searing hiss. *And before the two of you cry on each other's shoulders about o how miserable you are and oh how the House of Shadows of the Ethereal Lands has ruined your lives, I would like you to recall that I am here and that I have come with a third and more pressing matter.*

More pressing than our allies being attacked and overwhelmed? More pressing than us being attacked and overwhelmed?

I glanced at Prince Allomar again and hoped that in his nation there was a Ystren somewhere — domineering, opinionated, stubborn, but a chance to rally forces and take back what was lost. I didn't see any hope of that in his eyes.

"Yes, of course," he told the dragon in his heavily accented voice, but he seemed to deflate under their scrutiny, his shoulders slumping and his head bowing.

His warriors still stood strong — both men and women warriors — their heads held high and their weapons raised. They clearly didn't speak our language and didn't know what we'd told them. I felt my stomach flip knowing they would have to be told in a moment. Their prince turned to them slowly, opening his mouth, but before he could get a word out one of them pointed behind us with a cry.

CHAPTER 12

GET ON MY BACK! Now! Reshatharin roared and I leapt toward him but I couldn't get a grip. My good hand was sweating with fear and it slid on his tackle and of course my bad hand could not grip. To my relief, he boosted me up with his nose and as I scrambled into the safety straps, he began to rise.

By the time I had the straps buckled and could look down, everyone was scrambling into position.

Krullmark was mounted on Ursijek, the prince of Baojang had leapt onto the shoulders of Anyrwen Caohten Eeotjoy and the Baojang warriors, calling back and forth in their own language, were arrayed around her.

"*Can she carry them when she is injured?*" I asked, the others urgently. Even I had seen the deep cuts scored into her flesh.

My injuries are my own concern and none of yours! I will not have humans touch them.

I opened my mouth but before I could ask what the problem was, any words I had were snatched from my throat.

The Eefrit was back.

And he was not alone.

I squinted as I tried to look into his blazing form, but I couldn't believe what I was seeing.

Magic, Reshatharin said grimly.

Magic, Ursijek agreed as he kicked up and settled in a looping, defensive flight pattern beside Reshatharin. Together, they were circling the dragon below as if to provide cover and defense. Was that what they planned to do?

"There are too many of them for her to carry," Krullmark called to me and for a moment I thought he meant the girl sitting in the flames on the back of the Eefrit, not the huge dragon below. "She can take a lot, but not thirty-two. And their only mounts are horses."

I hadn't even noticed the horses.

You had a lot on your mind.

I blinked. He'd noticed the horses?

I was hungry. They smelled good.

He didn't really eat horses. He was just teasing me.

Besides, that was besides the point. The point was that the Eefrit was not alone. Somehow —

Magic, Reshtharin interrupted.

Someone was riding the fire creature.

Still magic, my dragon told me.

And they were racing across the open ground toward the rocks where the warriors of Baojang waited for them. On foot. Without a way to escape.

"Even if we loaded down our dragons we couldn't take them all," Krullmark called to me. "We can't run."

Was that even an option?

Yes! Reshatharin said, annoyed.

"We have to stay and defend them — or at least, I do," Krullmark called and finally, I ripped my eyes from the fiery Eefrit and to his worried face. "Your message is important. You should fly on without us."

He probably didn't see Ursijek rolling his eyes like they were on an axle.

Well, forgive me if I find his reasoning silly. The prince already told us that there isn't a government to deliver the message to," Ursijek said, snapping his jaws as he spoke in my mind. *He's just trying to get you somewhere safe so he can sacrifice our lives instead.*

I let my eyes snap back to Krullmark. It was so incredibly sweet. And protective. And strong. And *him.* Of course he was trying to save my life. Of course he was trying to sacrifice his. He was always doing things like this — caring for others above himself. Being ridiculously responsible. It was impossible not to love a man like that.

And that thought stole my breath for a moment.

Oh no, Reshatharin said, and to my shock, he put a wing over his face for just long enough to lose his stride and it took us almost a full count of ten to catch back up to Ursijek again.

Not now, Ursijek agreed.

I loved him back, I realized. Krullmark, not Ursijek. I loved him as he loved me. I hadn't realized but the idea of leaving him here while I fled brought it all crashing down on me. I didn't want to live my life without him.

This is worse than I feared, Reshatharin said grimly.

Well, I don't mind your company, Ursijek said. *And if they marry we will spend a lot of time together.*

Marry?

But there was no more time for them to freak out. The Eefrit had cleared the tree line and was rushing toward us, fire licking out in every direction. There was no avoiding him. There was no fighting his flames. And we couldn't run.

And somehow — due to magic, apparently — Violet was riding on his back, her lips spread back in a rictus of fear.

We were all about to die. This might be our last few moments on this earth.

I drew in a long breath, looked Krullmark in the eyes and called back, "I'm not leaving here without you."

He opened his mouth and I held up a hand to stall him.

"Not now, and not ever. I love you, too."

And then suddenly we were diving toward the Eefrit and Reshatharin was bellowing, and in my mind Ursijek said, *Nicely dramatic. If ever I give an impassioned plea to someone I want you to be in charge of it.*

The Eefrit was growing larger as we approached and Reshatharin roared again — whether to intimidate or to quell his own fear, I couldn't tell.

This was it. We had no weapon that worked against this creature. We were on our last dive. But at least we hadn't abandoned our friends. At least we hadn't run like cowards. At least I'd finally realized what was in my heart all this time.

And if I had to die, at least I'd die happy knowing I'd told him.

Oh, for pity's sake, Anyrwen Caohten Eeotjoy said, entirely ruining the moment.

A roar so loud it made me deaf blasted past me, burning my skin, slicing me with sudden pain.

I managed to twist my head around just in time to see Anyrwen Caohten Eeotjoy with her mouth wide open, the blast of it was what had burned me — burned with cold, not with heat. I bit my lip, wincing, trying to keep from screaming.

Reshatharin's sudden roar of triumph made me twist back again, just in time to see the cold slicing through the Eefrit. It sliced him in half — like a sudden strong burst of wind through a fire — and then suddenly there was a huge twist of white smoke and Violet was falling, screaming through the air, with no Eefrit under her anymore.

Reshatharin lurched forward, finding energy I didn't know he had, and we dove. We ducked under Violet at the very last second — just in time for me to catch her against my body and hold her there for a second time — as Reshatharin arrested his dive and turned it into an upward soar.

She didn't fight me this time. Didn't give me an evil look. Her eyes were huge, her mouth falling open.

"You have Anyrwen Caohten Eeotjoy with you," she said in a tiny voice. "The grandmother dragon."

"It would seem so," I said, having no idea what that meant.

You don't know what a grandmother is? Anyrwen Caohten Eeotjoy asked.

I knew that just fine. I didn't know what a grandmother *dragon* was.

It's going to be fun to show you, the female dragon said in a way that filled my stomach with dread. But Violet was having a completely different reaction.

She turned, looked at me, and then with pain tight around her eyes she gave me a very small bow and said, "This one is Fel Que'Tara and I live to serve, Honored of the Grandmother."

Well.

I hadn't expected that.

CHAPTER 13

We decided to camp the night on the hills. Hopefully, there would be no more Eefrits. Fel Que'Tara didn't seem to think there would be and neither did Anyrwen Caohten Eeotjoy but none of us felt quite ready to trust that — not even Prince Allomar who seemed to have an understanding with the dragon.

Fel Que'Tara had taken a seat at the head of Anyrwen Caohten Eeotjoy and we were happy for her to remain there where she was easy to keep an eye on. She was still our enemy. Even if somehow she was not an enemy to the female dragon.

I will keep her in hand, Anyrwen Caohten Eeotjoy said and she sounded almost as if she had agreed to babysit a troublesome child rather than to guard a prisoner. *None of you are to come near her.*

I tried to come near anyway. I needed to talk to Fel Que'-Tara, and she seemed badly shaken by her time with the Eefrit, shaking so hard I thought her teeth might rattle out of her jaw. But she would not speak to me and Anyrwen Caohten Eeotjoy would not let me within ten paces of her.

Mine, she said when I came near, gusting out long belches of frosty cold.

We had to settle for watching her carefully while Krullmark tried to tend my burns with aloe he brought from Dragon School.

"They are minor and they should heal, but they'll certainly sting," he'd told me gently, eyes full of concern, while Prince Allomar brewed tea and ordered everyone to sit around a fire together.

I wanted to talk to Krullmark — to say more about what I had said before, but though there was no chance right now I could tell by the way he tended my wounds that he had heard me and by the way his eyes twinkled when they caught mine, that he, too, would like time to talk.

Prince Allomar introduced his warriors to us as he brewed the tea and Krullmark worked, but the dragons kept talking over him so I missed most of the names. I bowed respectfully to each one, as was their custom, and hoped that would serve well enough.

They tried to kill me, those traitors, Anyrwen Caohten Eeotjoy was saying as I bowed to the second last warrior. *Me. Can you imagine?*

Reshatharin shifted awkwardly. I was pretty sure he'd imagined killing anything he'd ever seen. Maybe even me.

Not you.

Maybe even me.

Only for the barest of instants. I would never hurt you. But I've definitely dreamed of killing Ursijek.

You wish, Ursijek said, suddenly feeling the need to clean his teeth with a foreclaw.

A man named Jhairen Que'Shal led them. I was sleeping. We do that — grandmother dragons. That's why we're called that — because we sleep for a hundred years and when we come out you silly humans say you heard tales from your grandmother about us. Then we roam around. Have something to eat. Go back to sleep again. Who have we ever bothered this way?

Sheep? Reshatharin asked.

Other than sheep?

Horses?

Okay, there have been ... animals we ate. But we have not eaten humans in many sleeps.

Wait. Wait ... what?

The other dragons seemed to skip over that, asking her questions about her sleep but I was watching her from the corner of her eye as Prince Allomar's man — a steward perhaps? He was dressed as a warrior, too, but I saw ink stains on his fingers — passed me a cup of tea. Someone had fashioned quite a few from birch bark. It served perfectly well and warmed my hands immediately.

"We found the dragon on our way to you," Prince Allomar was saying and I realized he'd been speaking to Krullmark while I had been listening to the dragons.

I needed to focus or I was going to miss both conversations.

Ours is the most important, Reshatharin said.

Then he wold have to listen to it for both of us. I heard his laughter in my mind, but I focused on the prince.

"We were already in flight — on horseback. Since the troubles some hundreds of years ago when magic disappeared from Baojang and was only restored at the last moment, we lost our Sentinels and all other magical creatures and they never returned. Surely, you know this?"

"Neither of us is nobility," Krullmark said apologetically. "We were trained to ride dragons and deliver messages, but our understanding of foreign lands is limited. I have traveled to Ko'Torenth and the Bright Continent and know them a little, but I have yet to find your hospitality in Baojang."

The prince frowned unhappily. And I supposed that made sense. Our failure to understand his culture was as frustrating to him as it would be if he didn't understand dragons.

"With no magic creatures of our own, we rely on our loaned

dragons from the Dominion. But the dragons sent to us has been dwindling slowly ... until now we have almost none except the honor guard for the Prince of Princes."

Did we know that? The sour look on his face told me it was a sore spot, but Krullmark's politely interested expression had not changed at all.

I didn't know it, Reshatharin said.

"That guard — we relied to heavily upon them. And they turned on us — to a dragon — when the strange creatures flooded across our lands. Great turtles with cages on their backs. An undulating creature with many legs that matches its surroundings. Many of these rushed across the lands and with no more magic and no more dragons, what way had we to fight?"

I swallowed, feeling a tightness in much chest. What way, indeed? I felt like we were overwhelmed and we *had* dragons.

"But why did the Dominion stop sending you dragons?" I asked aloud.

The prince looked at me grimly and Krullmark shook his head — just a tiny shake, but a warning all the same.

The silence went on for too long and then the prince breathed out a long sigh and shook his head.

"Tonight is not the time to speak of such things. Or of many things. But there is one thing to discuss."

He turned to his people and translated his own words rapidly — or at least that was what I assumed he was saying since I couldn't speak his language.

"This dragon we met on the way, as I have told you. And she claims to be from a very strange place." He cleared his throat. "Please believe me when I tell you this strange fact — she speaks to me mind to mind."

"We are aware of this phenomenon," Krullmark said and the prince looked relieved.

"She told me she came into our world through a magic door."

We all turned to look at Anyrwen Caohten Eeotjoy. She preened, happy for the attention. Her tail was wrapped around Fel protectively.

It's true, she purred and I felt an immediate stab of ice down my spine, almost as if I could tell what was coming next.

"And this dragon told me that the strange creatures that have set our world on its head and destroyed Baojang and the Prince of Princes came also through this door."

Everyone hung on his words as he translated them rapidly and his warriors nodded, faces grim.

"And so we have only one course of action open to us — and now that we have met you, we implore you to join us in it." There was a long pause and then he looked us one by one in the eye. "We must close this door. We must keep other creatures from entering our world and upending it. And we must do this without delay. Are you with me?"

CHAPTER 14

"IT WAS THE ONLY OPTION," Krullmark whispered to me again as we huddled together a little way from the camp.

I'd made him walk even further toward the trees than he'd been comfortable with but I wanted to have a single conversation with him without having to deal with dragons constantly listening in. Prince Allomar's men were guarding Fel Que'-Tara. She had told them in a shaky voice that she didn't remember precisely where the door was located, but she could identify it for us when we found it and she kept looking at the female dragon like she both wanted her protection and expected her to swallow her whole. I would have found that more ridiculous if I hadn't seen what else dragons liked to swallow whole.

Cough, medusas. Cough.

As for Anyrwen Caohten Eeotjoy, she still refused to let us closer than ten paces to Fel Que'Tara and after our brief conversation she said it was time for the girl to rest and would brook no argument.

"I have decided to turn coat," she had said sulkily. "I shouldn't have to be questioned by my own allies."

But though it had been my hope all along that she would

see the need to join us, now that she claimed it was true, I was struggling to believe her.

Don't worry about her. We'll figure her out, Reshatharin urged.

He thought I'd gone off for cuddles and staring into Krullmark's eyes and he'd made kissy sounds as we left while the others snickered. He could think what he wanted. I needed a minute without the dragons. They were far too instantly excited about this turn of events. To them, this made perfect sense. There was a magic door. They would close it and be heroes. A dragon who breathed cold would help them. What more was there to say?

To me, there was much more to say.

"We cannot deliver the message," Krullmark said gently as soon as we were out of earshot. It really was comforting to have him near with his big bear-like body and those kind brown eyes. They crinkled around the edges with concern as he watched me. "And you know that if Ystren were here, he would agree that this priority trumps everything else."

Ystren. Had he known about this somehow? He'd been so vague about who to speak to in Boajang, but so certain we needed to go. I frowned.

"We're missing something," I said, biting my lip. But I didn't know what it was. I just had a feeling like I was being moved on a stones board into a position chosen by my enemy. "I've never heard of a 'magic door' before. It sounds like a made-up story."

"So do creatures that swim through the air with no real way to explain how they fly," Krullmark grumbled. "And Ystren made a door for us to walk through when you saved him at the Healing Arches. Maybe it's a door like that."

"He couldn't hold that door open for long."

"What about those portals in the warrens? They work like doors, moving people and dragons a dozen at a time."

I nodded and glanced over at him. We'd been going so hard toward a goal and so desperate to succeed that I hadn't stopped to think about how much we'd gone through. Krullmark had a bruise on one cheek and while he'd cleaned up at Dragon School he still looked worn and tired.

"We could ask Fel Que'Tara," I suggested.

"I wouldn't rely on her." His face looked tight. "I won't believe she's really on our side until she proves it."

"How?"

He looked me dead in the eye. "Sacrifice. Until she gives up something of value to prove she's with us, I won't believe her."

I changed the subject. I didn't think he was wrong, but I had trouble believing that Fel Que'Tara would ever sacrifice something she wanted ... for anyone.

"If we close the doors, won't that trap all these creatures here in our world?" I said, watching him out of the corner of my eye. He had admitted that he was with me on this quest because he loved me. Was it taking a great toll on him?

And what should I do about that? He was my best friend ... him and Reshatharin were. And he'd saved me again and again. Just thinking about him in danger made me sick. And thinking about him nearby made me feel safe. And I loved him. And I'd told him I did.

I swallowed and tried to focus on our discussion.

Krullmark shook his head, "We'll have to take that chance. We can't afford more of the enemy to come. If these creatures and their riders have destroyed two nations ... what could more of them do? Destroy all the world?"

"Maybe the key to fighting them is on the other side of the door," I said, still biting my lip. If he loved me and I loved him, shouldn't I tell him to go back to where it was safe? It wasn't right that his love should keep him in danger.

"Or maybe the key to destroying us is there, and if we close the door, we'll be safe," he suggested, having no idea what I was thinking. "We can't know everything. We can only make the best decision we possibly can and hope it is the right one."

I bit my lip. That advice worked for both the door and for me and him. He wouldn't go even if I asked him to, so I'd better not ask. And I did need him. And he made me feel like everything would be okay.

"What if we looked in the book?" I asked, reaching into my belt pocket and pulling out the Ibrenicus Prophecies.

Krullmark nodded. "There can be no harm in it. But the book is old, Spara. And the time of the Lightbringers is past."

"Ystren says he is raising them up again," I reminded him. "Maybe the time has come again. Maybe some of the prophecies in this book are for now."

"I thought you didn't like Ysten," he said with a wry look.

"I don't, but sometimes he's right."

He nodded slowly and cleared his throat. "See what it says."

I opened it randomly and read it aloud:

"*Do not wait. Do not doubt. Seize life while you still have breath and peace before it has dissolved like snow.*

From the mouth of the overlooked comes truth and from the hands of the oppressed springs mercy. Who can number them, for they are many. Who can count them, for they are endless. But I say to you, from the depth of your need draw out kindness and from the depth of your fear draw out hope. Hold them tight to your heart and offer them out with open hands and then whoever hears will understand and whoever seeks peace will find it and whoever binds up evil will see it severed."

I grimaced and looked up. "Raolcan claimed these prophecies led the Lightbringers in the time of Amel Leafbrought, but they are still powerful now. But how do you know if they are for that time or this time? This could be for any time. Hope and kindness are always good things."

And I was both surprised and not surprised when he took my hand in his, looking into the distance as he spoke.

"If they're always good things then they're for all the time."

I nodded.

"I wish I could send you home where you would be safe." His voice was tight and I laughed without meaning to.

He turned, looking hurt, but still holding my hand.

"I was thinking the same about you," I said. "Because your love for me dragged you here."

He was already shaking his head. "No. Don't ever think that. Love is a gift."

"A gift?" I said hesitantly. I should probably drop his hand, but I found I couldn't.

"Not just that I gift myself to you if you want me," he said, not looking at me. "It's a gift *to* me to be able to love you whether you want to join me in it or not. To be allowed to give to your wellbeing, knowing that you live and thrive — it's the best of gifts." Now, finally, he glanced at me a little shyly. "The best of gifts, Spara. Hold onto your hope and your kindness like the book says. And let me help you to hold on."

It was such a big thing to say. It made my heart feel full and overflowing and I opened my mouth, wanting to reassure him, too but he shook his head at me and I closed it.

"I don't want you to feel pressure to return my commitment," he said gently. "Especially right now on the brink of ... whatever this is going to be. Know that I am with you and will spend myself for your good. And look toward your work knowing you need give nothing back to me."

I squeezed his hand tightly. "Not nothing," I said, meeting his eyes with equal shyness. "For you are dear to me, too. You did hear me tell you that, didn't you?"

And the tiny smile that played around his lips. "I might have."

"Do you need me to say it again?"

"I might."

So I smiled, and I held his hand, and I told him all over again that his love was returned.

And by the time we went back to the dragons, I had stopped

worrying about what might happen to the creatures on this side of the door, and I had stopped worrying about whether the Ibrenicus prophecies could help us now, and instead I worried about Krullmark. I hoped the love he had for me in his heart wouldn't hurt him but only make things better.

How could it not? Reshatharin asked when he caught a whiff of my thoughts.

I felt my cheeks grow hot. How did dragons always know?

We can smell that you're in love.

He'd already said he could smell that Krullmark loved me.

And I can smell that you love him.

I froze at that. I was still getting used to it myself. I wasn't sure I was ready to hear other people talk about it.

But don't worry. Your secret is safe with me. Even if you did yell it out in the middle of a battle — which is a very strange way to keep a secret. Humans keep the weirdest secrets, you know.

And dragons keep none, I said in a huff.

We keep exactly the right number of secrets.

None.

He snorted and a puff of steam went up into the night. *Yes, of course. None. Keep thinking that.*

I nudged him playfully with my elbow, but as I drifted off to sleep beside him my thoughts were not so full of fun and I fell into a troubled sleep.

CHAPTER 15

I HAD FEARED we'd have to go slowly at the pace of the horses, but to my surprise it didn't work quite that way.

"I have made an important decision," Prince Allomar told us in the morning as we drank tea together again. "I will divide my forces. Anyrwen Caohten Eeotjoy has agreed to take as many of us as she can carry up on her back. The rest will follow with the horses. We will find the door from the air. Then we will guide the horse to it."

It was a reasonable plan. A good one, even, and while something told me that we shouldn't just go along with Prince Allomar or he'd get used to telling us what to do, it couldn't be denied that this was the best route to take.

We agreed and set out. Ten riders, including Prince Allomar, were on Anyrwen Caohten Eeotjoy's back.

I could carry more, she announced grandly to our dragons. *But I have limited it to those I like.*

It was funny think she had some humans she liked so fiercely and some she didn't when she'd only known them for a short time.

It has been more than enough time to judge, she told us as we lifted in the air. *We fly west today. Spread out, but keep in sight.*

Wave a cloth to get my attention if you see anything and I'll pass the word on to the next dragon.

What does the door look like? Reshatharin asked her.

Like a door, she said sharply.

Well, that's very helpful, Ursijek said wryly, but no one asked for more information. If she was unwilling to describe it further ... well, it must look like an obvious door.

In my mind's eye, I saw a door at the top of a flight of steps standing wide open with climbing roses grappling up its posts and through it one could see the ocean.

Reshatharin laughed at me mentally. *Do you really think that's the kind of place Jhairen Que'shal came from?*

He had a point. Mentally I revised my image to be dark and brooding, the door made of bars, the roses nothing but withered vines.

Better.

But that only made my stomach twist when I thought of where we might be headed.

Fel Que'Tara rode with the prince's men — all the better for them to keep an eye on her, Prince Allomar had said.

"All the better for me to keep an eye on you," had been her reply. She refused to say anything else and Anyrwen Caohten Eeotjoy was fiercely protective and refused to let her be pushed for more.

Reshatharin was far less concerned than I was.

Try not to worry. Whatever comes, I am with you.

And I was with him. And Krullmark was with me.

And I am with Krullmark, Ursijek said, his voice sounding distant. We couldn't even see more than a speck from his direction as the three of us fanned out through the clouds — me, at the northern tip of our sweep, Krullmark at the southern tip, and Anyrwen Caohten Eeotjoy flying straight down the middle.

Are all dragons and riders in this land like you, Anyrwen

Caohten Eeotjoy asked. *So ... sickly sweet? I swear I want to spit when I hear you speak to one another.*

Not all of us, Reshatharin said grimly.

Only the best of us, Ursijek agreed, and I was sure that Krullmark must be laughing the same as I was as we flew up and caught a draft and sailed west at top speed.

I spent my day focused, scanning the ground below and around us, trying not to miss the door when we finally found it.

I have a feeling it will be unmissable, Reshatharin said.

But that was the thing. The most important things in life were often very missable unless you knew where to look. And I did not know where to look.

I was getting used to long flights and by noon I had started to relax. Maybe this door would not be a big deal. Maybe it would be small and easy to close. Maybe there would be no one guarding it. Maybe all would be well.

But a few hours later, I knew that I was terribly wrong.

In the distance, we began to see movement. Not one or two moving creatures — deer or birds, or even a herd of sheep. Instead, it looked like the entire hillside ahead was moving. Like the way that anthills moved when you kicked them. As if the surface itself had come alive.

And all along the edges, licking along the treeline like a bonfire, were Eefrits. I counted one, two three ... ten of them. And the thought of the destruction ten fiery Eefrits could cause snatched my breath away.

I wanted to turn and run. My good hand, holding the saddle pommel, went slick with sweat. It took all my strength not to beg for reassurance.

The door must be near. It *must* be with so many strange creatures pouring across the landscape.

I scanned the horizon, but there was no sign of any structure far or close, so instead, I followed the line of people to the center of the clump where they seemed to be emerging from the ground itself.

Reshatharin kicked up a little higher, and the breath caught in my throat because well below us, down, down, down, was a massive pit that dipped directly into the ground. It glowed a faint, sickly-sweet pinkish color, and directly from the pit, crawling and struggling, emerged creatures in a flow like the tumbling water of a river. Medusas fell over Questrals, fell over Eefrits, fell over men trying to restore order, fell over horses, fell over everyone, and they all crawled up from the pit like the offspring of a great horror.

I gasped hard and in my mind I heard Anyrwen Caohten Eeotjoy say smugly, *I told you you'd know it when you saw it.*

But how did you close something like that?

Well, not from this side, she said grimly. *If you want it closed, you'll have to go to the other side.*

The other ... what?

It's a door. A portal. A tear between worlds. Why do you think our worlds don't mix? The medusas don't fly in a way that works in your world. Your dragons have very odd manners indeed. And even I — Anyrwen Caohten Eeotjoy — legendary that I am, feel as if my very skin might rub right off I itch so much from this place. Where did you think those gouges came from?

Well, if she knew everything about this place, then maybe she knew how to close the door.

Ha! If I knew that, I would have done it already.

Spara! Reshatharin said, and I looked up sharply to see him pointing at the great Pit. A pit so dreadful that I didn't know how anyone had given it such a simple name as "door." And from the "door" came a pair of Eefrits bigger than the other ten combined. I was just about to scream when a dragon shot through, pushing them aside.

And this dragon made Anyrwen Caohten Eeotjoy look

small. It was the size of a small village and the color of the emerald hills at mid-summer. Before I could even speak to it, it turned a tight circle and then lunged for the attack.

CHAPTER 16

Tighten up! Tighten up! Reshatharin screamed, dipping to the side and then half-diving, half-soaring so that we streaked toward Anyrwen Caohten Eeotjoy. I fought to stay on his back, hair streaming around me, my voice caught tight in my throat. When I managed to get my head turned around, I saw Ursijek doing the exact same thing with Krullmark. We converged on Anyrwen Caohten Eeotjoy at the same time and her voice rang in my ears.

Stick with me! Not too fast now!

We needed to swerve backward and retreat. We couldn't go through that door. Not like this! Not with this giant dragon taking wing before us.

"*Who are you?*" I called to the new dragon, but there was no response.

Up! Up! Reshatharin screamed, flapping his wings hard as he tried to lead the others upward and out of arrow range, to where he could control better what the skirmish looked like.

But no one followed and when I looked down, I felt like I had been frozen by Anyrwen Caohten Eeotjoy's breath because I didn't know what to do.

The grandmother dragon's jaws clamped around Ursijek's

neck in a sudden, vicious bite. I screamed with the purple dragon.

Krullmark stood in the saddle, yanking his short sword free, his balance precarious as the dragons twisted in the air together.

And there, on Anyrwen Caohten Eeotjoy's back, a second fight was raging — not dragon against dragon but human against human as half of Prince Allomar's warriors tried to subdue a mad, thrashing Fel Que'Tara, and the other half tried to tend to a fallen Prince Allomar. A dagger protruded from his back — one that looked like it came from Baojang, but it was obvious who put it there.

I had not been wrong. We should not have trusted the turncoat not to turn her coat again. And we should not have trusted the big female dragon who wasn't like our dragons at all and who had convinced Prince Allomar to leave the bulk of his forces behind and trust the rest to her care.

"*Stop! Stop this right now, Anyrwen Caohten Eeotjoy,*" I demanded with my mind, but being able to speak to dragons doesn't mean being able to order them and the grandmother dragon didn't so much as twitch at my words.

"*STOP!*" I yelled at the other, huge dragon and again, was ignored.

Fear tightened by belly and panic clawed up my chest. That was the only thing I had — being able to talk to dragons — and these dragons were not listening. What was I to do now?

I looked around us frantically, hoping for some kind of direction. The swarms of creatures had been stirred up by our arrival and some were shifting course toward us. In particular, the Eefrits were intent on attack. And in that moment, I realized that the dreadful pit — the door, I supposed — had opened right at the base of a Healing Arch. The arch was in ruins, nearly hidden by moving bodies, crumbled and worn by wind and weather, but it arched up to one side of the pit, like a sign showing the way.

I had used an arch before — tapped into its power before. I didn't know how I did it then but ... but ... what other choice did I have now but to try again?

The Eefrits surged forward.

Anyrwen Caohten Eeotjoy pushed toward them and toward the pit, dragging poor Ursijek with her.

A little help. Please! he cried.

Krullmark was up at his neck, hacking at Anyrwen Caohten Eeotjoy's muzzle with his sword, but her scales deflected his blows and she shook her head hard, dislodging him.

He fell and my heart fell with him.

His safety straps caught him, but he was dangling now from the saddle, unable to help as Anyrwen Caohten Eeotjoy flew them all directly toward the pit.

Whatever you're planning, do it now! Reshatharin called to me. He was turning in a slight circle as if he wanted to flee and wanted to attack and didn't know which to do. *You have a plan, right?*

I did not.

I don't know what to do, he said, his mental voice as panicked as mine. It was the first time I'd ever heard him admit to not being perfect. *I don't know what to do. If I chase after them, I risk you. If I run with you, we lose Krullmark and Ursijek and ... I'm not sure I'm faster than that big dragon.*

It surged toward us, impossibly fast. I hadn't even seen the people on its back, so large it was, but they surged forward now, scrambling to ready bows and spears.

Reshatharin was right. We wouldn't outrun them. Couldn't.

And I'd been in this place just one time before — a place so hopeless, so despairing, that there was nothing for it except to reach out and beg for hope, beg your faith might be met with ... something. Anything.

But there was nothing in my heart. Not a shred to make me think I could make any difference here. Not a shred.

If hope was the currency, I was impoverished.

Anyrwen Caohten Eeotjoy was so close to the pit now, dragging Ursijek, that it was hard to see her in the mayhem.

Ursijek screamed in dragon torment as she bore down, dragging him lower and lower and — I snatched my gaze away from him and from Krullmark dangling precariously from the safety straps.

Reshatharin roared and then — with me still undecided — leapt forward, heading straight for the monster dragon and his complement. The dragon was so large he was covered in moss and lichen as if he'd lain on a side of a mountain for a hundred years and been grown over. When he opened his mouth and belched, I flinched back.

A gust of ice burst from him so powerful and thick that we barely avoided it.

That was... that was...

This isn't good. This isn't good! Reshatharin screamed, but he hadn't stopped his headlong plunge.

I closed my eyes and tried to block out the chaos and the fear and the terrible sight of Eefrits being born.

"I don't know if this will work," I told Reshatharin. But I had to try. I had to try.

Please! Try!

And I reached with my last tiny flickering shred of hope — hope that my friends might live. Hope that the Dominion might be restored. Hope that love might not be snuffed out in the middle of all this violence. In my heart, I saw Reshatharin who had given everything to be my dragon, and Krullmark who kept giving up his own causes and rights to fly with me and guard my back, and Ursijek who had never complained about that even once, and Raolcan, gone now, but who had faith in a girl who was no dragon rider at all, and Alissi who never even told us she'd been hurt because she wanted to protect us. All of them — and so many more who had loved me all along. If that didn't give you hope — what could possibly do it?

I opened my eyes just as hope flared hot and powerful through me, blotting out fear, blotting out doubt, lifting me up.

A loud *boom* that shook the ground and then a light so bright and white that I couldn't see flared across my vision and a wave of wind hit us in the face.

For a moment, my hope soared. I'd done it! I was closing the door! I was keeping us safe!

And then, suddenly, the wind reversed, and began to suck us back toward the pit.

Uh oh, Reshatharin said, and it sounded hollow to my ears.

I watched in horror as the howling wind sucked back the nearest creatures, dragging them over the lip and into the pit.

And right behind them, it snatched at Ursijek and Krullmark and Anyrwen Caohten Eeotjoy with the warriors of Baojang and before I could even utter a cry they were over the edge and swirling down into it.

I screamed — I thought. It was impossible to tell. Every sound was lost the boom of the rumbling earth and the howl of the wind, Eefrits tumbling through the air and medusas and questral with them, and then the huge dragon was dragged backward, his strange eyes flaring with dismay.

I can't fight it ... I can't ...

And then we were being dragged forward, too, with the light of the Healing Arches surrounding us and the howl of the wind seeming to be endless.

I looked toward the arches, and to my horror, I saw the rocks were melting in place. It was being destroyed. The pit was slowly closing. And as it closed, it was dragging us toward it.

It's alright. It's alright, Reshatharin said in my mind, his mental voice breathy and terrified. *I'm right here with you. It will be alright.*

But it did not feel alright. I wanted to weep. I wanted to scream. I was supposed to be helping and now ... now what?

We've pulled out of worse situations before.

Had we, though?

And we are still together.

There was that.

Hold onto me, and I will hold onto you. And we will find our friends.

And then the world filled with white light and my vision was gone and I felt nothing at all except the sensation of falling and of clinging to the saddle and hoping we could survive.

DID YOU ENJOY DRAGON LEGACY: EPISODES 5-8?

LIKE YOUR FAVORITE TV SHOW, Dragon Legacy is written in episodes that can be enjoyed in a single sitting. You just read episodes 5-8 of the series.

If you liked the book, reviews are always a kindness or you can send me an email at sarah@sarahklwilson.com to tell me about it.

And if you liked this episode, you might want to go and binge read one of my **completed series:**

DRAGON SCHOOL: Amel is a disabled teen who comes to Dragon School hoping for a chance at life without being a burden to her family. To her surprise, she's chosen as the rider of a secretive purple dragon who sees far more than her disability. And when disaster strikes the school and her friends, it's a very good thing these two are friends because their help is desperately needed.

DRAGON CHAMELEON: Tor is a homeless orphan with street smarts and a bad attitude but when he meets a dragon in trouble and she chooses him as her rider, all his bad skills are suddenly put to good use and he starts to realize that maybe being a hero is exactly what's in store for him.

DRAGON TIDE: Seleska is happy with her island life, but when she finds a freshly hatched baby dragon, she throws it all away to protect him and help him save the magic of the world.

ABOUT THE AUTHOR

Sarah K. L. Wilson is a USA Today Bestselling author who has written almost one hundred fantasy novels and novellas. Sarah worries frequently that she won't be an able to write all the books she wants to in this lifetime -- as she has far too many ideas -- and is convinced she will have a long list to attend to in the next life.

With over 800,000 books sold or read in the Kindle Unlimited program, Sarah has her many fans to thank for her success and she remains their grateful staff and most enthusiastic purveyor of young adult, romantic and epic fantasy.

Sarah writes fantasy stories featuring practical heroines in the most impractical circumstances. She loves writing because it is the only way to make a living and give back to the world when your primary skill is an overactive imagination and a tendency toward violent daydreams.

Sarah can be found in the outdoors of Northern Ontario with her young boys and beloved husband, reading a book, or fending off her husband's pet turkeys with a straw broom.

You can find Sarah's books in paperback, hardcover, ebook and audiobook and they have also been translated into Italian, German, Turkish and (very soon) Russian.

You can find more out about Sarah at www.sarahklwilson.com.

www.ingramcontent.com/pod-product-compliance
Lightning Source LLC
Chambersburg PA
CBHW020336310726
48979CB00015B/2396/J

* 9 7 8 1 9 9 0 5 1 6 4 9 8 *